PRAISE FOR GRACE GREE

Beach Rental

DOUBLE WINNER IN THE 2012 GDRWA
BOOKSELLERS BEST AWARD

FINALIST IN THE 2012 GAYLE WILSON AWARD OF
EXCELLENCE

FINALIST IN THE 2012 PUBLISHED MAGGIE AWARD
FOR EXCELLENCE

"No author can come close to capturing the awe-inspiring essence of the North Carolina coast like Greene. Her debut novel seamlessly combines hope, love and faith, like the female equivalent of Nicholas Sparks. Her writing is meticulous and so finely detailed you'll hear the gulls overhead and the waves crashing onto shore. Grab a hanky, bury your toes in the sand and get ready to be swept away with this unforgettable beach read." —*RT Book Reviews 4.5 stars TOP PICK*

Beach Winds

FINALIST IN THE 2014 OKRWA INTERNATIONAL
DIGITAL AWARDS

FINALIST IN THE 2014 WISRA WRITE TOUCH
READERS' AWARD

"Greene's follow up to Beach Rental is exquisitely written with lots of emotion and tugging on the heartstrings. Returning to

Emerald Isle is like a warm reunion with an old friend and readers will be inspired by the captivating story where we get to meet new characters and reconnect with a few familiar faces, too. The author's perfect prose highlights family relationships which we may find similar to our own and will have you dreaming of strolling along the shore to rediscover yourself in no time at all. This novel will have one wondering about faith, hope and courage and you may be lucky enough to gain all three by the time Beach Winds last page is read." —*RT Book Reviews 4.5 stars TOP PICK*

A Light Last Seen and a Reader's View of Cub Creek

From a reader about Cub Creek and A Light Last Seen: "'In the heart of Virginia, where the forests hide secrets and the creeks run strong and deep,' is a place called Cub Creek. A place that has meadows filled with colorful flowers and butterflies to chase, and dirt roads and Cub Creek to jump over and disappear into the woods. A living and rural place that draws the reader to the setting and the characters who have stories to tell. A place with light and darkness and as unique as the characters who live there. When I opened the beautiful cover of this book, I stepped into the Cub Creek world and met the main character, Jaynie Highsmith. This is her story."—*Reader/Reviewer Bambi Rathman, February 2020*

A BAREFOOT TIDE

BAREFOOT TIDES SERIES ~ BOOK ONE
AN EMERALD ISLE, NC NOVEL

A BAREFOOT TIDE

BY

GRACE GREENE

Barefoot Tides Series ~ Book One
An Emerald Isle, NC Novel

Kersey Creek Books
P.O. Box 6054
Ashland, VA 23005

Cover Design by Grace Greene

ISBN-13: 978-1-7328785-7-0 (eBook) Release Feb. 2021
ISBN-13: 978-1-7328785-8-7 (Print) (Feb. 2021)
ISBN-13: 978-1-7328785-9-4 (Large Print) (Feb. 2021)
ISBN-13: 978-0-9907740-3-7 (Hardcover) (Feb. 2021)

Printed in the United States of America

DEDICATION

A Barefoot Tide is dedicated to my dad who was kind to all, interested in many things, and taught me it was okay to try and fail. I learned from him that the real failure was in not trying—and in not enjoying yourself while pursuing the quest.

ACKNOWLEDGEMENTS

Thanks to all who helped create this book beginning with my mother who shared her love of reading with her children, my father who showed me the joy of hobbies and projects, my husband who has always encouraged me, my family and friends who have done the same, including serving as beta readers to help me get the books right, my aunt and uncle who introduced me to Emerald Isle, NC, and my sister who introduced me to Cub Creek. Sincere thanks to Jessica Fogleman for her editing magic, and to author Karen McQuestion who offered her time and talent for reading and feedback. And special thanks to the readers who make the effort worthwhile.

BOOKS BY GRACE GREENE

Emerald Isle, North Carolina Series
Beach Rental *(Book 1)*
Beach Winds *(Book 2)*
Beach Wedding *(Book 3)*
"Beach Towel" (A Short Story)
Beach Walk *(Christmas Novella)*

Barefoot Tides Two-Book Series
A Barefoot Tide *(Book 1)*
A Dancing Tide *(Book 2) Coming October 2021*

Beach Single-Title Novellas
Beach Christmas *(Christmas Novella)*
Clair *(Beach Brides Novella Series)*

Cub Creek Novels ~ Series and Single Titles
Cub Creek *(Cub Creek Series, Book 1)*
Leaving Cub Creek *(Cub Creek Series, Book 2)*
The Happiness In Between
The Memory of Butterflies
A Light Last Seen

The Wildflower House Novels
Wildflower Heart *(Book 1)*
Wildflower Hope *(Book 2)*
Wildflower Christmas *(A Wildflower House Novella) (Book 3)*

Virginia Country Roads
Kincaid's Hope
A Stranger in Wynnedower
www.GraceGreene.com

A BAREFOOT TIDE

From rural Virginia to coastal Carolina ~ Sometimes the biggest risk is in playing it safe...

Lilliane Moore leaves the forests and rolling hills of her rural Virginia hometown, Cub Creek, to accept a temporary job as a companion to an elderly man who lives at the beach.

It's a risky move that's out of character for her, but her thirties are passing quickly—she feels like she's closing in on forty fast—plus she's got a hole in her roof and no AC. The big payday she's been promised for this short-term assignment will fix a lot of what's wrong in her life. The job is at the beach in North Carolina, in a place called Emerald Isle at the end of the Outer Banks. She's never seen the ocean before and she'd like to, but what's the catch?

Because there's always a catch, isn't there?

Taking a job in a home with someone she doesn't know and so far from her own home may be a risk—but the biggest risk for Lilliane may be the unexpected— including leaving the home and hometown to which her heart and past are irrevocably tied, and to which she must return—*no matter what happens while she's away.*

A BAREFOOT TIDE

CHAPTER ONE

On a Monday afternoon in June, Ms. Susan Biggs drove into the Fuel Up Fast parking lot. She bypassed the pumps and stopped her car in front of the convenience store, almost blocking the entrance. When she came inside, she ignored me completely and walked directly back to the drink coolers.

I was busy assisting customers, so other than sparing her a quick look and noting her too-blonde hair and very blue suit, I didn't give her much thought—never guessing that within thirty minutes of her walking into the store, my world would be overset.

For my almost twenty years of adulthood, my life had been pretty much the same day in, day out. I'd always believed that if I worked hard and took care of my responsibilities something better would come along, as if belief alone could make it happen. Over those years, I'd gained fine lines at the corners of my eyes and found a few gray hairs among the auburn strands, but otherwise? Nope, nothing. And definitely no sign of improvement—not in jobs, love, or my future.

Hal walked past where I stood at the cash register. He was headed to the manager's office in the back. He gave me a nod, saying, "Good morning, Lilliane."

He always said my name right. My parents had kept the *e* on the end because I was named after my grandmother and that was how she'd spelled it, but that *e* tended to confuse people. Hal always remembered to say my name as if the *e* didn't exist. Hal was a good guy and a good boss. I appreciated him.

The woman in blue was returning to the front of the store with a tall bottle of expensive water. She set it on the counter in front of me without greeting or conversation. I was good with that because other customers were queueing up to check out. No time to dally.

I rang up the bottled water but before she managed to slide her chipped card into the reader, her phone played a tune. In a heartbeat, she pasted the phone to her ear and turned her back to me and the counter saying, "I told him I . . ." Her voice dropped as she walked away.

Walked away.

My hand was frozen in midair, still pointing at the credit card machine. The customers who were lined up and waiting, starcd at her, then at me. Supremely annoyed, I made a huffy noise and pulled my hand back.

Loudly, I called out, "Ma'am?"

She was standing in front of the milk and soda coolers now. Her back was to me, and she was speaking low into her phone. She leaned closer to the cooler door, using it as a mirror, patting her hair, and then smoothing the bright blue slacks and suit jacket, all the while talking. The rest of us, in our jeans and T-shirts and workday clothes, didn't exist for her.

Making an angry, frustrated noise loud enough to be heard by everyone, I voided the transaction. I didn't bother to call Hal back out from his office to approve it first. What was he going to do if I broke a rule? Fire me? *Hah.* He'd already told me I was being laid off at the end of the week.

I didn't blame him for that. He didn't have much of a choice about it, but . . .

The next customer, a regular, stepped up without hesitation, his well-worn wallet already in hand as he slipped out the bills to pay for his extra-large coffee and danish. The blue woman paid no attention to any of us.

Keep an eye on her, I told myself. If she thought this was some slick way for her to slip out without paying, she had another think coming. I'd been doing this job on and off for a long time, too long, and I knew all the tricks. This wasn't about Hal or the convenience store or even the bottle of water. This was now between me and her.

By the time she ended her call and noticed the rest of the world again, I was finishing up with the last person in line. I reached for the voided slip I'd tucked under the stapler, ready to speak a whole slew of harsh words at her. Again, what was Hal gonna do if I was rude? Would he let me go today instead of at the end of the week? For once in my life, I would experience the satisfaction of unloading my anger on a customer who'd crossed the line. This arrogant woman deserved it if anyone did.

But before I could vent all over her, another woman walked in. Gwen. I knew Gwen. She was kind and very smart. Vaguely embarrassed that she might have read such ugly intent on my face, I tried to smooth the anger away. The blue lady was lucky. She'd never know how close she'd come to being unleashed on.

Gwen caught my eye, gave me a tiny wave, but then walked right past me to join the woman.

They greeted each other with a smile and a hug. The expression on the woman's face said Gwen was *expected*. These two had planned to meet up here.

Seriously?

As I watched, they started chatting. I stood there behind the counter, annoyed, holding the voided receipt that no one else gave a darn about.

I was curious. They seemed an odd pair for friends. Early fifties. I could guess that much from knowing Gwen. But Gwen's curly hair had gray in it, and she wore simple, sensible clothing, much as you'd expect with a visiting nurse. This other woman was . . . well, not at all like that.

Gwen had visited my Aunt Molly on a regular schedule to assess her health—that's how I'd gotten to know her better. I'd taken almost daily care of my great-aunt for a couple of years before she passed. A few times, I'd stayed over when her grandson and his wife were out of town on vacation. I'd never had a real vacation myself, though once I'd taken Aunt Molly along the Skyline Drive clear down to the Smokies. She'd wanted to visit her last living childhood friend before she grew too feeble. It was Gwen who'd convinced my cousin that his grandma was up to the trip. I drove her car, and we both enjoyed the scenery. Plus, we'd driven over to Asheville to see that Biltmore place. Molly had treated me to a tour ticket. The tour was amazing, and I bought us each a Christmas ornament as a keepsake. We'd had a great adventure. As much as I loved Cub Creek, I enjoyed seeing different sights too. But that had been a couple of years ago. Aunt Molly had been smart to go on her trip while she could.

Gwen and the blue woman were still chatting over by the coolers and occasionally casting glances my way. It ticked me off, especially when I heard my name. Finally, I waved the receipt with big, exaggerated motions.

"Whenever you're ready, ma'am?"

Gwen flashed me a surprised look, then a quick smile. She touched the woman's arm, murmuring something to her in a low voice, and then they moved toward me.

"Lillie," Gwen said as she approached me. She had a big smile on her face, but I sensed tension in her smile and definitely in her eyes. Gwen was the only one who called me *Lillie*, and I wasn't sure why I allowed it, but I did.

She continued, "There's someone I'd like to introduce you to. This is Susan Biggs. Susan, this is Lilliane Moore." She turned to face me full-on. "Lillie, Susan is an old school friend of mine. She called the other day and happened to mention she needs someone who is good with the elderly for a couple of weeks."

I saw where this was going and pushed away from the counter. "I'm not in the eldercare business. I helped my aunt out. I was paid, yes, but that was more a family thing than otherwise. Sorry. Not interested."

Ms. Biggs frowned.

Gwen said gently, "Hear me out. It's short term, with some nice perks."

Everyone was always so eager to plug me in where it was most convenient for them. I was the unencumbered one. Unencumbered, in fact, by children or a spouse, or even by a working air conditioner, a reliable heating system, or the money to fix them. Not to mention the hole in my roof that was still patched with a blue tarp. I had a working vehicle only because Aunt Molly had given me hers when she'd surrendered her driver's license.

On the other hand, I did have a home with working appliances, a car that ran, and a job. *Job? Scratch that.* My job was ending because revenue was down at the Fuel Up Fast, and Hal had to let one of his people go. Since I had no family depending on me, I was the unencumbered one and thus the most reasonable choice to be let go.

As usual, I was the most convenient person to be assigned the task that no one else wanted—or to be let go altogether, as needed.

Without thought—or maybe acting purely on emotion and without any kind of dignity—I flew out from behind the counter and headed for the glass doors, slamming through them to get outside. Anger drove me. Maybe fear did too. Because I wasn't getting any younger. I wasn't getting any smarter or better trained either. When I stopped moving, I found myself just around the corner of the building, and I came to my senses there. I was embarrassed at what I'd just done. My hands were shaking. I gripped the key pendant through my shirt. The pendant was hanging on a silver chain around my neck. Dad had made it for my mother long ago. I wore it almost all the time. Holding it helped calm me.

"Lillie," a soft voice said.

Embarrassed, I released my hold on the key and crossed

my arms instead.

Gwen said, "I'm sorry I presumed. I thought this was an opportunity you might enjoy. Hal had mentioned to me that . . . well, that you were leaving the Fuel Up Fast. He's very sorry about it, I know. He hates to lose you, but that doesn't help you. Plus, you are way overdue for a break. To get away, even for only two weeks, paid . . . When Susan told me she needed someone right away, someone she could absolutely trust—she was venting, not asking for a recommendation, but I thought of you."

Fixing Gwen with my best stern, no-nonsense look, I asked, "Why? Why me? I know *you* trust me, but I don't know her from any other stranger. Why is she willing to pay me, on your say-so, to go sit with someone for two weeks? Tell me straight out, what is this about? What's the catch?"

Gwen shook her head slowly, saying, "No catch. I promise." She paused, perhaps wanting to see my reaction. I held it in, waiting.

She continued, "It should be easy work. I understand that Mr. Dahl is fully capable of tending to himself, but he's elderly and can't stay alone. It's a live-in job. He needs a reminder to take his meds, someone to cook simple meals and to wash clothes. Light housework. But it's not a twenty-four-hour-a-day babysitting job. You can go out between meals during the day. See the sights. Have some fun. The pay should be quite good."

Okay, that didn't sound so bad. Maybe I'd overreacted. My face felt warm.

"There's more, though," Gwen said.

Here it comes, I thought. *Now the catch.*

"It's out of town."

She'd kept her voice neutral. What did that mean? Out of town? She'd also said new "sights." *And paid,* my brain reminded me.

I could go sightseeing on my own. Face it, Aunt Molly, dear as she was, hadn't been fleet of foot. *On my own.* Out of town might work fine. *Unless . . .*

Unless it was somewhere really bad.

"Where?" I asked, suspicious.

"At the beach. About seven hours from here. The Outer Banks."

She waited for my response, but my brain was busy echoing the word *beach* over and over.

She prompted, "Have you been to the beach before?"

"When does she need me?" I asked.

"Monday of next week."

When I'd fled the store, I'd stopped too near the dumpster. The waste truck had emptied it this morning, but the semipermanent thin coating inside—the accumulation of years of trash—held on to its aged reek and responded to the hot day. A few feet away from me, oil spots marred the parking area. Crumpled cups, where folks had missed the trash cans, had caught in the edges of the grass. Just summer at the Fuel Up Fast, thank you very much. At least the air-conditioning was pumping inside the building.

And as of Sunday, I wouldn't even have that. I'd be home without AC.

"Mr. Dahl, you said? What if he and I don't get along?"

"Then you'll call Susan and tell her. She'll find someone else." Gwen touched my arm. "To be honest, I hear he can be difficult, but he also likes to be alone, so you won't be at his beck and call." She smiled. "I don't know him, and I don't want to say too much, anyway, because I want you to make up your own mind about this job and about him."

Gwen softened her voice. "This isn't a long-term answer for you, but don't you deserve a break? A change of scene? Susan usually goes through an agency, but the last few people didn't work out well. She needs someone she can trust while they find another long-term person. You are trustworthy and capable." She placed both hands on my arm. "But if you'd rather not, you aren't obligated in any way. You aren't being asked to do this as a favor to me or to anyone. Susan will find someone else. Or she won't. But that's not your problem."

I nodded. Too many words were swirling in my brain. If my present job had been secure, or if I had another job in sight, I might've said no outright despite the temptations of seeing new sights and extra cash. Likely I would've favored the sure thing—the thing I knew—over the risk of something new.

"May I introduce Susan to you?"

What harm could it do? "Sure," I said. They were only talking two weeks. At the beach. Paid. I'd be a fool not to consider it.

Susan Biggs joined us. She must've been hovering just around the corner. Her manner was overbearing, though perhaps not intentionally. She seemed rushed. Intense. I could see she was trying to be nice, but it didn't come naturally to her. Apparently, she needed me more than I needed her. Which gave me pause. How awful *was* Mr. Dahl? Also, she'd taken Gwen at her word for her excellent reference of me. As we spoke, I saw shades of doubt in her eyes, especially when I said *cain't*, or *get* came out sounding like *git*. That reassured me, since it indicated she wasn't willing to take just any old warm body.

"There'll be plenty of free time. A housekeeper comes in twice a week for cleaning and cooking. Lots of time to read. Are you a big reader, Lillie?"

"Lilliane, please." The reading part threw me. Felt like a non sequitur to the conversation we were having. "I don't read much. Never have."

"No?"

"No, ma'am. I rarely read, not for pleasure, certainly. But if Mr. Dahl likes having a story read to him, I can do that. I *can* read."

She made a strange noise, and I could tell she was strangling a laugh. Why? I waited for clarification on the reading part, but she said, "No, that's fine. Reading stories won't be necessary." She changed the subject, asking, "What would you charge? For two weeks live-in. No heavy cleaning or cooking. Just light duties like reheating and tidying up in between. Mr. Dahl is very independent but needs someone around."

My daddy would've said, *What's it worth to you?* So I asked, "What are you willing to pay?" I smiled in that moment, remembering him.

Had Ms. Biggs misread my smile? I thought she might have, because she glanced over at Gwen. Maybe she didn't want to appear cheap or unfair in front of her old school friend. When she looked back at me, she named a figure that was more than what I'd earn at the Fuel Up Fast in two months, even with full-time hours.

With that kind of payday, I'd be able to get a new window AC unit installed, and maybe afford one upstairs too. I could get the roof fixed and get rid of that blue tarp. I could even start repairs on the heating system. Winter was only a few months away.

I tried to look dead serious. "I won't wear a uniform."

"Heavens no. Mr. Dahl would not allow that. He doesn't want anyone to know he has an aide, especially a live-in one. He's very private. And proud." She pushed. "Can you be there Monday?"

"I can."

"Will you promise that you won't just leave if he gets cranky or you get a better job offer? Please. If you decide not to stay for whatever reason, call me. I'll do my best to find a replacement as quickly as possible, but it was ridiculously hard to—" She broke off. "The last aide left abruptly."

I looked askance, questioning my decision again.

She hastened to add, "We discovered she was dishonest."

"Oh. Well, no worries about that. I'm more honest than most folks would like."

Hal came outside and yelled around the corner, "You coming back in to work or what?"

I'd totally lost track of cars and customers coming and going at the pumps and into the store. "Almost done, Hal," I yelled back, and he left us.

Susan handed me a business card. "My phone number and email. Mr. Dahl's address is on the back."

I accepted the card, and she gave me a blank look, perhaps thinking I'd presto pull out a handy dandy card of my own. When I didn't, she extracted another card and a pen, too, from her purse. She turned the card over to the blank side. With her pen poised, she asked, "Your number?" As she wrote it down, she asked, "Can I text you?"

"Best to call me," I said. My data plan wasn't unlimited. Didn't want to risk her blowing it up.

"Okay. Got it. Monday morning, then?"

"No. I'll be driving down. I don't know exactly how far it is, or how long the drive will take, but even with leaving early I won't get there before afternoon. If I run into trouble or traffic, it could be much later."

She gave me a long, blank-faced, thinking stare, as if I were speaking a foreign language. Her expression changed as light dawned. She said, "I'll make a reservation at a hotel near the beach. You can drive down on Sunday and be there rested and fresh to meet Mr. Dahl on Monday morning. On our tab, of course. Will that work?"

"Sure."

"Excellent." She nodded and turned toward Gwen. "I have to be in Richmond in an hour, so I must get back on the road. Next time I'm up this way we'll do lunch. My treat."

"Drive carefully," Gwen said. "Have a great trip."

Quick hugs and waves were exchanged between the two women, and then Ms. Susan Biggs drove off. Gwen had gotten into her car but stayed behind. I went over to her open window.

Gwen asked, "Are we good?"

"I was surprised."

"I wish I could've given you a heads-up, but I didn't want

to get you excited about something that might not work out. Susan moves fast once she makes up her mind, doesn't she?"

I handed her Ms. Biggs's card. "Write your phone number on the back for me. Just in case."

"Just in case?"

"In case this ends up being as crazy as it sounds. If I need you, you'd better come rescue me."

She laughed and leaned toward me, returning the card and patting my arm. "This is going to be such a nice change for you, Lillie. Enjoy yourself. You've earned a break. You did right by Ms. Molly. You always do. You're that kind of person, and that's why I thought of you immediately when Susan mentioned—by chance, and by way of complaint, actually—that she was looking for someone stellar she could trust. You deserve a little fun for a change. Enjoy the trip. Enjoy the ocean."

Gwen left, and I stood there alone, feeling a little stunned until I noticed the gas pumps and thought of that tall bottle of water.

What were the odds? I sure hoped Ms. Biggs had settled her tab before taking off.

If not, I knew where to find her. At the beach.

I looked at the business card. And smiled.

Yep, that's where I'd be too.

CRSO

When I was a kid, I had one of those folding maps, the kind you used to see in racks at gas stations and convenience stores. The paper rustled when you opened it, and it was tricky to refold. I don't remember how I happened to come by mine, but it was probably my father's. I loved poring over the mysteries of its lines and symbols and unfamiliar place names. With the tip of my finger, I traced the contour lines of the Blue Ridge and the shoreline of the Atlantic Ocean. I asked my dad why we never followed those lines to see where they went and what it all looked like in real life. Daddy patted my hand and said, "Lillie, we are blessed to be where we are. We'll stay right here."

So I had put the map away. I didn't mind. But I did keep it, tucking it under my mattress near the pillow end of my bed. For the next several years, I fancied that at night I traveled in my dreams while still being safe and snug at home.

Back then, I believed I had the best of both worlds. Of *all* worlds.

I grew up in the foothills of the Blue Ridge Mountains. I lived my life close to the earth and generally went barefoot because my good shoes were saved for school and church. When the weather turned bad, I wore the older scuffed-up pairs with their worn-over heels so long as I could squeeze my feet into them. My daddy worked hard at various jobs. Momma clipped coupons, and she canned food, some for us and some to sell. We didn't have extra cash, yet I never went hungry and didn't understand that we were poor until I was nearly grown.

My parents were loving, and I adored them. Our small family dwelled amid the rolling hills and shady, winding roads and dark creeks of my hometown of Cub Creek. On clear days we might catch glimpses of the distant mountains in the gaps between the hills and trees around us. And whether the view was of nearby hollows or far-off mountains, they looked like snippets of fine-art watercolor paintings. The beauties of this landscape were like gifts sent straight to the soul. My life satisfied my heart.

Harder realities intruded in my life as I grew older, but even so, I was happy until I lost my parents.

At the time, I was eighteen and of legal age, and so I simply stayed where I was, grateful to have our family home and able to manage on my own. But it was lonely. I tried marriage once. Big mistake. I didn't like to talk about Joe and me, except when cautioning a friend or coworker on the verge of making the same error. Marriage never fixed what was already wrong in a person's life. You were just adding someone else's miseries to your own. My momma taught me not to act in haste. To think things through before making big decisions like marriage or anything else. Better to be alone than stuck with the wrong person or an unfortunate outcome. The one time I didn't heed her advice, it derailed my peaceful life for a while.

Momma had a wealth of cautionary tales that she happily shared with me throughout my growing-up years, all accompanied by appropriate expressions of sympathy or amazement. I'm sure some of her stories came to her from her mother, and I'd added a few new stories to the mix in my turn. My favorite thing was to share them when it was my turn for storytelling at the local library. I had a flair for it, like I was born for it.

Momma and I were often teased about our inability to speak without moving our hands, and even our bodies. We laughed about it many times. Momma said it was part and parcel of the same thing. It was story. It was life.

I knew countless folks in and around Cub Creek. Living in a small town in the country meant we knew a lot about each other's current events and family histories—sometimes too much. It was nearly impossible to keep a secret. All things considered, I had lots of friends, but of the friendly variety rather than super close. I could be friendly with most anyone, but I was a close friend to few.

After I lost my parents, the next twenty years had passed with little change except for my brief adventure into my ill-fated marriage. I always assumed a better future lay ahead, that someday a really good job would come along or I'd find love with a man who could stay employed and encourage me in the things I valued. It wasn't until I met Ms. Susan Biggs on that June afternoon that I had to open my eyes and admit I was mistaken about all sorts of things, including those assumptions.

The earlier excitement I'd felt when Ms. Biggs had offered me that job at the beach warred with aggressive second-guessing. I carried a glass of iced tea out to the backyard and sat by the cold ashes of the firepit. It was June and too hot for a fire, but I could cherish the breeze that rustled the leaves in the forest around me as it rushed up the knoll to finally hit the clearing. It brought freshness, and sometimes fresh thoughts.

I had asked myself over and over what had possessed me to agree to this madness. As I sat there, the back of the white clapboard house two stories high was before me. My dad's huge wood and metal patchwork shed stood behind me. Was I trapped or protected? I'd be a fool to leave. And yet . . . there was a world out there. I'd like to see more of it than just Cub Creek and Asheville.

And I continued asking myself that and similar questions later that evening as I sorted through my clothing with packing in mind.

Jeans, T-shirts, shorts—all of it well worn. My pink terry robe looked almost new. It had been a gift from Aunt Molly. It would cover my mishmash of worn-out nightwear in case Mr. Dahl had night-wandering issues.

Per Gwen, Mr. Dahl was ninety, but he was in good shape for his age. When I mentally replayed my conversation with Ms. Biggs, I realized she hadn't specifically said all that much about him. She had been more focused on me. But if I got there and found I'd been misled in any way, I'd exit ASAP and Susan Biggs could deal with it, inconvenient or not. Another odd thing was that she was listed on her card as a business manager. What did that mean? Was that like a CPA? Or maybe a business agent for like an actor or such? If Mr. Dahl was ninety, then he'd had this daughter pretty late in life, because she was fifty at least, gray or not.

Suddenly filled with another rush of doubts, I sat on the edge of the bed and the neat piles of clothing toppled. And then I had a thought, like one of those little gifts you get sometimes. I slipped from the bed down to the floor and dug deep under the mattress.

It was still there.

Thirty years or so. Not the same mattress, of course, but when I'd gotten this one, I'd stowed the map back under it, for memories and old times' sake. Slowly and carefully, I unfolded the old, creased paper and spread it out on the floor. I traced the highway lines from Cub Creek to Richmond and down to North Carolina and the ocean.

I probably needed a new mattress. For certain sure, I needed an updated map. Because I was going. Doubts or not. But first I had to take care of a few things.

CRBSO

Joe ran an auto shop out of his garage, a freestanding three-bay building he'd had built years ago, and he was making a surprisingly good living with it. The next day after work, I drove over and explained I was taking a trip.

"Where to?"

"The Outer Banks. Per the map, it's way down at the end. A place called Emerald Isle. I've never been to the beach before."

He was bending into a car's engine, finishing up whatever he was doing. He glanced over to where I was leaning against my car. "Wow. Nice vacation."

I was struck again by how inviting his brown eyes were. Had good hair, too, and had kept in shape. Most of the time he was well intentioned. But he wasn't someone a body could count on for more than an oil change or so.

Shrugging, I said, "Well, it's a working vacation, but you know how it is."

"Indeed I do. We find our fun as we can." He wiped his hands on an orange rag. "But there's worse places to go, work or not."

"I know that's true." I laughed.

I touched the hood of my car and gave it a soft pat. It didn't look like much, but the day Aunt Molly gave her to me, I nearly fell over crying in gratitude. I'd driven Dad's old truck until it flat-out died and then had to plunk down money I didn't have for a used car that cost me still more in repairs to keep it on the road. The last time Joe had fixed that car, he'd warned me it was at its end. So getting Aunt Molly's car, old or not, was a blessing. I'd done my best to keep it in good working order, even over letting other things, like my home AC, go. Sweating was free, but food and shelter weren't, and without the car, I couldn't get to work to earn money.

"Is she in good enough shape to make the trip?"

"I'll take a look soon as I finish up here. How's that sound?"

"Thank you. You're a good friend."

"As are you, Lilliane." He smiled one of those slow, lazy grins he was known for. Always gave my heart a tiny thump before my memories kicked in to restore my good sense.

"Think I'll wait out on the porch."

"Nice breeze today. House is unlocked. Help yourself to something from the fridge, if you care to. I'll get right to work on the car."

He checked the tires and oil and such, and he did it for free, while I rocked and dozed on his front porch. Finally, he gave the verdict. "I believe she'll do fine. Just don't push her too hard."

"Thank you, Joe."

"Happy to help, Lilliane. If you need anything else, let me know."

"Will do," I said with a goodbye wave. Joe had a good heart, but he was a much better friend than he'd ever been a husband.

I dropped by the library to speak to Debra. I found her over in the children's section tidying up. This was my favorite part of the whole place. Every month or so, I took a turn at the children's story hour, but instead of reading to them, I took them on fanciful trips of spoken words.

"I'll be gone for a couple of weeks. A job, actually."

"Out of town?"

"At the beach, in fact. Outer Banks." Hearing myself say the words was starting to feel more normal.

"How exciting."

"I expect to be back before the next story session."

"We'll figure it out if you aren't. The kids, and more than a few parents, will miss you, but the new experience will do you good. Put your mind to having a wonderful time." She laughed. "And you can tell us fabulous stories about it when you return."

Gwen dropped by during my Thursday shift at the Fuel Up Fast and waited. After I finished up with my customer, she came to the counter. She was smiling big-time and holding a camera.

"This is for you to take to the beach. It's an older camera. I don't use it anymore." She pushed it into my hands. "You can keep it."

"I don't know how—"

"It's easy. You can't change the lens, but it does telescope." She took it back into her hands to demonstrate. "And here, on the side, is where the memory card goes in." She flipped open the little door on the side and pushed the card to show how it came out and went back. "This card is empty now and will hold a bunch of images. You turn the camera on right here."

"It's digital, Gwen. I appreciate your kindness, but not only do I not know how to use it—"

"You'll figure it out. It's easy."

"But I don't have a computer that I can download the pictures to."

"Don't worry about that either. Just take the photos. I'll help you get them downloaded when you return. You'll be so glad you did."

"My phone will take photos."

"You mean that it *can take* photos, but you don't bother with it, do you?"

I shrugged. "The picture quality is poor. Plus, it burns up my battery in nothing flat."

"Then do this. Take this camera and use it with my blessing."

Her earnestness melted my resistance. "Okay. Thank you."

She said, "If you need me, you call anytime, day or night. But you won't because you are going to have the best time of your life."

CRSO

Hal gave me my last paycheck on Friday before the workday was done. "I thought you might need the cash for your trip," he said. "I wanted you to have your check in time to run by the bank." He added, "I paid you through tomorrow, but Ann here has volunteered to cover for you."

Ann grinned. "You'll need tomorrow to finish packing and such."

"You can't do that, Ann. You have your own obligations."

"No worries," Hal said. He lowered his voice. "She's getting paid too. The owners just wanted to give you that day's pay as a bonus."

"Wow. Okay, thanks, y'all."

Hal threw in extras, including some bottles of water and a bag of pretzels for the trip. "Important to stay hydrated when you're traveling, Lilliane." He handed me one last thing, a bottle of sunscreen. SPF 30. "Make sure you use it," he said. "You're not used to the beach. Sun's different there. Stronger."

"Thank you so much, Hal."

"Come visit when you get back. Tell me how it went."

He smiled, and his cheeks went a little pink. "If I can get the owner to up the payroll, maybe we can bring you back on board."

"Will do. Thanks for the water and snacks."

"My pleasure."

On Saturday, I carried my dieffenbachia over to my neighbor's house. It was a bit of a stroll back down the dirt road lugging the plant that had once been small and now wasn't. I was near to regretting not driving it over to Patsey's house, but then I would've missed the walk. Her house was tucked back a ways into the trees, just as mine was. I loved the walk, the trees, the birdsong—all that went with it—and today, if felt poignant saying a temporary farewell to the landscape of my life.

When Patsey answered the door, I held the pot out and asked her to water it for me. "I'll be gone two weeks. Do you mind?"

She seemed surprised, but why not? I never went anywhere. She took my plant and asked where I was going.

"To the beach," I said.

"Yeah? I've been to the beach. My in-laws take us along every August for their week at Sandbridge. Course that's in Virginia, but when it comes to sand and waves, a beach is a beach is a beach. You'll love it. Make sure you bring a good sunscreen. And a hat." She set the plant on the end table, saying, "Hold on." She dashed off.

She was back in a quick minute waving a straw hat at me. "This'll keep that sun off your head." She set it carefully on top of my hair and clapped her hands, saying, "It's perfect." She took hold of my shoulders and turned me around to face the wall mirror. "Did you know how good you look in hats?"

My protest rose automatically, but I squelched it. Patsey was right. I did look good in a hat. Who knew?

I thanked her, saying, "I'm all set now, I guess."

"You betcha. Go have fun, Lilliane. Have fun for all of us."

CRITO

Before leaving early Sunday morning, I did the usual house check that everyone everywhere does when leaving home for a trip—making sure the windows were closed, with no toilets left running or burners burning. I loaded the car, then went out back to the shed.

Dad's shed. His workspace. It was space Dad had cleared in what had been our old barn-shed and he'd done whatever was needed to keep it standing and dry inside. I pulled the tiny key from my necklace pendant and unlocked the padlock. It had been a while since I'd looked in here. More than a while. I had chosen to leave his old workshop and projects mostly undisturbed. As a result, the smell was musty, heavy with the accumulation of dusty years.

I stood in the doorway with the daylight behind me, my shadow stretching ahead and merging into the dark interior. The only lights inside were the reflections off the metal surfaces. I'd seen enough. All was as it should be. I slid the large metal door closed again, fitted the hasp and reinserted the lock, and pushed it until it clicked. Carefully, I tucked the key back into the pendant holder. The key was small, easily lost, and the last one I had.

All would be fine, I told myself. I'd only be gone for two weeks. Hopefully, Mr. Dahl would be as billed—independent and only needing someone around. A companion. With plenty of time for myself, I'd have some fun and make good money while doing it.

I'd make fine memories, too, to bring back home with me.

After one last check of the house doors—*Yep, they're still locked*—I headed for Short Pump. All the stores anyone could ever hope for were located there. One of those stores would have a swimsuit that would fit even me.

Why? Because I need one.

Why? I asked myself again for no better reason than to hear my inner voice speaking the answer and feeling that delicious excitement—*Because I am on my way to the beach.*

CHAPTER TWO

As the miles rolled away between Virginia and North
Carolina, the annoying Ms. Biggs started calling. Finally, I
pulled over at a rest area near the state line to park before
calling her back.

"I'm on my way," I said.

"You didn't answer. I was concerned." She sounded on
edge.

"No need to worry. Had to wait until I could get off the
road."

There was a long, silent moment. I knew she was doing
that thinking thing again.

I explained, "Had to pull over to make the call. No
Bluetooth."

"Of course. I didn't think of that." Her tone was
changing as the edge in her voice softened. "I'm in a
scheduling crunch, so I do need you here tomorrow morning
promptly, as we discussed."

"I understand. I'll be there. If there's any kind of
problem, you'll hear from me immediately."

"Excellent."

We muttered quick goodbyes and disconnected. After a
trip into the building for the restroom and a short delay to
check out the array of slick, colorful brochures about places
to go and sights to see—because I might get to take another
trip sometime—I was back on I-95 in no time.

CRSO

Coming from Cub Creek where the forests overarched

everything—whether a cleared field or a curvy road—the first thing I noticed about the inland coastal area was the light. Bright light. Light with the strength of the sun and tinted by the blues of the ocean, though the ocean was still miles away.

In Cub Creek, it was the trees that folks noticed most. The smell of the leaves and the wood, both living and decaying, scented the air. The deep shadows beneath the ancient oaks and swaying pines gave atmosphere. The leaves in spring could ache your heart with that new green that was so sweet, so vibrant. Those same leaves could charm you in autumn with their crisp, clean textures in the colors of pumpkins and cranberries.

But here, soon after I left the interstate and headed east, I knew I was nearing the ocean long before I reached it. The land flattened, and the light swelled to fill all the open spaces. There were trees, yes, but they were lower and looked different, less noticeable, as the blue sky and the strong, clear light filled up all the space a person's eyes could take in.

I'd dismissed the suggestion that I'd need sunglasses, counting it an unnecessary expense. Now I understood.

As I waited in a small traffic jam to cross a high-arching bridge ahead, I noticed the car was running a little hot. I turned off the AC and rolled down my window. Heat rushed in, but it felt good and I breathed it in. I smiled, feeling like the top dog—the one whose nose always pokes out the half-open window, beating out the lesser members of the pack. I aimed my nose at that blue sky and breathed in again. Not a greenery smell. It was a smell of heat. Of salt. I came from a land of fresh water only. The difference between them was apparent in the air around me.

Suddenly thirsty, I grabbed the open bottle of water, one of those that Hal had given me, and took a long drink. Anxiety? Yeah, maybe some. Crossing that bridge might be a sort of point of no return. A not-coming-back kind of thing. The city of Atlantic Beach was on the far side, and I could hardly wait.

I laughed at myself, took another deep breath, then noticed the car in the lane next to me.

That car, also waiting, was dark blue and with such a high sheen that it was almost blinding. The person in the passenger seat was a young woman. She was wearing dark sunglasses and turned toward me. I couldn't see her actual eyes, but I felt them. On me. Dismissing me. On my car. She would be able to see the left front fender, and she'd see the dents and dings. Even the *s-h* of the word that Tammy's son had carved in the paint.

Tammy lived down the road on the other side of Patsey's house. When I'd complained, she'd been real apologetic about it. Embarrassed, too, but mostly because she had to admit they couldn't afford to get the scratches fixed. She had a marker, though. Not quite burgundy, but close. Together we'd colored in the scratch. Didn't fix it, but it seemed to diminish the obviousness of it somewhat. Maybe. But in this bright light? With no shade or leafy filters? That woman, behind her dark glasses, wouldn't have to use much imagination to figure out what Junior's new word of the week had been. And to understand his lack of respect for private property. Poor people's private property, that is. Junior would never be allowed anywhere close to rich people's property.

So, it was what it was. I refused to act like anything was different about my car than hers. Both cars had four tires and a working motor. What else mattered?

The traffic began moving. Her lane moved first and faster. Thank goodness.

Two weeks, I reminded myself. *Only two.*

Make the most of it. Enjoy it. Don't waste time or energy on what is different between my life and anyone else's. I'd never been a negative or jealous person, and I wasn't planning to start now.

CRICO

Had I been fearful that Ms. Biggs would choose to put me in a high-rise hotel with confusing concrete parking garages? Maybe, but there didn't seem to be many of those. As I drove through Atlantic Beach, lots of stores, shops, and restaurants lined Fort Macon Road. Bogue Sound was to my right, and the ocean was a couple of blocks over to my left, and both were mostly out of view. What I saw from the main road were condo buildings and houses. I kept my attention on crosswalks, stoplights, and traffic as I drove through. I was headed beyond Atlantic Beach. The hotel where Ms. Biggs had made a reservation for me was in a place called Pine Knoll Shores. My eventual destination, Emerald Isle, was a few miles more. I wouldn't be going there until the morning.

I found the hotel without difficulty. It had multiple stories—six or so, depending upon whether you counted the ground floor. I spied views of the ocean beyond. But the parking was just a normal, paved lot, and I sighed in gratitude.

I'd never stayed in a hotel before. People could laugh, but it was true. When I walked into the lobby, it appeared pretty grand to me. And clean. Families were walking through, and everyone looked happy. The man at the desk had my reservation. He said it was already paid for and gave me a key and a bottle of water. *Nice.* I'd add it to my stash.

"Fourth floor?" I asked.

"Yes, ma'am. The elevators are just around the corner. Our dining room opens at seven a.m. for breakfast and serves until ten a.m. This ticket is for a complimentary meal tonight and another for the morning."

"Seriously?"

"Yes." He smiled. "If you need anything else, please let us know."

I might not have stayed in a hotel before, but I knew enough to understand that the meal tickets were extras, and Ms. Susan Biggs had paid for them. I appreciated that.

I'd brought two tote bags inside with me, and now I carried them to the elevator. The floor had wet, sandy patches left behind by small feet, and I was excited. I should've asked the man at the counter the most direct route to the beach.

Fourth floor. I double-checked the room number, and when I opened the door, I stood, transfixed. I had a balcony and a view of the ocean stretching away into the distance as far as the eye could see.

I dropped my bags and went straight to the sliding door and opened it. The wind blew in carrying the scents of the ocean. I nearly tripped over the threshold in my hurry to get to the railing.

The ocean was blue. Or gray. Or blue-green. It kept changing as the whitecaps rode the waves to shore. I could also see a gorgeous pool directly below. Chairs and tables were arranged around it. A few were occupied. There was also a long wooden walkway from the pool area that crossed over the dunes and grasses. Then the sand. Then the ocean.

The hot breeze brushed my face. Holding tightly to the railing, I closed my eyes and felt the cooler threads of ocean air woven in among the warm.

I could hardly believe my luck.

As I changed from my jeans to shorts, got my flip-flops from my bag, kicked off my sneakers and slid my feet into them, I was finally noticing the room. The huge bed had a fine-looking spread and big fluffy pillows, and the bathroom was big and bright.

I shoved the room key in my pocket and took a long drink of water before setting the bottle aside. I didn't want to be burdened with hanging on to it. I checked my pockets for hair ties, then said aloud, "Here I come, ocean."

First time.

The words rang in my head like a kid's song. I added silly lyrics, thanking Ms. Susan Biggs, who, whether she realized it or not, and overbearing or not, had set me up in the perfect room.

I danced down the hallway. Instead of waiting for the elevator, I skipped down the stairs. I found the way out with no trouble, and there was the pool and a gate, and next I was crossing that wooden walkway. All new. All first time. As soon as I hit the sand, I took off my flip-flops and secured them to my belt loops with hair ties.

The sand beneath my feet felt glorious. I'd walked barefoot most of my young life and a goodly bit of my adult years. But this sand was sun-drenched, not rich earth. The grains slipped and slid, hot beneath my feet, shifting like a living thing, until I reach the cool, damp part. The ocean was rolling toward me, the swells crashing and then rushing forward as they thinned to delicate fringes trimmed with bits of foam, ending moments before they reached me. I backed away, totally eager, but also fearful.

Around me, a few solitary folks were sunbathing or passing by. I edged a few steps closer to the water, noting the little clear bubbles that emerged from the sand. What were those about? Small birds with stick legs and twiggy feet left prints as they moved away from me. Step by step, I moved closer as the waves rolled toward me until those foamy fringes touched my toes. I tingled. A new wave rushed in over my feet and pulled the sand from beneath, and I stumbled backward.

And there were shells. All sorts of colors and shapes. Many broken, but beautiful still. I felt like a kid, plucking a purple one from the sand, brushing at it, rinsing it. I followed a wave out to grab a shell that was just in sight, but the next wave came in quicker than I'd judged, and suddenly my shorts were wet. I jumped back, laughing as another, bigger wave followed it.

Thus did I spend my first visit to the ocean.

I would never forget this. Never. The next time my turn came to stand before the children at the library and tell them stories, I'd remember this. The giddiness of it. The newness. My arms waving in alarm as if I might take flight and the little birds watching me curiously—I would tell them about this experience.

Suddenly, I missed them all. I missed my people, the ones I would've run into at the grocery store or at work or at the mailbox row on our little road and would've paused for a chat or a longer conversation. Not because I was lonely but because I wanted to tell someone about all this. To share this mystery and the wonder of it that none of the people passing by or lounging in the sand around me now would understand. To them, it was ordinary. So I kept the nearly overwhelming sense of it—while it was still new and glorious—close inside me and felt it warm me throughout. I'd save the feelings in my heart and brain and share it later when I got home. I'd tell them about this adventure and make it live for them too.

After a long walk up and down the beach, and with handfuls of shells collected and piled beside me, I stretched out on the dry sand, my arms back behind my head, and watched the sun go down. I'd never seen such an unfettered horizon. Back home the trees hid that meeting line between land and sky. I watched the light clouds shift and the color streak around the sky in ribbons of pink and lilac as banks of clouds began to gather. It left me breathless.

Before full dark, I brushed the sand off my arms and legs and returned to the hotel. The sun sets late in June, and the restaurant looked like it was wrapping up service. I asked at the desk if I could get food to go.

He offered me a menu. "You can tell me or order from your room and we'll bring it up."

I gave him my order and my room number.

I could learn to like this. A lot.

When my meal arrived, I sat on the balcony with my feet up—soles bare to the night breeze—and ate my grilled cheese and fries high above the sandy beach, suspended somewhere between the night full of stars and the dark Atlantic beyond.

CHAPTER THREE

It was Monday and I was due at the Dahl house by ten a.m. Not having GPS, I was relying on the paper map—a new one I'd bought for this trip. I checked it again before leaving the hotel. The best route to Mr. Dahl's home was simple and straightforward—directly west. Bogue Banks was actually an island where the main roads ran east–west, instead of north–south like most of the Atlantic coast. The island was connected to the mainland at each end by a bridge. I had arrived at the east end when I crossed over to Atlantic Beach. I'd spent the night about halfway along the island in Pine Knoll Shores. Mr. Dahl's house in Emerald Isle was west of that. In fact, if I missed the turn into his subdivision, I'd know soon enough because—per the map—I'd run out of road and dry land.

My plan was to arrive at the house promptly, meet Mr. Dahl, and get this job off to a good start. I'd chosen to wear my khaki pants and a nice button-down shirt, hoping to look reasonably professional.

Despite being morning, the day was heating up, and the humidity was already thick. Even so, I kept the car AC off because the motor had run a little hot on the trip down. Ms. Biggs had sounded nervous on the phone yesterday, and I didn't want to take a chance on a breakdown. It was only a few miles to the subdivision. My hair was pulled back in a ponytail, so no worries about the wind from the open window making a mess of it. This was the height of the beach season, and the traffic was heavy in places, so I tried to focus on the road and not be distracted by the coastal landscape and the colorful rental homes and duplexes.

As I passed the more commercial area, the road changed. Instead of the straight-as-an arrow road I'd driven on through most of Bogue Banks, now it was curvy and winding, with trees and green foliage crowding on both sides. Made me feel almost at home. When I spied the classy-looking sign set in a low stone wall I knew I'd found the right place—Sunset Shoals. The entrance was framed by deep-green shrubbery and overarched by low, reaching trees,

Live oaks. Imagine me knowing the name of those trees. Must've seen them on a TV show. Probably one of those reality shows about buying houses at the beach.

I turned onto the narrow road. It was nicely paved with asphalt but unmarked by traffic lines, which, to me, screamed *private*. A small guardhouse came into view. The narrow road circled around it, offering the chance to turn around and go back. I stopped at the guardhouse, a little nervous. Susan hadn't mentioned this. What if the guard took one look at my car and refused to let me in?

He did look—at me, the car, and I was certain his gaze paused on that gift from Junior.

"My name is Lilliane Moore. I'm here to see Mr. Dahl."

"ID, please?"

I fished my driver's license from my purse. He examined it, looked at me, then looked at a clipboard. "Yes, ma'am." He made a checkmark and flashed a smile, then returned my license along with a cardboard pass. "Keep this on your dashboard. Drive straight ahead. You'll come to the houses. The house numbers are clearly marked, but if you aren't sure or get turned around, come back here and I'll help you figure it out."

"Thanks." I drove forward, somehow feeling validated. The man had been nice, respectful. It felt like a good start.

⊂⊱⊰⊃

The road ran back, picturesque and overshadowed by

the numerous live oaks with homes set like postcard views among them. This was a coastal woodland, a forest of low, contorted tree trunks that thinned as I drove. They were twisted and hugging the ground as if trying to crawl away from the ocean. Not just windblown, but wind-blown-over. Clearly healthy, though, since they had plenty of leaves and handsome bark. Ocean winds had sculpted these trees over decades, perhaps centuries.

Then the trees thinned out significantly—the beach was near—and I saw houses ahead. Large homes with fences or walls and tall plantings between them.

I don't know what I'd expected. Not this.

All of the houses looked huge to my eyes. When I arrived at the house number Ms. Biggs had given me, I stopped the car for a moment before pulling into the driveway. Because of the multistory stuccoed walls, the tall fences, and the mature landscaping, I couldn't see the ocean, but the house must have quite a view from the back side. Did one old man live here alone?

The driveway widened into a concrete parking area—pristine concrete with no oil spots. I hesitated. My car didn't belong here. I didn't either.

There she was, Ms. Susan Biggs, closing the front door behind her and hurrying down the steps. Lots of steps. The house was raised. I'd heard of that. The area under the house was used for parking and whatnot. Couldn't see that from here because of the false ground-level panels—breakaway walls, that was it—that would give way without causing structural damage, in case of flooding.

Ms. Biggs had exchanged her blue pants and blazer for a paisley dress and heels. The paisley was nice enough but lacked the flair of the blue. As she rushed over, I briefly imagined throwing the car into reverse and driving off. I didn't. I shifted the gear to *P* and called out through my open window, "Where should I park?"

She gestured toward the garage. I pulled in and found a

spotless room. One other car—a very shiny, expensive one—was parked there. Otherwise, it was almost empty. Of anything.

The next little while was a blur of me apologizing for the oil spots that would shortly mar Mr. Dahl's garage floor, Ms. Biggs remarking that it didn't matter, but that I was lobster-red and she couldn't believe I was driving without AC, and throwing in snippy remarks that indicated she'd been worried I wouldn't show and was now maybe a little sorry I had. By her facial expressions, I could see she was doubting the whole arrangement. There was a sharp edge to her tone and gestures, and my own temper was feeling frayed.

It got worse when I climbed out of the car. Sweat stains were blooming through my blouse and khaki pants. The creases from where I'd been sitting in the car were deeply wrinkled and damp. Impossible to ignore. The wet clothing was sticking to my skin. I resisted tugging at the fabric.

With dignified composure, I said, "I'd like to freshen up before meeting Mr. Dahl."

That seemed to calm her.

"Excellent idea. Do you need help with your suitcases?"

"No suitcases. Bags. I can manage them." I grabbed my tote bags. "I'll come back for the rest later."

I don't know that I'd ever seen such dismay as I witnessed in Ms. Susan Biggs's face as she stared at my tote bags. Not plastic. I was at least that much aware when it came to ecology. These were reusable fabric bags I'd collected from various vendor giveaways through the years. I stared back.

She said, "Come with me."

Ms. Biggs led me along a dark interior hallway and into a gorgeous kitchen of light and glossy surfaces that proclaimed *clean* in near angelic tones. I wanted to ask questions and touch the stone counter and the stainless appliances and look in the cupboards, but she was talking as we walked and never paused in her stride. Her heels clicked lightly on the tile floors as she moved, like a tap-tap beat that I had to match. I wanted to look around. But I was equally glad she kept me in motion. I was rather anxious, myself. Totally uncharacteristic for me. A first trip to the beach was one thing, but it was obvious that now I was in over my head. Out of my depth. No way that my toes could touch bottom here. Swimming references and clichés circled in my brain like song lyrics you hear and then can't shake. *Ugh.* I was losing my mind.

"The foyer is this way."

Suddenly we were in a large oval room—larger than any foyer I'd ever stood in except at Biltmore. As we turned toward the stairs, Ms. Biggs gestured to the left, saying, "Mr. Dahl's study," and then led me up the wide stairs.

No carpeting here or anywhere. Large tile on the foyer floor and rich, dark wood on the stairs and in a living room and dining room that opened off it. The handrail was smooth as silk. I gripped it firmly because the generous proportions of the stairway and even the treads sort of threw my balance off. Ms. Biggs went directly to the only open door in the hallway. It was near the head of the stairs, with only the railing between.

"This will be your room. It's the most central guest room to wherever Mr. Dahl might be." She gestured toward the railing. "You'll have an easily accessible view of the foyer and the study doors below from up here. You can see or be there immediately, should you need to." She gestured toward the open bedroom door and invited me in.

She said, "Mr. Dahl should be home in about thirty minutes. I'll introduce you to him and then be on my way."

"Which room is his?"

"Not up here. He moved down to the main floor last year. His bedroom adjoins his study."

She started to leave the room. I touched her arm.

"Wait, please, I have questions. For instance, what does

43

he like to eat? I can cook, but maybe not what he's accustomed to. What medications does he take? Is there a list of emergency contacts? Doctors?"

She gestured toward a desk on the far side of the room. "That's all in the folder. As far as meals go—and grocery shopping, for that matter—leave that to Bertie. She cooks his meals and leaves instructions for final preparation. She knows there are two of you to cook for now. You'll follow the prep instructions she leaves and perform the cleanup after. Please add anything to the grocery list that you need, and she'll get it when she goes shopping."

"You haven't said where you're going. Will you be reachable in case of emergency?"

"I'll be reachable, yes, but I'm not your first call. My assistant's number is on the first page in the folder. Please read through the folder carefully." She pointed toward a door. "Your bathroom is there. Meet me downstairs as soon as you can."

CRSO

Nice bathroom. Plenty of counter space, and everything, including the floor, was shiny, but nothing was personal—rather like the bathroom in the hotel.

I splashed water on my face and patted it dry. I tried to refold the hand towel so that it looked unused. I told myself I was being foolish. As I ran a brush through my hair, I considered the strangeness of this situation.

Being a companion or an aide for an elderly family member like my great-aunt was different. No special clothing had been required. No nicey-nice manners were needed. Just love and respect and a desire to be helpful. Seemed to me that should hold true for Mr. Dahl too. But Aunt Molly had lived in a regular home—not a huge place like this—and she'd loved me. These people didn't know me.

I could hardly blame Susan for her reaction. But she'd

better not be thinking I'd misrepresented myself as some sort of super-duper home-healthcare professional. Because if she did, we were going to have words.

Susan. Hah. For the first time, I'd thought of her as *Susan*—without the surname. *Good.* I was finding my way. Maybe Ms. *Susan* Biggs was a little less intimidating now.

I tried to hurry as I shook out my clothing from the bags. Everything would be fine on the bed for now—and an amazingly inviting bed it was. I could hang and fold the clothing later. Aunt Molly's flowered skirt—practically unworn when she'd given it to me or since—didn't look too wrinkled. The gathered skirt disguised a lot of travel rumples and went well with a yellow sleeveless shell. With my sandals, I'd do. I stripped off my wrecked shirt and pants and donned the skirt and top. I checked my appearance in the full-length mirror. *Good enough.*

When I left the room, I paused to look over the railing. The stairs were directly below me, as well as a good view of the huge foyer below. There were other doors up here on this floor, all closed. One of the doors was quite large, and I was stunned to realize it was an elevator. An actual elevator. In a house. But there was no time to investigate. Susan's shoes were clicking on the tile floor below as she paced the foyer.

"I'm here. I'm ready. Is he home yet?" I asked as I held the railing and descended the stairs.

She gave me a look, and though her sigh was silent, I heard it anyway. Didn't matter. My wardrobe was what it was. I'd done my best. I wasn't buying a whole new wardrobe for a two-week temporary job.

Besides, this was the beach.

"Mr. Dahl's running late, but no worries. He's with a friend who'll see he gets home. I have a flight I must catch. Mr. Dahl understands that you'll be here to greet him when he returns. It's all set, and you have the information. I suggest you review that and familiarize yourself with his habits and with the house while you wait. *But* stay out of Mr. Dahl's study. He's very picky about that. Very protective of his privacy and independence. I hope you'll support him in that. Keep—"

In disbelief, I interrupted. "Are you saying you're leaving this very minute?"

"There's no need for me to stay. You seem capable, and I know Mr. Dahl is." Susan strode right out the front door. I followed. A car was idling outside, the engine running, waiting for her. It looked like one of those hired cars, the fancy kind.

"Wait!" I called after her.

She paused at the foot of the porch steps and looked back up. "I have to get to the airport. Everything is in the folder. If I've omitted anything . . . But I haven't. I'm very thorough. If you have a question that isn't answered, call me if you can't reach my assistant."

I shouted after her, "I'm not sure this is going to work between me and your father!"

She inclined her head as if she hadn't heard me right.

In a more normal voice, I asked, "What if your father hates me?"

"Merrick Dahl isn't my father. He's my client. I'm his business manager. I thought you understood that. Well, I'm sorry for any miscommunication. You'll do fine with him, and he'll be fine, too, as soon as he becomes accustomed to you."

I was nearly speechless. "Miscommunication?"

"No worries, Lilliane. I have full legal authority to hire and fire on his behalf." She started to turn away, then paused. "One thing I'd like to reiterate—you'll see my notes about this in the folder, but just to be clear—the security at the gate and in the neighborhood is usually sufficient to keep trespassers out. Occasionally someone will show up asking to meet him, or pretending they're already friends with Mr. Dahl. Don't allow them into the house or on the property unless you're sure. Always clear it with Mr. Dahl first. When in doubt, call security." She smiled, waved, and climbed into the back seat, and the car drove away.

CRS&O

The open, two-story foyer was the heart of the house. I followed Susan's advice and wandered through the rooms on the first floor. The double doors to the study were closed. Locked? Maybe. I'd been told to stay out, so unless Mr. Dahl told me otherwise, I'd do exactly that. A large, professionally decorated living room was on the opposite side from the study. A formal dining room was situated between the living room and the kitchen.

There was another room on the study side of the foyer, but that door was closed too, so I left it alone. As I followed the hallway from the foyer to the kitchen, I found the elevator, as well as a stairwell that led down to a basement-type area adjacent to the garage. This lower level allowed stairless access to the pool and patio. The access on the main level, with the stairs, was fancier. I wanted a better look outside, but first, I poked through the cabinets in the kitchen. In the fridge, food had been prepared and packaged. Instructions for reheating were taped to the dishes. Over on the counter was a list of grocery supplies and cleaning items. My guess was that Ms. Bertie was a stickler for order. Okay by me. I searched the drawers and cupboards and found pots and pans and dishes and silverware—everything I might need.

Every little noise grabbed my attention. Was Mr. Dahl back yet? Each time, I hurried to the front of the house and saw no one and nothing. I rushed back through the kitchen and out to the driveway. No one.

This constant watch was annoying. Finally, I went upstairs and grabbed Susan's folder and took it out by the pool to read through the information. As eager as I was to see the beach, sitting by the pool would have to be enough until after I'd met Mr. Dahl.

CRIGO

The umbrella-topped glass patio table was mostly in shade but with a lovely breeze, so it was pleasant. I could hear the ocean, even smell the saltiness, but with the fence and the shrubbery I couldn't see it. Rising above that foliage at the back of the yard was a small peaked roof topped by a weathervane.

Have patience, I told myself. I'd go exploring after Mr. Dahl returned. Presumably our meeting would go well, and I'd officially agree to stay. If not, then Susan's day would take a downturn.

I settled at the patio table with Susan's notes and opened the folder.

The pages were closely typed. She must've dictated them and had her assistant type them up, because the image of Ms. Susan Biggs, Business Manager, sitting at a keyboard creating a document like this with its dense paragraphs and extra, unnecessary words just couldn't come together for me.

Reading had never been my strong point. I could manage better now than as a child, but it was far from fun.

I propped my feet up on a patio ottoman. An alert pendant was clipped to the folder. I presumed Mr. Dahl had one too, and I slipped this one over my head and around my neck. One push at his end and it would be buzzing at mine. Flipping through the pages, I scanned the thick blocks of text and bulleted sections. His medication list was short. Not much for his age. Blood pressure pills, a few vitamins and supplements. There was a list of upcoming appointments with his doctor, to the barber for a haircut, and with the dentist for a dental cleaning. There were notes about Ms. Bertie and a groundskeeper and a pool person. *The groundskeeper* . . . I looked around. Nice foliage and hedges and such, but the grassy part was so small it could be cut in a quick minute.

Ms. Bertie appeared to be key to the running of this house. On her two days here each week, she did laundry and housekeeping, food shopping, and meal prep for the week. Susan wasn't joking when she'd said my part of the actual work would be light and easy.

Maybe Gwen was right. This could be good. Two weeks at the beach, and meanwhile my bare feet were propped on the patio ottoman beside this gorgeous table and umbrella, on this lovely terrace and next to this pristine pool. The surface of the water shimmered in the breeze. That same breeze smoothed my hair and cooled my neck. I wiggled my toes and put my head back, the folder on my lap. I moved a hand to secure it lest the breeze disturb it. I closed my eyes and took a deep breath of the fresh air that started in the ocean and crossed the sand and . . .

CR&SO

"Here she is!" a man yelled.

I jumped up too fast. A rush of lightheadedness knocked me back into the chair.

Pressing my fingers to my temples, my forehead, and to the back of my neck, I tried to orient myself. I must've dozed off, and now a strange man was standing here beside me. Must be Mr. Dahl . . . no, not *this* man. He wasn't elderly. Couldn't be more than in his early forties. He'd yelled to someone—*that* must be Mr. Dahl.

Where was he? I struggled to my feet.

The man reached out as if to steady me. I waved his hand away. He had longish dark hair, and he was tall and dressed in a flowery Hawaiian shirt and tan shorts. Definitely not ninety or anywhere near it. His eyes were a light brown. Almost topaz.

Perhaps I was staring. He looked amused. A rude man. But I was lucky. Fact was, anyone could've wandered back here. Thank goodness he wasn't a serial killer—assuming he wasn't.

Another voice—a raspy, cranky one—came from the doorway at the top of the steps. "Sleeping on the job, huh? Already. Hardly arrived. Not worried about making a good impression."

That was uncalled for. I frowned and ignored the man who'd awakened me. Instead, I focused on the wizened creature half-shadowed in the doorway above.

When it came to Mr. Dahl, I might not know exactly who I was dealing with yet, but that worked both ways. He didn't know me either. But he would.

Directing a short, no-nonsense stare back at the dark-haired man with the light eyes, I said, "Excuse me." Leaving him behind, I went up the steps, chasing after my new charge.

I caught him in the hallway.

"Mr. Dahl? I'm Lilliane Moore. Pleased to meet you."

The old man made a rude noise and walked away. The click of his cane on the tile floor was a lot like Susan Biggs's shoe heels tip-tapping. Just slower. Like *Aunt Molly* slower. He disappeared into the shadowed study, and the tapping stopped.

I was surprised to realize I had the folder with me. I pressed a hand briefly over my eyes. I'd been in that bright light by the pool for too long. What time was it, anyway? I didn't pause to check.

I followed him. The other man was somewhere behind us. But he'd been rude waking me like that and putting me at a disadvantage in front of Mr. Dahl. I wasn't giving him any more satisfaction or amusement than he'd already enjoyed at my expense.

He could see himself out.

I wasn't anyone's daggone butler.

Chapter Four

The study doors had opened noiselessly at the old man's touch.

Not locked.

He'd left them open behind him as he went directly to his desk and around to his well-padded leather chair, where he eased himself down.

My eyes were adjusting to the interior light, and I paused on the threshold to get a better look at him. He was olive-complexioned—from many years of sun, was my guess. His thick eyebrows could've overwhelmed his eyes if not for their own dark, piercing quality. I felt that stare even from several feet away. Mr. Dahl was very thin and would've been tall if not for his stooped posture. His hair was thick and gray and neatly trimmed.

The windows in this room were covered by fine sheers over wide-slat wooden blinds, so though the blinds were open, the light was heavily filtered. Mr. Dahl's desk was positioned near the window. Nearby was the usual stuff you'd expect in an office, like a printer and such. In the corner opposite his working area was a round wooden table with three leather upholstered chairs around it. Three of the room's walls were covered by bookcases. Built-in cases of real wood. Not the kind you'd tote home and assemble with a lot of complaining. These bookcases were beauties.

"Don't just stand there," he said. "Come in where I can see you." He added, "Davis? You still here? You can stay or go as it suits you. We're done, aren't we?"

I didn't hear Davis's answer because as I'd stepped onto the carpet, I'd become acutely aware that I was barefoot. I'd left my sandals somewhere, probably out there by the pool. And thank goodness. Because what I felt under my feet was unlike anything I could ever recall. The carpet, in gorgeous shades of blue and aqua and lilac, seemed to go on forever, both wide and deep. In my lifetime, I'd walked on hot roads, sharp rocks, and twigs. I'd walked on springy grass lawns and soft gray dirt that was as silky fine as powder. Yesterday I'd walked on that warm, shifting sand. But the soles of my feet had never experienced this. I'd always heard good padding made all the difference under a carpet, but I'd never tested the truth of it. I held in a long, moaning, *Ahhh,* but just barely.

"What's wrong with you?" he asked. His voice was sharp.

Cranky old man.

That younger man, the one called Davis, was standing nearby and was also staring at me, but with some kind of amusement on his face. When he caught my eye, he made a point of looking down. Did he find my out-of-fashion hand-me-down skirt amusing? No, he was staring at my feet.

My feet were way short of a pedicure, but I'd never worried about having pretty feet before, and I wasn't about to start.

I ignored this incredibly rude man and looked at Mr. Dahl. "Nice carpet."

He frowned, and then his face cleared. "Well, that's a new line. Haven't heard that one before." He waved his hand in a dismissive gesture. "I'll be in touch, Davis."

"Let me know if you need anything, Merrick."

Mr. Dahl nodded. "I hear you."

Davis looked at my feet again and grinned. As he walked away, I noticed that he, too, was barefoot.

I laughed inwardly, silently. Maybe that shirt wasn't so very awful after all. At least it was colorful. On the other hand, the elderly man sitting behind the desk was dressed in a cream-colored suit that seemed like it needed a panama hat to complete it. He was eyeing me like a bad bargain.

"I'm Lilliane Moore."

"So you said. I'm Merrick Dahl. Susan told you that, of course. What else did she tell you?" He was waving those skinny fingered, big-knuckled hands again. "I don't need a keeper. Stay out from underfoot. I have things to do. I'll let you know when I want your assistance."

At first, I felt a surge of anger, but then I thought better of it. Instead, I said, "Excellent, because I've got things to do myself. After all, I've never been to the beach before."

He stared. I didn't blame him. I'd sounded like an idiot, but with a purpose.

I shrugged. "Well, except for yesterday. I stayed at a hotel on the beach last night. For the first time . . ." I heard the genuine excitement creeping into my voice. I couldn't help it. "I walked on the beach."

"You don't say?"

I ignored his mockery. "So if you're good on your own, I might go check out the beach here. See if your beach is as nice as the one I visited yesterday. Do you need anything before I go? Maybe a drink of water?"

He continued staring.

"Well, then, if you're all set, I'll go see the ocean." I turned, doing my best to execute a carefree saunter across that delightful rug, away from him and toward the double doors.

"Where're you going?"

I stopped, but I was grinning inside. Point scored. I half turned back toward him. "Is there something I can get you? Would you like to talk or something?"

"Nah. You'll need the code for the gazebo gate—1120 to exit and enter. Same for the doors that have a key code contraption. Do you already have it?"

I hesitated. My move had been countered.

"My birthday," he added. "To make sure I don't forget it. The code, that is." He cleared his throat. "Pull the gate closed behind you, so no tourists wander in thinking we're some kind of blasted hotel or looking for a toilet."

I pointed toward the door, crooking my arm to indicate a left turn toward the back of the house. "That way?"

"Yes, ma'am. Out back and down the steps. Or take the elevator to the garage level and you can exit that way."

A smile forced its way out. "Thanks. I'll be back shortly."

"Take your time. I'll want supper at six p.m."

"Understood. It will be ready." On impulse, I touched the alert pendant. "I've got this on, in case it's needful."

He grunted. "Better you than me. Never wear the thing myself." Without waiting for my response, he added, "A word of advice. You might want to wear shoes. Those boards get hot."

I laughed politely. "I'll be fine, but thanks." I exited and crossed the foyer to the back hallway—going right back toward the pool area. I presumed the weathervane I'd seen earlier had a gazebo under it, so I'd head that way.

Altogether, I was encouraged. It seemed to me that Merrick Dahl and I had had some sort of meeting of the minds. He was rude, and I was sometimes cranky. I suspected both of us were competitive and could be manipulative—for good purposes, of course. So maybe this arrangement would work between us. Surely we could get along well enough for two weeks.

We could discuss that alert pendant later.

And my new AC? Practically paid for already.

☙

Out the door, then down the many steps to the ground level—and now I was passing beside the pool with it's lovely, very tempting lounging area in the shade of the house where I'd enjoyed my unplanned nap, and next to it was a screened porch area. Beyond me, I could see at the far end of the yard, amid the thick greenery, a gazebo top peeking out.

I picked up my pace.

The gazebo itself was tempting, with seats and a spigot for washing sandy feet, and with the foliage, it had a feel of privacy. The four-foot-high gate had a code box with numbers to punch. A thin, spry adult could've climbed over the gate, or a beefy adult might have been able to knock it down, but that would've been deliberate—not just a stranger hoping to find a shortcut through to the road.

Mr. Dahl had a wooden dunes crossover here too, much like the hotel had, but this was his very own private one that started at the gazebo and covered quite a distance, but it would deliver me directly to the beach. It had a slight rise about midway along. When I stepped past the gate, I saw similar walkways up and down the beach. The landscape they protected looked arid, like small sandy hills dotted with shrubby greenery.

At first, the boards felt warm to my bare feet, but with each step, they grew hotter, and soon I was running along the walkway. *Ouch, ouch, ouch.* Perhaps it was the optimist in me that caused me to quicken my pace instead of turning back to fetch my sandals.

Or pigheadedness.

Mr. Dahl had suggested shoes, hadn't he?

I hoped no one was watching me *ouch* my way along that crossover. If so, they were having a good laugh. When I reached the sand, I kept running. I never paused until I reached the water. I held up my skirt and plunged my feet in, nesting them down into the wet sand.

As my feet cooled, I began to feel vaguely guilty. My sense of triumph at not allowing Mr. Dahl to intimidate me was warring with the very real of responsibility of this job.

Should I have stayed and insisted we chat? I could've hung out at the house until I felt more confident about leaving him alone.

Well, I was here now—only for a few minutes—and the

sand was soothing to my poor feet. I looked both ways. It was a beautiful beach. Only a few people were out here. Weekday? Time of day? The beach stretched in both directions, with nothing to block access that I could see. I'd read in a brochure that Emerald Isle alone had twelve miles of unbroken public beach. Now that was a heck of a morning jog.

Which was definitely *not* my cup of tea.

A woman was lying facedown on a blanket sunbathing, either asleep or oblivious. Down the other way, not too far from me, another woman was seated in a beach chair under a striped canopy and wearing a turquoise straw hat, reading. She must surely have seen my Olympic sprint to the water, but she gave no indication of it.

I turned my attention back toward the vast body of water before me. The Atlantic. And I was standing right here on the edge of it. Life had been growing and thriving in it for uncounted time. In more recent centuries, pirates and explorers had been sailing along these shores, and—considering the span of time—almost a blink of the eye later, there was me. None of them ever imagined that one day a certain Ms. Lilliane Moore of Cub Creek would be cooling her unpolished, unmanicured tootsies in that same water and contributing to a constant restirring of the molecules.

As I stood clutching my dead aunt's skirt up around my thighs to keep it from the waves, I fantasized about adventure and history, while nearby that woman was reading under that canopy, fully dressed and with hardly a bit of flesh exposed. Both of us could probably use some lessons about proper enjoyment of the beach.

I started working my feet loose. This was a beautiful, quiet beach. I missed a little of the raw newness I'd experienced yesterday. The lady under the canopy looked like she relaxed out here regularly. Maybe that's why she'd brought a book along. I'd never understood reading for pleasure. As with jogging, reading wasn't my thing.

As I freed my feet, I moved them in the water to rinse them off, which was pointless, because as I walked away, I picked up more sand. And the woman was suddenly waving at me. Was she waving at *me* or someone else? Or just being friendly?

She called out, "Girl? Over here! Mind giving me a hand?"

Still clutching at my skirt to keep the fabric from touching my wet, sandy legs, I walked to her. As I got closer, it was clear she was much older than I'd thought. Her slacks were rolled up to just under her knees, and her shins and feet were even paler than mine. She was wearing sunglasses, but even so I could see she was at least in her seventies.

In my best customer-friendly voice, I said, "Hello. How are you?"

"I'm fine. I guess I am, anyway. Hard to tell some days."

"Yes, ma'am. I feel the same at times."

"Not likely," she said low and under her breath. More loudly, she added, "Yes, well, I'd like to go home, but I dropped my cane. Also, I need a hand to get up out of this chair. Just a boost. My granddaughter helped me get set up out here, but she's not coming back for a while." She held up the book and glared at it. "Story ended. I tried to slow down the reading, but that last page was done way before I was ready to let it go."

I retrieved her cane and handed it to her. I offered her my hands.

"The sand is the problem, you see. Can't get leverage." She took one of my hands but kept the cane in her other hand. "Just steady me in case the sand shifts beneath my feet."

"Where are your shoes?"

"Up by the path."

She gripped one of my hands, and I put my free hand on her arm, just in case. She pushed down with her cane as she rose to her feet, and the two of us just stood there for a moment. A bit breathless, she said, "I go by the path. Those wooden things get too hot, and the boards try to trip me."

"Hot? No joke. I found that out the hard way."

"I'm good now." She pointed with her cane. "We'll go that way."

We started walking. I presumed someone would come back later for the chair and the canopy.

With a quick side glance, she assessed me. She kept her hand on my arm as we moved through the loose mounds of sand. "I'm out here most days. I haven't seen you. Haven't seen a moving truck either, so you must be here visiting someone."

I started to speak. She shushed me. "Let me guess. Hmm. Let's see. Might you be the Landons' older daughter? She hasn't been to visit since they moved in."

"No, ma'am."

"Well, then, are you Johnny Byrd's stepdaughter?"

"No, again. My name is Lilliane Moore."

"I'm Miranda Wardlaw. Pleased to meet you, Miss Moore."

"Lilliane, please."

"Who are you visiting? Or are you permanent? Or renting for a week? Careful you don't burn. You are always welcome to join me under my canopy."

As we stopped for her shoes, I was prepared to let the conversation end naturally and politely. I could see my way through the dunes to the Dahl house and it was time to get back. The path was a longer route than the crossover to get back to the house, but it would be gentler on my feet.

"Well, I see you looking across the way at Merrick Dahl's house. You mean to tell me that's who you're visiting? He's the most ornery man I know. Just plain, no-excuse-for-it rude. I should ask how closely you're related to him before I say such. Unless you're here as an aide or a nurse, in which case, if you haven't already learned the truth about his dark nature, then you soon shall."

She said it all with such energy, I nearly laughed. I

remembered what Susan had said about how Mr. Dahl didn't want people to know he required live-in assistance.

"So what is it, Lilliane Moore? Are you forced to put up with him by accident of birth or as a means of employment?"

"Accident of birth?" I laughed.

"A niece or a cousin?"

I laughed again. "A very distant cousin."

"Well, one day you'll have to join me on the beach and tell me all about how you came to be spending time with this man. How long are you here for?"

She was certainly nosy. "Two weeks."

"Make sure you have plenty of fun. I can tell you're a sensible, kindhearted woman. You might have to put up with Merrick Dahl, but at least you have a beach to enjoy." She shook her head. "Don't let him monopolize your time. That man can talk like nobody I know—not that I've exchanged words with him in many years. But dogs don't change spots. He'll talk your ear off, or he won't spare a word for you. Wasn't all that sociable before, but hasn't been worth a pin since—oh, here's my granddaughter coming this way." She looked past me and waved. "Isn't she a cutie? Oh, to be eighteen again." She patted my arm and released me. "Thank you so much for your help."

CRLSO

"Where do you prefer to eat?"

He looked up from his laptop to where I stood in the study doorway.

"Kitchen? Dining room? Out by the pool?"

"Bring my food in here."

I pointed at the round table in the corner. "Why don't I set that up for us? We can chat over our meal."

"Chat?" He looked horrified. "Why should we chat?"

"We're going to be spending two weeks together. We should talk a little, at least."

He gave me a longer look. "Why? Didn't Susan's notes tell you what you needed to know?"

Not the reaction I was expecting. I frowned. "Well, I did read through them. I think I got the most important points. But . . . it was . . . dense. Hard to stick with. I was reading it when . . . I fell asleep by the pool."

His chest jolted, and his arms moved in reflex. His cheeks turned pink.

I started toward him thinking the worst, and then I realized, when he started making actual noises, that he was laughing. I waited, truly unsure what to do.

He shook his head. "Everyone's a critic, ain't that right?"

"She meant well," I said. "Some of the stuff in between the important parts . . . I confess I skimmed that."

He laughed louder, and now I laughed too. I couldn't help it. I was so relieved that he wasn't having some sort of seizure, and that maybe there was a real person concealed within that rude persona, someone I might be able to connect with.

"I have to check the oven. Ms. Bertie left chicken with gravy and those small red potatoes. Looks delicious. I'll be back with the food when it's ready." I didn't repeat the suggestion of us sharing the meal at the corner table. I'd just do it and make him kick me out if he felt that strongly about it. I was pretty sure that since he found me so witty, he wouldn't. At least not for this first meal on this first evening.

෴

I returned with the plates and utensils and the first of the food dishes, then went back for the rest. I brought a tall pitcher of ice water, as well as the small glass of wine that Susan had noted in her instructions.

If he usually ate alone, then he might not welcome too much chatter, so I made sure not to talk too much at first. But sitting there politely and quietly when there was a dead-silent living being sitting across from me made me restless and caused my attention to wander. Those bookcases were the most overwhelming thing in the room. Books lined three walls. Books, books, and more books. Some of the bindings looked old, in a dignified way. Some shelves held colorful, dust-jacketed books that seemed more modern. Suddenly a shift in the light caught the spines of those colorful books, hitting one of them just right, such that even from where I was sitting, I could read the name. The book was *Twilight Fire*, and the author's name was Merrick Dahl. I squinted, sure that my eyes must be playing tricks on me.

I glanced at his face. He wasn't looking at me looking at those books, but I knew he was aware of it. I pushed my chair back and walked over to the shelves where the colorful, flashy books were arranged.

Next to *Twilight Fire* was another book, *Moonfire Chase*, by the same author. Merrick Dahl. And others. Several shelves of them.

Turning to face him, I asked, "Are these yours? There isn't another Merrick Dahl, is there?"

CHAPTER FIVE

He didn't answer.

I repeated my question. "Are these your books?"

He lifted his face and met my gaze with his own, very cool expression framed by those bushy eyebrows. "I own them, yes. Do you mean to say, did I write these books?"

"You know exactly what I meant."

"Then you should be more precise in your language."

"I don't know when I've seen someone try so hard to avoid answering such a simple, obvious question." I put my fist on my hip and pointed at the books with my other hand. "That is, unless you happen to have the same name as the author of these books, and you purchased the whole collection to fool people." I said it in a serious way, but of course, I was teasing. I put my finger directly on the spine of one of those books as I silently dared him to warn me about touching them.

Keeping my eyes on him, I slid the book out from between its fellows and flipped to the back cover. I might not be much of a reader, but I'd seen a book or two in my lifetime, and I knew there was usually an author photo on the back of the book jacket. I was all prepared to make a big fuss when I saw the expected glamour shot, but I faltered. The man in the black-and-white photo was decades younger. Half a century, even. He was maybe in his late forties in this photo. There was a distinct Humphrey Bogart look in the pose and in the intensity of his expression.

I looked over at Mr. Dahl and said in a softer tone, "I guess you've been writing a long, long time."

His aloof expression slipped a little. "That is very true."

I held the book in my hands, astounded, not by his apparent fame, but that he'd written a whole book, and he'd done so over and over. "Have they made any movies from your books? Something about the names sound familiar."

"*They* did." He said *they* like he had some specific no-good folks in mind. "Long, long ago."

I retook my seat at the table, still holding the book. "I'm impressed."

"Don't be."

"Are you kidding me? Why not?"

"I wrote because I had to. Story finds expression. That's how it is."

"Don't you need a muse or mermaid or something like that?"

He spit out a little of his wine and grabbed for a napkin. His face turned red. I was trying not to laugh.

He pointed a bony finger at me, jabbing it in my direction. "You said that on purpose."

"I did. I confess. But I am also sincerely impressed. Just sticking with a project"—I flipped through to the end—"for three hundred and fifty plus pages. That takes dedication. Not just because you're *driven* in some way. Easy enough to become undriven by other, shinier distractions. So bravo, Mr. Dahl. How many books have you written?"

"Thirty or so."

"Wow. Are you working on one now?"

"Now? No. I'm old. I haven't been under contract for a new book in . . . I don't know . . . a quarter of a century."

"Why?"

"Pardon?"

"Did you lose interest?"

"I got old."

I made a rude noise. "Clearly, you are still clever enough to write. That said, it's okay to not enjoy doing something anymore. To choose not to do it."

"Oh well, then. Thank you so very much. I was earnestly

hoping to gain your permission to *not* do what I *don't want* to do."

I ignored his tone. "I'm not much of a reader, else I might have recognized your name. But I might give one of the books a try. This looks thriller-ish? Are your books scary or gory?"

"Some think so. I leave it to the reader to decide."

"Mind if I take one to read? Are these like collector's editions or such?"

"You are welcome to *borrow* that book to read, but please *do not* share your thoughts on it with me. Those books are my past."

He sounded less like he was challenging me and more just plain tired.

"And *do not* turn the corners of the pages down to mark your place."

"I'll take good care of the book. As for critiques—as I said, I don't read much, so my opinion would be uninformed. Not helpful." I shrugged and smiled. "Maybe I'll simply enjoy it."

"If not, then you can wait for the movie to rerun for the gazillionth time."

I laughed gently. I stood, placed the book on my seat, and gathered the dishes and assorted trash together to carry to the kitchen.

When I returned, I said, "Would you care for some dessert? Ms. B didn't leave anything specific, but I noticed ice cream in the freezer."

"No, thank you. Help yourself, of course." He rose slowly. I stayed handy, but he didn't need my assistance. "I believe I'll retire early. Watch some TV. Perhaps even read a bit."

"Mr. Dahl, I have to ask you—where do you sleep? Susan said it was down here, but I haven't seen a bedroom. I'd like to know where to find you if you happen to need me."

He pointed toward the fireplace on the right-hand wall.

A door was next to it. Another was on the other side. "That door goes to the hallway and the gym. The other door goes through to my bedroom."

"Gym? In the house? How cool."

"I don't use it. Not in years. Feel free to make use of it, if you like."

"I'll take a look, but I'm more of a doer and not so much of an exerciser." I wiped the tabletop. "You moved down here to sleep because of the stairs? Why not use the elevator?"

"I've lost interest in walking even that far for no better reason than to sleep. Sometimes I don't sleep well and wake during the night. If you hear me rambling about, ignore it. Do not try to babysit me. I get up and do this or that until I'm drowsy again. I suit myself. And I can tuck myself in."

"Mr. Dahl, how late do you usually sleep?"

"What did Susan say?"

"She said you eat breakfast at eight a.m."

"Don't disturb me before nine a.m."

"Yes, sir."

"And don't call me *Mr. Dahl*. If anyone happens to be around, they might think I need a sitter or a nurse. Just call me Merrick."

"Oh, that's good, because I ran into one of your neighbors today when I was down at the beach."

I swear his ears literally perked up.

"I helped her back to the road via a path she showed me. A very nice lady. She asked where I was staying. I'm afraid she guessed here. I told her—we had a bit of a miscommunication—that I was a distant cousin here for a visit."

His mouth twitched up at the corner. Almost a half smile. "Miranda Wardlaw, sounds like."

"Indeed. That's exactly who."

It pleased him to have guessed right. I could see that.

He said, "She's nosy."

"I hope you don't mind the lie. It wasn't intended. As I said, it was a miscommunication, and I let it stand."

"Remember, Ms. . . . Remember, *Cousin* Lilliane, that I wrote fiction for a living. I know all about making things up. Perfectly fine with me, so long as you stick to the facts when it's between the two of us."

"I'll go make some hot tea. Good for the digestion." And I walked out without waiting for him to say he didn't want any. Mr. Dahl—*rather, Merrick*, I corrected myself—as my Daddy would've said, Merrick was prickly, but more gruff and bluster than rough and tough.

I'd already put my personal stash of teas in a corner of the kitchen cabinet over by the fridge. *Momma's tea* was how I thought of it. She'd been a fan of hot tea in fancy cups. Daddy had preferred plain old iced tea. I liked both. For after dinner, hot tea was best. I chose two bags of dandelion tea and two of honey spice. One bag of each went into the cups, and when the water was hot, I poured it in. I put spoons on the saucers, along with two tea biscuit cookies each—my mother's preferred shortbread cookie that she'd called biscuits, always with a pretend English accent. Daddy would say she'd read too many fancy romances. And we'd all laugh.

I carried the after-dinner snack back to his study.

Merrick wasn't there. The door to the room he'd identified as the bedroom was cracked open. I went over to the door and called out, "I have your tea."

No answer. I peeked in. It was a nice room. Paintings and photographs—correction, *photographic works of art*—filled the walls. Several caught my eye, in particular a painting of a woman dancing on the beach in a blur of color and light. Her bare arms, her bare feet, were the most concrete things in the picture and immediately drew the eye. The clothing was a swirl that mixed with the beigy sand and the blue-green water. Aside from the artwork, there were no knickknacks. The furniture was minimal and included an adjustable queen-size bed. Bet that cost a fortune. The room was done up in neutral colors. Pretty bland and anonymous—the only color being in the artwork, and I wondered if that was on purpose. To, in effect, set off the art. There were two doors. One was likely a closet, and the other was certainly a bathroom. Both were closed. I yelled, "I'm taking my tea out to the pool area. I'll leave yours on your desk."

He didn't answer, and I let him alone. I wasn't about to pester an old man going to the bathroom. If he didn't need my help, then he didn't need my conversation at such a time either.

It was warm outside, and still broad daylight, but the patio area was shady, and the cool breeze from the ocean mixed with that of the fresh, chlorinated water of the pool. Altogether it was pleasant, and it smelled clean, for sure. The pool and patio area was large. There were blocks of landscaping nearer the tall white privacy fencing and gazebo. And beyond that, the blue sky stretched forever. If I dragged a chair across the grass to the back run of fencing to peek over, there'd be prime beach and crashing waves. I could see it in my head. Not a bad view, and the sounds of the ocean provided a low background rhythm.

The houses on either side were at an angle, and with the landscaping and fencing, it felt almost totally private. I had to walk well out into the yard to see them. Even then, I could only see the upper levels, and they looked as quiet as this house was.

Day one wasn't quite over, and not even a full day here—which surprised me. It felt like I'd squeezed a lot into a few hours of living. And now I was sitting by the pool, my feet propped up on the ottoman and a book in my hands. I ran my fingers over the title, tracing the raised lettering. I was curious to read the book, as if reading it might give me a sneaky glimpse into my charge's mind.

Reading had never come easily to me. Momma had said that each person came with special gifts and special challenges. Reading was my challenge. I could read, yes, but the idea of pleasure reading had always seemed an oxymoron to me. On the flip side, though, I could tell a whopper of a story. Maybe it would be different reading a book while at the home of the person who'd written it and was even now brushing his teeth and donning his jammies as he prepared for bed.

Even if I didn't like the book, Merrick Dahl would never know. As far as he was concerned, I considered his writing fabulous, and I'd never say otherwise.

I read the author biography first. That was an old photo, for sure. Not strictly handsome in his younger years, but distinctive. And likely demanding. You could tell it by those thick, dark eyebrows and the set of his strong jaw. It seemed strange to be meeting the subject of the photo now for the first time, several decades after this black-and-white image was taken. A huge swath of time accompanied by change. It gave me pause.

Time always passed, with or without you.

He might be a grouchy jerk, but as long as we could get along—and I suspected we'd do fine, based on our short acquaintance thus far—it wouldn't matter. In fact, he might feel the same about me.

I opened the book and skimmed the stuff in the front pages. The dedication mentioned people I'd never heard of. The acknowledgments was the same. Finally, I came to chapter one.

Settling back in my seat, I prepared to dig in. And I did for a short while.

I'd seen action movies, treasure-hunting movies, spy movies, plenty of dramas and romance. I enjoyed a good scary movie or TV show but had no use for horror, likely because I lived alone. But an "action" story was different, especially when it came to reading. I had to reread the first page three times to get a fix on what was happening. Basically, it opened in a city where a guy walks into a restaurant and starts a conversation with another guy, and then the plate-glass windows shatter as something explodes out on the street and the glass shards fly in, impaling . . . I shut the book.

Wow.

I let the words I'd read play out in my head, but as if it were on my internal TV screen. I got my bearings, then tried to read it again, but still no good. I needed a translator—or a movie screen.

Reading for pleasure, they called it. I shook my head.

Persistence. That had been the big message from my teachers. Read more. Keep working at it. *Reading will get easier for you, Lillie. You'll have better comprehension.* I tried harder, and over time my reading skills did improve somewhat. I'd managed well enough in school until my senior year, when I'd dropped out after losing my parents. But it was never fun. I looked back at the colorful cover that promised entertainment.

I needed the movie version.

Determined, I dove back in.

"Your tea is getting cold."

Startled, I jumped, but grabbed the book before it could fall and get messed up.

"Mr. Dahl. Merrick. Did you enjoy the tea?"

He made a noise. I couldn't tell whether the verdict was good or bad. I assumed it wasn't an outright condemnation. He was wearing a navy-blue robe that coordinated with his pajamas and slippers.

"I returned the cup and saucer to the kitchen," he said.

"Would you like to join me here? Or if you'd like something more to drink or a snack . . ."

"Relax. I'm done for the day. If my younger self could witness me saying that at seven thirty in the evening, he wouldn't believe it. You're young. If you want to go out or amuse yourself somewhere, feel free."

"Oh, thank you. I was reading the book, but I might take another stroll on the beach before sunset."

He made another noise. He shook his head. "You have a house key, right? Don't forget the key code for the gazebo gate. Important to lock up. Doesn't happen often, but from time to time some idiot fool will find their way into the yard or the house. Public persons seem to be fair game."

"From fans, you mean?"

"Fans?" He shrugged. "Less so, these days. Mostly it's folks who have a notion to make a buck off me. Maybe writing a magazine article—one of those 'whatever happened to . . .' stories or wanting an endorsement for their own novel. Even after all these years of me being out of the industry, a few people still remember my name."

"Susan Biggs warned me about letting people in the house without your approval. Is that why?"

"Likely. There's still rights available, and occasionally someone wants to do something with them, and they try to go around my agent and get to me directly. I'm old, feeble, and fair game, I guess."

His voice had gone from being a bit puffed with pride to something that sounded forlorn. I decided to offer up a detour.

"Well, you certainly have a lot of experience, so maybe you could help me with something. You may not write new stuff now, but—"

His manner turned harsh as he interrupted. "So that's it. All that stuff about not being a reader and seeming surprised about my books was just a ruse. Keep whatever you were wanting to achieve by being here, all devious and ulterior motives, to yourself. Pack your belongings up and—"

"Whoa." I interrupted him this time. "I don't lie, Merrick. And you can save the outrage, because I don't waste my time or anyone else's with more manipulation than can be accomplished by a pleasant word and a courteous smile." I smiled as if illustrating the word, remembering, as I added, "My mother used to tell me that. I can almost hear her voice again right in this moment as I'm talking about it." I picked up the book. His book. I held it up like a show-and-tell object.

Distraction could be a handy tool. Momma had also told me that.

"I never read for fun. I stopped reading anything optional after I left school. But I *can* read. So I was surprised when I tried your book and it was a no-go. Maybe it's just not my cup of tea . . ." I paused and laughed. "That pun wasn't intended, I promise. But the thing is this—I had trouble sorting out what was happening at the start." I pulled the book closer to me and focused on the cover. It showed a man running, his figure dark with a huge, threatening moon shining down on him from behind.

"All of that action happening right on the first page— was that on purpose? When a show comes on TV, there's promos and glimpses and maybe even an intro that sets the scene before a big boom. But with this, one moment I'm reading the words 'Chapter One,' and in the next instant glass is shredding everything within the blast range."

All I received in response was a blank look.

I shrugged. "Sorry. Stupid question, I guess."

He frowned. He shuffled over to the chair opposite me and sat, still frowning. If movements could be considered grumbly, his were.

My question was sincere, but only intended to divert his mood from slipping further. It hadn't worked, so I was ready to move on. Before I could, he began tapping his fingertips on the glass-topped table. His face looked rather like a thundercloud.

"They say there are no stupid questions." He grunted. "They lie."

My feelings were ruffled after all.

He added, "But that isn't one of them."

"Oh."

"It's actually a worthwhile question, but I don't know how to answer it." Now all his fingers were tapping, beating a soft rhythm against the glass. The movement reminded me of typing or maybe piano playing. When he resumed speaking, I wasn't sure he was actually talking to me. "Is this about writing craft? Writing fashion? *Fashion* meaning that storytelling changes over time in terms of what's considered acceptable by the industry or the audience. Some authors transcend that, usually by some combination of skill, talent, and luck. Most don't. Or is it about the approach to the written form of entertainment versus the silver screen?" He went silent.

He was really enjoying this. Like an old professor too long out of the classroom. I sighed. Too loudly.

Immediately, his gaze shifted and skewered mine.

"Now what? Did you want an answer, or were you just criticizing?"

Goodness, but he was touchy. And behaving badly.

"Actually, I think my question was wrong."

"How so?"

"I'm thinking that the answer was simply that I'm not a thriller kind of gal." I shrugged. "Not the fault of the book or the author or how well it's written. Just not my thing."

"Genre."

"Yes. That's it."

He reached for his book. I grasped it more tightly.

"I'm not done with it yet. If you don't mind, that is. Sometimes things that are new don't seem a good fit at first, but I'd like to give it another try. Persistence, you know."

I thought I saw a glimmer, a connection again, in his eyes. His fingers had stopped tapping, and his shoulders relaxed from their hunched position.

Hugging the book, I asked, "Anything I can do for you before I go down to the beach? I'd like to watch the sun set." I smiled. "Care to come with me?"

"Nah. I've lived at the ocean for too many years for it to be worth the effort."

"Oh." I sighed. "It's all new to me. Yesterday was the

first time. Ever."

He stood slowly, and I walked alongside him until he entered the study.

"Good night, Merrick."

He turned back and gave me a look. He said, "First time at the ocean? You said that earlier. Were you serious?"

"Yes, sir. First time ever to see, smell, or to dip my toes in saltwater or to walk on that shifty sand. Or today, to burn the soles of my feet on that wooden crossover thing."

"Where are you from?"

"A beautiful, shady place just this side of the mountains called Cub Creek."

He grunted in acknowledgment. "You like what you've seen of the ocean thus far?"

"It's amazing."

"Burned feet and all?"

I grinned. "I'll be better prepared this time."

"Should've taken my advice." He grunted and went inside, apparently heading back to the bedroom.

First day. Not perfect. Not great. But not bad.

Not bad at all.

I went upstairs to do a quick change. Shorts and flip-flops this time. No more hotfooting it.

 CRSO

The planks of the crossover had started losing their heat as the sun's angle shifted with the passing of the afternoon. Another lesson learned. Still, it was a warm walk, and splinters were a possibility I hadn't considered before, so I was glad to have my flip-flops.

There was at least an hour of daylight left, so I took my time. The dunes on either side of the crossover were topped with some sort of tall grasses and low, scrubby bushes. Still had a desert look to me. But no trash. No littering here, not even blown in, so someone must be keeping the neighborhood clear of litter.

Where the crossover rose in a gentle grade to a higher point, I paused to take a slower look at the houses from the ocean side. I couldn't see the subdivision road for the houses and fences, but it was clear that Merrick's house was on a curve near the end of the main subdivision road. Houses were on either side of his house, but the angles and the landscaping provided a lot of privacy. There was also the discreet, unofficial-looking path between the houses that Miranda had shown me.

From that same vantage point, when I turned my back to the houses, I could see only the beach landscape and the ocean. The shore. The sand. The waves rolling in. And the sound of the waves along with the salty air—it overwhelmed me again—perhaps more so than the first time because now there were no worrisome distractions about my new charge or burning boards. Just the Atlantic.

I left my flip-flops in the sand near the crossover and enjoyed kicking my way through the dry sand until I neared the firmer sand at the ocean's edge, and I kept going until I entered the water.

The waves hit me at shin level and splashed my knees. My shorts were dry for the moment, but I saw a bigger wave coming, and like a kid who'd thought they were bigger and braver than they actually were, I lost my nerve and tried to dash back toward the dry sand. I was amazed at the drag of the water on my feet and legs. Running against the pull of the receding wave was like running in slow motion. Weird and delightfully new.

I walked along the shoreline, picking up shells to examine the colors and silky textures. Creatures had lived in these. There was a woman and a child on the beach, and they were packing up to leave. That feeling of being alone in this wide openness with no sturdy trees rooted in the earth and providing screening and shelter to God's creatures, but instead of shelter, here were the shifting sands, the thundering ocean, and the sheer vastness. It matched something deep inside me. I wanted to do as I'd done the evening before when I'd lain in the sand and watched the sun throw out the ribbons of color in the sky before being swallowed by the ocean. My brain felt almost lyrical. It was a heady feeling. I was grateful that I didn't have to explain it to anyone. Just me. Unencumbered and glad to be that way. Perhaps for the first time in my life.

My toes in the wet sand, my vision following the streams of color—I felt a prickling along the back of my neck and spun around to see a man. Distant, but there.

The woman and the child were gone. The man was standing where the path met the sandy beach, still a ways from me. He was wearing shorts and a light-blue cotton shirt. And he was staring at me. I stared back. I was intensely aware of the ocean at my back and the absence of anyone else in sight, and the dimming daylight.

He raised his hand in a wave and began walking toward me.

CHAPTER SIX

Who was he?

Susan had said to be wary of strangers showing up at the house. Did she mean on the beach too? I knew, after almost forty years on this earth, to be wary of strangers, especially males. At the Fuel Up Fast, even. I had nothing against a friendly chat, but counters were puny barriers. Most men under fifty could come over them in a split second if they wanted to. Cameras weren't helpful, except in the follow-up investigation.

So I stared and gave him that look perfected by generations of teachers and moms, and certain psychopaths. The *make-my-day* look. The body language, too—that was another thing I'd learned in my various jobs. Stand like you were ready to rumble, and maybe even looking forward to it. My feet shifted to get a stronger purchase on the sand, my legs bent slightly at the knees, and the muscles in my legs and arms tensed.

But as I stared, I noted his hair was dark and longish, and the overall image rang as familiar in my head. I remembered.

Davis. That's what Merrick had called him.

This was the man who'd awakened me rudely earlier today after I dozed off by the pool. He'd embarrassed me in front of my new employer. But that jerk had left hours ago. Now he was back? And down here at the beach? Why? I thought again of Susan's warning.

"Lilliane?" He stopped a few yards away. "I'm sorry, I don't think I heard your last name. I came by to drop something off for Merrick, rang the bell and no one

76

answered. I was leaving when I noticed someone down here on the beach and thought it might be you."

His words sounded good, but his hands were empty. Plus, I doubted he could've seen me out here from the house. He would've had to come at least as far as the path. Looking for me.

"Davis?" I asked him.

"Yes, that's me. I'm sorry for disturbing you. When no one answered the door, I guessed Merrick was either already in bed or not in the mood for visitors. I don't usually come by this time of evening, but he'd asked me about a book I was working on, and I wanted to drop it by."

"You changed your shirt."

A hint of bemusement crossed his face. He touched the fabric. "I did."

"And you saw me here on the beach?"

"Sorry. I realized how creepy that sounded even as I was saying it."

Okay, maybe I was believing him. Didn't mean I'd drop my guard, but I relaxed a little. "He does retire early. You are welcome to leave the book, of course. I'll see he gets it."

"I left it outside the house where you or Merrick will find it."

Then why had he felt the need to disturb me here by the ocean?

I didn't ask the question aloud, though, so it was disconcerting when he added with a slightly embarrassed smirk, "I guess it was the bare feet that did it. Made me think you might be down here."

Was that a criticism? I said, "As I recall, you were wearing bare feet too."

He laughed. "I wear my bare feet often. Never really liked shoes."

"Did you grow up in the country?"

"Nope. Beach all the way. My family lived on the Florida coast."

His manner was friendly and nonthreatening, but I needed to stay smart and not trust so easily. It was time to go in, anyway. My evening solitude had been spoiled.

He seemed to read my mind again, as he said, "You probably came down here to enjoy the sunset. I'm sorry for disturbing you."

It occurred to me that this man—this Davis—was exceptionally canny about reading expressions and body language. A very observant man. Most men weren't. It made me even more suspicious.

Laughing voices could suddenly be heard nearby, and we both looked. A teenage couple was emerging arm in arm from the path and onto the beach. My distance vision wasn't as good as it used to be, but I thought the teenage girl might be Miranda Wardlaw's granddaughter. The couple ignored us, but the distraction provided me with the perfect opportunity to break off the encounter with Davis.

I moved away from the water and toward the path. Davis moved with me, but he kept his distance. I'd found most men weren't especially intuitive, but this *Davis* was different. Which might be interesting in other circumstances, but it was also unsettling if he was going to be hanging around the Dahl house.

I reminded myself that I wasn't required to be friends with the friends of Merrick Dahl. I was an employee. I had free will.

Davis Whatever-His-Name-Was was a little too slick and easygoing for my taste.

He followed, and even though the light was fading, my concern was minimal because the teenagers were within sight and sound of us and the road was just a short distance down the path.

As we reached the house, I saw his car in the driveway. I stopped beside his vehicle and waited.

There was a fractional pause before he opened the car door. He said, "Tell Merrick I'm sorry I missed him. That I'll give him a call tomorrow."

"Will do." I held my position without yielding. *No invite* was what I telegraphed.

He lingered another second or two, then got into his car. I stayed in the driveway and gave him a quick wave as he drove off. I felt victorious. Stupidly so. Had this become my life? A series of contests of wills across convenience store counters, or outlasting the people who'd let me down, or protecting myself from a near-stranger—who was easy on the eyes and probably totally harmless? What was I protecting myself from?

Not protecting myself, I corrected. In this case, I was protecting my charge, wasn't I?

Yes. Absolutely.

ΩΒΕΟ

There was no package on the front porch.

I'd left my flip-flops at the end of the crossover. I only had the one pair and two weeks of needing them, so I ran back via the beach path to reclaim them. Thus, as it turned out, I was there precisely at the moment in time when the high clouds turned a heart-achingly beautiful shade of violet. And the sun, disappearing behind the horizon, threw out those last stark rays of light like gilded hands grasping to save, or bid farewell to, what was left of the day.

I stood there, flip-flops clutched to my chest, and cried. I didn't know why I was crying, but I let it happen.

In the dark, after both the sunset and my own storm had passed, I returned by way of the crossover and gazebo. At the pool entrance, I eased the door soundlessly shut behind me. In the foyer, I listened. No sounds. The study door was open, but there was no sign that Merrick had gotten up since going to bed. I wished I could peek in to check on him, but his bedroom door was closed. For some charges, that wouldn't matter. But Merrick had a strong sense of privacy and independence that wouldn't mesh with even a well-intentioned nursemaid. Besides, he had his alert charm—his choice whether to use it—and I had mine. He also had a monitor in both his bedroom and office that would allow him to communicate with the monitors in the kitchen and in my own room. So, yes, stuff could go wrong, but he could also reach me, if needed.

I left the study and went to the kitchen for a tall glass of water, intending to take it out to the table by the pool. Through the window, I could see the top of the table umbrella and a snippet view of the pool.

The morning I'd left home, I'd stopped to shop for a swimsuit and had purchased a navy print one-piece that I might be bold enough to wear in public. How did I look in it? Good or bad? Who knew? But it fit, and considering the challenges, I think I looked pretty decent in it. Besides, people of all sorts of sizes and shapes wore bathing suits. I wouldn't stand out. No one would even notice me. Plus, I could always hang out in the deep water, if necessary.

This would be the opportune time to don the swimsuit and give it a try. The pool had low lights burning in the sides just below the level of the water. It was enough for me to see by. I couldn't actually swim, so I would only be wading, anyway.

I trotted up to my room and pulled that swimsuit from the drawer. Squeezing into it almost convinced me to abandon the whole idea. But Momma always said, "Do new stuff like you mean it, and most folks will never know you were embarrassed or afraid. They'll just think you're bold and brave."

Pulling a T-shirt on over the suit helped.

The water probably wouldn't hurt the alert fob, but it was different with my key pendant, especially given the pool chemicals. I unfastened the silver chain and set it carefully on top of the dresser, arranging the chain so it wouldn't tangle and the pendant was neatly laid out. Couldn't help thinking of my parents, of course. They'd certainly find my current situation fascinating.

I grabbed Aunt Molly's terry robe on the way out. It could almost pass as a beach cover-up, so I took it as a just-in-case.

Back down the stairs, with a quick peek into the study to reassure myself that nothing had changed with Merrick—still no sign of him—I went out to the pool. The underwater pool lights gave the water a low, gentle glow. When the breeze touched the surface of the water, it shimmied, and the lights under the water seemed to ripple and dance.

A package was on the patio table. The one Davis said he'd left? So he'd come all the way around the house to leave it back here? Even the side gate had a code, so apparently he was trusted with the number.

I didn't get the feeling that Merrick spent much time out here, so had Davis come around back thinking he'd find me here?

Instead of a book, Davis had left a large manila envelope holding a fairly thick stack of papers sealed inside. I picked the envelope up, and it flexed. Yes, definitely papers. I set the envelope back on the table. When I went back inside later, I'd put the package on Merrick's desk.

At the pool's edge, with the watery lights below me and the stars popping out overhead, I took in the night. The stars and the moon played peekaboo among the moving clouds. From somewhere distant, a voice called out. An unknown door slammed. Mere night noises. The houses on either side had limited views of the backyard. There was nothing to indicate anyone would notice me, or even care to watch the show.

My T-shirt joined Aunt Molly's robe on the chair. I stood at the half-circle stairs leading down into the shallow end of the pool, rested my hand on the rail, and put my toes into the water.

It was warm.

Years ago, I'd been in my cousin Lisa's pool. It was aboveground, round, and maybe two feet deep, and it was set up in the shade. Talk about cold. Nothing quite beat well water when it came to chilly. My recent encounters with the ocean had also been on the chilly side. But this water had been heated by the summer sun all day long and was glorious. I kept my grip on the railing and waded in step by step.

I stood there about armpit-deep, moving my arms and feeling a little floaty, but kept my feet on the bottom. Maybe next time I'd be more adventurous. For tonight, I experienced the water around me and the night sky seeming deep and mysterious doing its universe thing high above me.

After a while I turned back toward the house and began walking out, feeling the odd combination of pressure against my body, slowing me, but with a floaty sensation. When the water dropped below my waist, suddenly the buoyant feel was gone and the water created a huge drag, like that wave at the beach had done. Walking felt awkward.

As I reached the steps, I saw I had company.

He was seated in one of the chairs at the round patio table. My clothing was in the chair next to him, just as I'd left it, but Merrick Dahl hadn't been there then and now he was.

I tried to smile pleasantly as I climbed those steps. "Couldn't resist," I said to him.

"Glad someone is using the pool. I pay that pool cleaner a small fortune to maintain it."

Walking around the other side of the table, I picked up Aunt Molly's robe, glad it was terry since I hadn't thought to bring a towel with me.

Merrick asked, "You've been in a pool before?"

"You're asking because I said I hadn't been to the ocean?"

"Yes."

"I have been in a pool. Years ago. My cousin had one,

but not like yours. You have a lovely pool, and I'm glad you've kept it up so I could enjoy it tonight."

He was holding the envelope that Davis had left.

"I'm surprised to see you up," I said.

"My sleep was interrupted."

"How so? Not by me, right?"

"No." His fingers tightened on the envelope. "I had a dream."

"A nightmare?"

"No. Not good or bad. Just . . . disturbing. I don't know why. I haven't had one of those dreams in a long while. Maybe years."

I nodded. "Sometimes it's better to get up for a while to put some distance between you and the dream to help it pass. Shall I fix you some tea? Decaf. More of the dandelion brew?"

"No."

"Tell me about the dream. It might help. Talking about a dream can help loosen its hold over you."

"No, I don't recall enough of it, and it wasn't all that interesting anyway. Other people's dreams never are."

I shrugged. "I might disagree, but it's up to you."

He'd sounded so glum. Thinking of Davis and that envelope Merrick was holding in his arms, I said, "Let's talk about something else, then."

But instead of mentioning the envelope, he said, "Tell me about the place you call home. This town that's so remote you'd never seen the ocean. You have people, right?"

"Not so remote. Richmond is an hour east, and Charlottesville is less than an hour west. And I have people. Friends. A few cousins of varying degrees, though I rarely see them anymore. My parents are gone. I lost them when I was eighteen." I smiled. "They loved each other. I was very blessed."

"You lost them at the same time?"

"When they died, they went together. Thankfully, I was

old enough to manage on my own."

"Did they leave you money? How is it that you stayed there and didn't travel?"

"No money. I've always had to work. But I did travel once." I added, "I went with my aunt on a road trip along the Skyline Drive. She wanted to visit an old friend, and we also toured Biltmore. Now that was a house—huge and so fancy."

"Is that the aunt you took care of?"

"Aunt Molly? Yes, my dad's aunt, so my great-aunt. Her grandson and his wife both work at the college in Charlottesville, so yeah, it was a job, but I enjoyed being around her too. Family that I was close to, you know?"

"I'm sorry for your loss. It must've hurt to lose her?"

I frowned. The usual expression of sympathy framed as a question seemed odd. "Well, yes and no. She was in her nineties and not as independent or capable as you. When she started going downhill, she grew feeble so fast—she told me it was because she was ready. I stayed with her in hospice." Despite myself, I had to reach up and press the back of my hand to my eyes. "It may sound strange, but it was actually good to be able to say goodbye, not like with my parents."

Without a murmur of apology or sympathy, he asked, "How did they die? You said together."

Humph. I'd thought we were just chatting. It had stopped feeling that way. This seem more like an insect being examined prior to being pinned in someone's collection. Back home no one would've asked something so personal. They would already have known. And knowing, it would not have been spoken of to me. Certain things were just too personal or too painful to pull out any old time, as if it were tea-party chat.

"Not tonight," I said with finality in my tone. I nodded toward the manila envelope. "Davis left that for you. He said to tell you that he'd give you a call tomorrow."

It was his turn to *humph*. We were no better than two cantankerous geezers exchanging stories and grunts.

Merrick surprised me by explaining. "He wants me to read it. *His newest manuscript.*" But he said the last words with an expression of distaste.

"He's a writer? A bad one, apparently."

"No, it's not that. Practice makes better, and all that, but no—he wants to use my name to help sell it."

"But if he wrote it . . ."

"As an endorsement."

"Like one of those snappy quotes you see by famous writers on the cover?" I considered it. "Is that a bad thing?"

"No, nothing wrong with him asking. Endorsements are fine."

So then what is the problem? But I let it go. "Tell me this. Is Davis his first or last name?"

He laughed. Merrick Dahl laughed out loud for the first time, and the sound had a quality of mirth that I never expected to hear from this cranky old man. I smiled, and then we laughed together, even though I had no clue whatsoever as to what we were laughing about. It didn't matter.

When the laughter stopped, I stood, but the good feelings remained with us. I said, "Wait here. I need a snack before bed, and you must need a bite too by now. I'll be right back. Unless you'd like to join me in the kitchen?"

CR&SO

I showered before putting on my pajamas. It had been a long day. Hard to believe that just over twelve hours ago I'd arrived at this house, had followed Susan Biggs around on a whirlwind, breathless tour, and had been abandoned by her because she had to catch a plane. To where? Who knew? Not me. And then I'd met Merrick and Davis, but I still didn't know whether Davis was his first or last name, and I had discovered my new charge was a famous author. I'd seen my second sunset over the Atlantic and squeezed into my first swimsuit in how long? Maybe twenty-five years? About the same time Merrick had stopped writing novels.

Wow. Just wow.

I crawled into bed between the clean sheets with their expensive thread count and a feather comforter that must've fallen straight from heaven. I needed that delightful feather comforter because the AC worked here. Bliss.

The blinds were raised in the window nearest the bed so that when I was ready to switch off the lamp on the nightstand, I'd see the sky. It connected me to home. I always preferred to sleep with a clear view of the night—the dark nights of the forests and hollows where the stars and planets reigned and reminded you that your actual place in the universe was small—that occupying that space was a gift and should be used well for the short time you dwelled in it. Earthbound landscapes changed depending upon where one was, but the sky spoke to eternity. It was the same whether I was here at the beach and far away from all I'd known or snug in my simpler bed at home.

Merrick's novel *Moonfire Chase*—whose colorful cover along with its own slew of author endorsements promised a thrill on each page—awaited me. Propping myself up against the pillows, I picked up his novel and once again opened the cover.

CHAPTER SEVEN

Reading more of *Moonfire Chase* didn't happen—and no wonder, after such a day. My eyes kept closing, despite me. Finally, I gave up, cut off the light, and snuggled down. The stars were bright outside as I considered what tomorrow might bring. I'd be meeting the housekeeper, Ms. Bertie, and sparring with Merrick and . . . the beach . . .

I remembered nothing after that.

In the morning, I woke early. Predawn. Ready for my first full day on the job. I'd meet Ms. Bertie today. Would Merrick and I get along okay? All that passed through my mind, mostly unheeded, as I rushed to wash up and dress.

I was in a hurry because I had a date. With the sunrise.

Leaving through the back door, I crossed the yard, walked through the gazebo, and then along the crossover until I reached the high spot. I leaned against the railing to watch the sun peek over the Atlantic horizon. Gwen's camera was hanging by its strap around my neck.

It would be fun to give it a try—and all the better to have photographs as souvenirs. I found the on button and made sure to remove the lens cap.

The breeze was blowing from the Atlantic toward the shore. A change in the hue of the dark as the sky lightened almost imperceptibly warned that the dawn was not far away. The incoming breeze carried a mix of cool night and the forecasted heat and humidity. A flock of seabirds—I didn't know what kind, but they looked ancient, like those dinosaur birds with the sharp wings and long, pointed beaks—skimmed a few feet above the rolling waves. Every so often one or another dipped into the top of the water, and I realized they were after breakfast. Funny, but I'd never really thought about fish in the ocean. Farther out, yes, but not so close in. Maybe one day I'd get brave enough to go into the waves above my knees and maybe even go underwater. I'd open my eyes and see fish and maybe crabs, and who knew what? There was a whole unknown, unexpected world hiding under all that water—a world I'd never considered.

The sun rose as expected, and I enjoyed the beauty, but in the end, I was more awed by that wondrous, yet eerie landscape just before the arrival of the sun's rays. It was time, however, for me to move on. The workday was beginning.

At least I wouldn't be starting the morning shift at the Fuel Up Fast. Gwen had been right. I needed a break. When I returned home in two weeks, I'd make a point of letting her know how right she'd been and how grateful I was she'd thought of me.

⚮

Susan's notes had explained that Ms. Bertie came every Tuesday and Friday. I had the idea from what Susan had said during the whirlwind tour that Ms. Bertie or one of her relatives had come over daily after the last aide was let go, but that couldn't last and was part of the reason, along with that trip she was taking, that Susan was so motivated to get a new, trustworthy aide in place. I viewed myself as more a companion than an aide. But it was the same tune, otherwise.

Ms. Bertie was already in the kitchen. I stopped just inside the doorway. She flashed a quick look over her shoulder and then went back to assembling casseroles.

Not pausing in her work, she said, "You must be Lil-li Ann."

"Lilliane."

She cast me another quick look. "That's what I said."

"One word. Not Lil-li Ann. Lilliane." Plus, she'd said it

with short, clipped syllables, Lil-li, so I made sure to say it slowly and clearly.

"Beg your pardon."

She sounded a bit huffy. I didn't want to start this relationship off with hurt feelings. So much easier to get the job done with good will on both sides.

"No pardon needed." I was still standing in the doorway trying to decide what I thought of this woman. Her gray hair wanted to be a buoyant mass of frizzy curls, but she'd pulled it back into a tight bun with a little net over it. She was short and relatively broad across the shoulders and hips. And she was wearing a uniform that totally looked like a uniform. No pretense here. Not scrubs or anything like that. This was chef-like, but without the hat. Very professional.

I added in a conciliatory tone, "It's just one of those things. People get it wrong, and it's simpler to tell them up front. But it's not important."

As if I hadn't just spoken about the name thing, she said, "I'm putting the meals together. The laundry is already in process. I assume you'll wash your own clothing?" She paused, but not long enough for me to answer. "If you'll strip your bed every Tuesday morning and put the sheets in the laundry room, I'll have them washed and back on the bed before I leave that day. Tuesday is the main laundry day. On Friday, I catch up on anything extra that Mr. Dahl needs. On Tuesday, I perform light housework, but I do the majority of that, especially the heavier cleaning, on Friday. I don't do any of the outside work."

Whatever she did or didn't do, Ms. Bertie had certainly done all the talking. Even so, I felt a little breathless just listening. And impressed. She added, "I've already put Mr. Dahl's breakfast in his study."

"What? Is he up? He said he sleeps until nine or so."

"That's what he says, but it isn't what he does."

I caught the note in her voice this time—the invite to ask. I moved a few steps closer and asked, "Really?"

"Oh, you'll find out. Yes, you will." Ms. Bertie was slicing a steak into thin strips.

That lady could handle a knife. Involuntarily, I took a step back.

Under her breath, she muttered something. I tried to reengage.

"Is he actually up now? If so, I'd better check on him."

Ignoring my words yet again, she said, "Take a look at that list, Lil-li. See if I missed anything."

Sigh. Lil-li it was, apparently. I picked the list up from the table. I scanned it while thinking about her accent. It was so faint, but the way she turned some of her vowels and hit her consonants hard made me think of Mrs. Nachek, one of my regular customers at the Fuel Up Fast. Ms. Nachek had a stronger accent and talked a lot about the old country. She was super old herself.

Eastern European? I tucked that bit of info into my pocket. Never knew when details might be handy or offer an opening.

I smiled, remembering how Aunt Molly sometimes called me a detail collector. Said I had a nose for other people's business, including secrets. Sometimes it was true. But most times catching and storing all that info was just a waste of brain cells.

"List looks good to me, Ms. Bertie. But I'm sure you have a better handle on Mr. Dahl's needs than I could ever hope to have. You've been working with him for a long time, as I understand it. My stay here will be pretty short."

The action stopped. She held the knife poised above the beef for a fraction of a second before resuming the even rhythm of *slice . . . slice . . . slice.* But I could see a shift in her body language. She was interested in something I'd said.

"Two weeks," I added.

She didn't take the bait.

I said, "Well, let me know if there's something you need me to do. I'm going to check on Mr. Dahl and see if he's up and about."

What was her deal? Was she worried that when I left, she or her helper would be back on the hook for daily duties? Aides fired. Susan rushing off. Ms. Bertie making odd little remarks. I filed it all away, but given my short stay here, the bits and pieces weren't likely to be useful. Might make good stories, though. Not like what Merrick, and possibly Davis, put onto paper, but stories to tell—always with the names changed to protect the guilty and the innocent—or a good tale when the job was boring or quiet, or around a campfire. Even for the little ones at the library. I could imagine describing Ms. B to them and how she couldn't, or wouldn't, get my name right. Even Ms. B might find it funny. I'd love to hear her laugh. Would it be as amusing as Merrick's laughter?

I liked stories. Always had. They gave the appearance of personal interaction but under the guise of being "made up" without the outright sharing of personal, revealing details. Maybe writing and reading stories was different than speaking them aloud, but maybe those things also had a lot in common. Maybe Merrick and I had that much in common too.

I'd never thought of reading in that way. For the first time, I wondered how much I'd missed by not being able to climb into a book and truly enjoy a story.

In the study, Merrick was seated at his desk. His plate contained toast crumbs, partially eaten fresh fruit, along with a small dish of untouched prunes, all piled together and topped with a crumpled napkin and tangled plastic wrap. I stood in front of his desk.

I said, "You misled me. You've been up for a while. Not how you described your mornings, or how Susan described them either."

He grimaced. "I woke early. Didn't break any laws."

No point in responding to that remark directly. "I was up extra early too. I went out to enjoy the sunrise."

He glanced up. "Oh? First ocean sunrise, I suppose."

His tone was a little too thick with mockery for my liking. I wasn't here to be slammed.

Dropping any attempt at being pleasant, I said, "I'll take your plate. Would you like coffee or tea? No? I'll be back later when it's time for your medication." I picked up his plate and started to walk away.

"Wait," he said.

I turned back to face him but didn't speak. I wasn't inclined to be chummy at the moment.

"I am unsettled this morning. Slept little or dreamed a lot. I'm not sure which."

My annoyance softened. He was a ninety-year-old who'd had a bad night. I couldn't stop myself from saying, "Should I call your doctor? What can I do to help?"

"How about some tea?"

"Tea? Sure. What kind?"

"What you made yesterday will be fine."

"All right then. I'll be back shortly."

"We'll talk about that question from yesterday."

Goodness, I had a jolt. I'd forgotten. What question? Something about writing, right? Something I'd come up with to distract him.

I dragged my feet as I walked down the hallway, suddenly tentative about disrupting Ms. Bertie's domain. *Shoulders back,* I told myself. *Hold your head high.* The kitchen was not only *her* domain. I had a certain amount of responsibility for a sliver of it—on behalf of the living and breathing person whose name was Merrick Dahl.

The woman was wrapping up the prepared meals and stowing them in the fridge.

"Ms. Bertie? That list. I need to add something to it."

"What's that, Lil-li?"

Lil-li. It grated. "Tea. I need to add dandelion tea and honey spice tea to the list. I get a particular brand, so if that's possible, I'd appreciate it. I'll note the brand. I'm not generally picky, but when it comes to tea it's important to be aware of how and where it's grown. For impurities and such, you know. It's for Mr. Dahl." I was just running on, increasingly nervous in the face of her stare.

"Mr. Dahl doesn't drink tea."

"He does now."

"I'm sure he won't mind me getting it for you, though. No problem."

"I brought my own." I went over to the cabinet by the stove and took the boxes out. I showed them to her. "These. But with two of us drinking it, it won't last even a week. So . . . if you don't mind?"

I saw surprise in her eyes. Barely there, but I caught the glint of it. I smiled. Kindly.

"He asked me to fix him some now." I reached for the kettle I'd used before. "Hot water is fine, but one of these days—when my ship comes in, as they say—I'm going to splurge and get a brewer with those temperature controls and auto cutoff." I was chatty, trying to be friendly. But she'd stopped listening. She was copying the tea info onto her list. She looked outright puzzled and was muttering in a low, breathy voice.

Pretending that I wasn't listening in on her private mutters, I stood on tiptoe to reach the mugs on the second shelf in the cabinet near the stove. Gorgeous, colorful mugs. The same ones Merrick and I had used yesterday. As I got a hold of them and set them on the counter, Ms. B came close and I thought she was going to slap my hand. I looked at her, surprised. Her face was flushed.

"Is it okay to use these?"

"Coffee cups and saucers are over in that cabinet." She pointed.

"We used these mugs before. I know they don't quite match the saucers, but he seemed okay with that." I finished rather lamely, "They're colorful."

She struggled a bit before saying, "Yes, of course." She

gave herself a shake. "Never mind me." She tucked the list in her uniform pocket. "I'll go to the grocery store and cleaner's now and be back in time to serve him lunch. You'll be here for lunch?"

"Certainly."

"Where would you like to eat? Here in the kitchen? By the pool?"

"In the study with Mer—Mr. Dahl."

She stared again. I began to see that Merrick and I were upsetting her routine. I understood. I never liked it when someone came in and changed my routines around. Routines were important. Involuntary. Like breathing or blinking your eyes. Routines left the brain free for more important stuff. I smiled. Important stuff like observing the housekeeper or staying a step ahead of one's elderly charge.

"Mr. Dahl dines alone," she said.

"I imagine he'll tire of me soon enough. I don't have anything interesting to contribute to a conversation. No doubt, he'll return to his usual habits pretty quickly."

As the tea steeped, I remembered. "Oh, the cookies." I retrieved that box from the cabinet. "These too. Could you get some at the store?" I showed her. "We have them with our tea."

"Indeed."

"Would you like some?" I opened the box to dole out two each.

"No, thank you."

I used the spoon to remove the tea bags. "I need to tell you something, Ms. Bertie."

"Yes?" she said stiffly.

"You are an amazing cook. That chicken we had for supper yesterday was outstanding. I've never been a good cook. I can barely handle simple dishes. So I absolutely appreciate someone who has a gift for it."

Her cheeks pinked up. She looked pleased.

I added, "If there's anything I can do while I'm here,

please let me know."

She nodded with a hint of a smile, and I was pleased that maybe I'd unfrozen her just a little.

I loved a challenge. I loved positive results even more.

Super careful not to lose a drop of tea nor a cookie crumb, I moved down the hall from the kitchen to the foyer and into Merrick's study. He wasn't there. A newspaper was in a disordered jumble of pages on the floor beside his desk.

My teacup went on the end of his desk. I set his tea on the blotter in front of his chair. I presumed he'd want to drink it here. And chat here. Chat about what? Maybe he was just feeling down after a poor night's rest and wanted some company.

I carried one of the chairs from the table over to the desk and sat to wait for him.

He'd left his cell phone on the desk. It looked like a nice one. One of those big ones. I couldn't help noticing things, like when things were different or had been moved or changed. It wasn't a conscious effort, and it was harmless, but unless you were getting paid to notice such things, it just felt nosy.

Not that it took a detective to spy Davis's manila envelope on the desk and to see it had been opened. Neatly, yes, and done carefully so there was minimal wrinkling. Either the pages hadn't been taken out or had been slipped back into the envelope with great care.

Sounds of movement were coming from the bedroom now.

Merrick came into the study slowly and using his cane. Was that apprehension on his face? Or just general dissatisfaction? Clearly, he had something on his mind, even if it was just feeling wonky after a poor night's rest. He dropped into his big leather swivel chair. The chair gave a big squeak for such a scrawny man. He stared at the tea and saucer, touched the handle of the cup, and moved it slightly without picking it up.

"You seem preoccupied. Is it the lack of sleep from another disturbing dream? Is anything hurting or bothering you?"

He pulled his hand back. "No. Just too many thoughts."

"Want to talk about them?"

He grunted and reached out again, but this time for the cookie. "No, Lilliane, I was thinking about your question and how best to answer it."

Seriously? That question again? It had only been intended as a distraction.

"Don't worry about—"

"Hush. You asked it. Now you must allow me to answer it."

"Yes, sir." I picked up the teacup and sipped. I replaced it on the saucer, folded my hands, and said, "I'm all ears."

He grunted again. "Clichés. You seem to have an unfortunate predilection for clichés."

I shrugged, slightly annoyed by his criticism. "Most people share a common understanding of what a cliché communicates in a given situation. It's an efficient way to communicate a simple concept."

He stared.

My cheeks warmed. Probably flushed. "I heard that somewhere. Sounded smart. Made sense."

He cleared his throat. "There is truth in that. I learned to deplore clichés in the writing craft. Much like never ending a sentence with a preposition. Did you know there's no actual grammatical rule against that? And there's the overuse and underuse of commas. Don't get me started on semicolons."

He wasn't really wanting me to respond to all that. I kept my mouth shut this time. He paused for a sip of tea, and I did the same.

"It's good," he said.

I smiled. "Ms. Bertie was surprised you liked tea."

He squinted at me. "Madam Bertie is smart and capable."

"I believe it."

He said firmly, "Don't change the subject again."

Flippantly, I said, "Where I come from, folks can have more than one conversation going on between them at the same time."

He waved his hands in jest, as if surrendering. "You win." He picked up the last bit of his cookie. "Tell me, then, about this place you're from. I believe you said it was a small town in the country? A place where people don't go to the beach?" With a superior look, he popped that last bite of cookie into his mouth and settled back in his chair. "Now *I'm* all ears."

Another sip of tea gave me a moment to consider what he was actually asking. "Cub Creek," I said. "It's a small town west of Richmond and east of Charlottesville, in the foothills of the Blue Ridge Mountains."

"Yes, I know where Richmond and Charlottesville are located. Please continue."

"People there do most certainly go to the beach. Many go every summer. Don't judge them by me. I've never gone much of anywhere. Beach vacations cost money. While I enjoy new sights, I've never done more than think about it."

"Except for that trip with your aunt."

"Yes."

"So, then, what do you do there? In that Cub Creek place?"

"I work different jobs. I garden a little. Grow tomatoes and cucumbers in season. Momma canned and pickled, but I don't do that." I shrugged. "Never liked how the heat and steam would come up and make my hair cling to my face. It was itchy. A misery. Though Momma never seemed to mind." I stretched a little, changing position, a little uncomfortable to hear my home accent grow ever stronger as I remembered those early years. Here in Merrick's study, the twang was distracting.

He was staring at my hands, and now he moved his ever

so slightly, as if mirroring mine. Was he conscious of it? Or was it mockery? I might have stared back too openly because he looked at his hand suspended near his face, then brought it down, saying, "I hope you don't mind. I was noticing how you move your hands when you speak. When you get into the story."

"Sorry."

"No, not at all. I know many people who 'speak with their hands,' but it's really just gesturing as they are speaking normally in the course of their day." He tapped on his desktop with his fingers. "It's different with you in that I don't see the gesturing generally."

"It's a storytelling thing, I guess. Or a learned way of storytelling, maybe. I've always done that. I don't hardly notice anymore when, as you say, the story gets rolling." I shrugged. "I wish it meant more. I've thought it would be fun, for instance, to be able to do some genuine sign language while sharing a story."

He asked, "You have other family?"

"Some cousins and distant family." I shifted in my seat again. He'd kind of spoiled the chat for me with his question bringing attention to my hands. "Is this an interview? What's up?"

"You don't like to talk about home?"

"Where did you grow up? Where's your family?" I stopped, embarrassed. I'd sounded aggressive. Defensive? *Why?* "Sorry. Normally, I can hold up my end of a conversation just fine. I guess it's the questioning mode that puts me off."

He nodded. "Don't blame you there. I would feel the same. I was curious."

"Why? Why are you interested?"

"Why not?" He opened his hands and spread them wide. "It's good sometimes for an old man to sit and chat. I spent my life writing stories, and sometimes I like to hear stories told by others. Days like this, especially."

He seemed sincere, yet I sensed subtle manipulation.

"Okay. But you've been forewarned that my life is pretty boring."

"Thank you," he said.

He sounded sincere, as before, and this time when he put his head back against the chair, he closed his eyes. Perhaps he really did just want a story in preparation for a post-breakfast nap.

Where to start? I sighed, reaching up to tuck some stray hairs back behind my ear. What did he really want? Not my biography, for sure. "My parents were born and raised in Cub Creek. They married young. Dad spent some time in the military but didn't stay long. He was a crack shot, and I think he had some idea of being a sharpshooter, but they put him in the motor pool. He had mechanical skills and learned more, but he always said that if he was going to work on motors and be covered in oil up to his neck, he could do that on his own time without any bossy types shouting at him." I shrugged. "So between him and the army, as he told me, they decided to sever their acquaintance."

I smiled, almost forgetting Merrick was sitting a few feet away. I was watching the light streaming in through the windows behind him. The streams caught the motes and dust, highlighting the area behind him. I gestured toward them, moving my fingers much as the motes danced.

"I remember Daddy working inside his shed out back, with that wide door slid open and the daylight slanting in and touching his shoulders and back, lighting up his ginger hair as he bent over the front end of a fuselage."

Merrick made a noise. His eyes were open. I nodded.

"You heard me right. He had a hobby. Daddy, that is. He collected spare parts of things. For a while, it was old cars and ancient farming equipment. Did all kinds of things with metal. But what I remember most was the airplane." I laughed. "More than an airplane. He called it a bomber. If he'd ever succeeded in completing it, it wouldn't in a million

years have fit in that shed, but that wasn't the point, I guess."
I laughed. "Or, knowing my dad, he would likely have
enlarged the shed, though it was already huge and built like
a tank." I stopped and winked. "A pun and a cliché all in
one."

"I caught it." He squinched up his face in a momentary
show of distaste, but quickly went on to ask, "How'd he get
started on assembling a plane?"

"Oh, you might be surprised what folks have hiding in
their junk piles and old grown-over fields out in the country.
The fancy furniture and glassware they find in the attics and
cellars goes to the antique stores if it's in decent shape, or to
the flea markets if it isn't. The other stuff tends to be cast off,
and nature tries to hide it over the years. In this case, Dad had
done a job for a man who was short on money but wealthy
in junk. Dad saw the propellers peeking out from behind an
old hay baler, made a deal, and he was off to the races."

"Did your mother complain?"

"Momma? Oh, no. She said he didn't spend much cash
on that stuff, and the hobby kept him home and happy instead
of out and up to no good. On nice afternoons, after she was
done with her canning or laundry or whatever, she'd sit out
there in the shed with him and read or chat while he tinkered
or such. They were childhood sweethearts who never lost the
joy of each other. Plus, the plane came with a story. Oh, not
a story as such—not a story at all without some help from the
teller. But Mr. Price's father had served in World War II, and
somehow he'd shipped parts home. That's what Mr. Price,
the younger, told my dad. We spent many hours speculating
about exactly how that might have happened."

Merrick made a noise. I took it for encouragement to
continue.

"Yeah. Like how much would postage cost for such a
thing? Would a box suffice? Or would you need to cushion
it with those popcorn foam things? For sure, it would break
the post office scale." I didn't wait for an answer, but went

on to say, "What's left of it is still in our shed."

I stole a peek and saw he was still watching me.

"Yes, all these years later, I still live where I grew up. Never moved out. Never had a reason to." There was a long moment of silence between us, and then I stood, saying, "Enough for now, I think."

Merrick was silent, watching me as I gathered up our empty cups and crumpled napkins. I felt a little wooden, as if my brain needed to cut off the influx of memories. I hid my discomfort by keeping my voice cool and polite.

"I'll get this mess out of the way. Ms. Bertie will be back by lunchtime, so if you don't mind, I think I'll take a walk and maybe put my feet in the sand and sea again. Do you mind?" I didn't wait for an answer. I said, "There are times . . . well, just now the past feels mighty close. Heavy. I need some air and a little time a . . . away." I said to him, "Hand me your phone."

He did, and I programmed my number into it before returning it. "Call if you need me. I'm going for a walk."

"Thank you, Lilliane."

"If you want to chat again later, I'm fine with that. Just need a break."

He nodded.

I left.

After abandoning our dishes in the kitchen—*Sorry, Ms. Bertie*—I went out to the pool. I didn't stay. Unsettled, I wandered around the house and down the driveway to the road and eventually along the path back to the beach. I went straight across the sand and only stopped when I reached the water's edge.

It was cooler there, as I'd learned. The reflected heat from the dry sand made the beach proper seem extra hot, but down at the water's edge, the air was cool, like a trapped bubble of onshore breeze—perhaps a healing breeze riding in atop the incoming tide. It touched my body and psyche as the water washed over my toes, my bare feet—even as it shifted the sand from beneath them and then piled it on top, digging me in deeper. Eventually, I would have to move. The moving sand would, itself, force me to action.

My brain asked, *What happened in that study with Merrick?*

I'd felt something crack inside me.

Not fully cracked, but a slight fault had been revealed. Something related to telling Merrick about my mom and dad. About the home I'd grown up in and still enjoyed. One tiny snippet from my childhood. No secrets. Nothing I couldn't have told anyone. So why did I feel slightly shaken?

Only slightly?

Yes. Really, no more than that. Was that what homesickness was? I seized upon that. Yes, I'd never been homesick before.

Homesick. That would explain it. I sighed in relief.

It wasn't my stories. I'd been telling those for as long as I could remember. Of course, that had been back home in Cub Creek, where the foliage and shadows softened the harder edges of life.

A person could hide there, even out in plain sight.

The light was different here at the beach. Maybe that, or maybe just the simple act of being in a new "here" made the difference—revealing flaws in the ordinary and risking potential crashes I could never have anticipated.

It was up to me to determine the boundaries and my responsibility to keep them. Or not.

Merrick Dahl was my charge and my employer. I'd known him for less than twenty-four hours. Was he my friend? Truly? So quickly?

In the end, though, I was just myself, Lilliane Moore— small-town woman who gave everyone the benefit of the doubt, at least on first meeting (unless they woke me rudely by the pool), who worked hard, missed her loved ones, and would tell stories to anyone with a heart to listen.

I really didn't know how to be anyone else.

CHAPTER EIGHT

By lunchtime, I was back to being my usual well-balanced self. I helped Ms. Bertie get the food to the table. I saw she was confused—and maybe a little amused, too—over the change in dining arrangements as Merrick and I settled ourselves at the corner table in his study.

She hesitated near the door. "Well, then, if you're all set, I'll get back to work?"

"This looks and smells delicious," I said.

Merrick added his words to mine. "Ms. B is an amazing cook."

"Well, then." She fairly glowed as she left us.

I looked at Merrick with a conspiratorial look and said in a low voice, "It's just this simple—that woman can cook."

"Indeed."

We dug into the food, but as we slowed, I treated him to a taste of good-natured inquisition, this time directed at him.

I asked, "How did you end up here in the Outer Banks?"

Slicing into his turkey burger, he said, "Marriage."

"Seriously? I expected you to say that you retired here."

"Nope. Never would've done that. Maybe New York. Maybe even Texas." He shrugged. "*She* wanted to live here. When she left . . . I never got around to moving. Figured I was old. A *senior*. That I might as well stay. If I'd known I'd still be hanging around here more than twenty years later, I might have done differently."

"I'm sorry it went that way."

"No reason to be. It was my choice. I should've had better sense than to marry at that age."

"How long were you married?"

"Five years." He looked at me. "What about you? You mentioned you were married?"

"Yeah. Joe. Nice guy. Nice to everyone. Even to the guy who asked him to lend a hand with robbing the local liquor store."

"Oh?"

I sighed and shrugged. "He assured me—promised me—over and over that he hadn't had anything to do with it, until he was charged, and then he confessed. He only had to do a little jail time, but as far as I was concerned, the marriage was done."

"Oh."

"Yeah, but he's doing well. It was long ago now. We're friends. No one in town holds it against him. He's that kind of guy."

"Oh," he said again. But his jaw worked.

I could see questions were coming, and I remembered the need for *boundaries*, so I stood, saying, "I'll clear the table now. Anything I can do for you? What do you usually do in the afternoon?"

He shrugged. "A little of this or that. I might email friends or take a short walk—very short. Might even watch a little TV or take a nap."

Out of nowhere—even surprising myself—I said, "Or read Davis's manuscript?"

He gave me a sharp look, then looked away. "Likely so," he said. "No need to concern yourself."

Well, then. Should I consider myself dismissed?

"Good enough. I'll be around if you need me."

Merrick made a noise and raised his hand. I assumed it was a *see-you-later* wave.

I stopped in the kitchen and found Ms. B.

"I think Merrick wants some quiet time. I'm going out for a short while." I wrote my phone number down. "Call me if you need me."

CRBO

I did go out, but not far. Where *would* I go? A stroll on the beach, a walk along the street…. Other than that, the day passed much as the day before had, including conversations with Merrick at mealtimes. He seemed to enjoy my stories, but I tried to keep them less personal. And that evening, Merrick joined me at poolside again for tea and cookies. But the hours between stretched long, and I felt restless. I wished I had hobbies like knitting or such. The beach was beautiful, but I wasn't used to an idle life. I needed more.

CHAPTER NINE

Merrick and I began Wednesday in the study with our usual light breakfast and banter, though he seemed less engaged. I did some easy tasks during the morning, and by lunchtime I had the table set and food dishes steaming on hot pads. Over our meal, we had our usual, almost sparring conversation, but nothing in depth. Merrick seemed distracted and kept glancing toward the desk. I said nothing about it because that restless feeling from the day before was still hanging around me—until I noticed Davis's manila envelope on the corner nearest us. Had Merrick finished reading it? If so, was Davis coming by to pick it up, along with Merrick's feedback?

I found the idea lifted my spirits.

But I was wrong.

As we finished our meal, the silence grew more pronounced. Awkward. I couldn't place what was different about this meal and our interaction. Was it me or Merrick?

Trying to lighten the mood, I launched into a story about a crazy squirrel who'd spent one summer dropping nuts down on me from the oaks high above, but I was stopped midsentence when Merrick cleared his throat.

"On another subject," he said, but then he stopped speaking.

I waited.

He stood abruptly, steadied himself, then crossed to his desk, where he picked up that manila envelope. He brought it back to the table, saying, "I was hoping you'd do me a favor."

The envelope looked much the same as it had two days before. Perhaps a bit more crunched, but not much.

"Davis left this."

"Yes, I recall."

"I have a request."

"Name it." Hasty me. Always eager to accommodate.

"I'd like you to read it and give me your opinion."

I leaned forward, nearly knocking over my drink. "What? We've already discussed that I don't enjoy reading."

"That space on the shelf where *Moonfire Chase* used to sit is still empty."

I shrugged. "Sorry. I'm going to put it back where it belongs. I thought as long as it was handy on the nightstand, I might give it another try, but no, I don't think that will actually happen."

"Because you are not a thriller reader."

"I'm not a good reader. I don't enjoy reading."

He ignored me. "This is not a thriller manuscript."

"Didn't you say that Davis writes thrillers like you? Hence, he wanted an endorsement?"

"I did say that. But this isn't a thriller. It's different than what either he or I writes. Very different. I want another opinion before I discuss it with him." He placed the envelope on the table between us and took his seat.

"I don't know anything about writing. What can I possibly tell you? Also, I can't imagine Davis would be thrilled about me reading it."

"He won't know. We won't tell him."

I must've looked suspicious because he added, "We wouldn't want to hurt his feelings. Writers can be very sensitive. Harsh criticism can damage their confidence."

"Like cause writer's block? I've heard of that."

He almost smiled. Apparently, I was on target.

"This is more like a . . . a heartwarming story. A relationship story. More like a Nicholas Sparks novel than a Merrick Dahl."

"I've seen a couple of movies made from Nicholas Sparks's books." I nodded. "They were quite good."

"Then this is probably the perfect approach. If you wouldn't mind helping me? At least give it a try." He pushed the envelope in my direction.

I reached for it, sure this favor was bound for disaster, but it wasn't such a huge ask, was it? A few pages, and then I'd return it to him with, *Sorry, I tried . . .*

He added, "We'll keep this our secret. Right?"

"Sure. No problem. But if I don't like it, I'm not promising to finish it."

"That's only the first three chapters. What we, in the industry, call a partial. If you find it boring, just say so. No harm done."

I took the envelope into my hands.

He cautioned, "Don't leave it lying around. Davis might drop by, or Ms. Bertie might see it. She knows Davis, of course. I would feel badly if she saw you with it and mentioned it to him."

"I understand." This felt odd and awkward. Stealth reading? No worries, I told myself. I'd get started right away. The sooner I began, the sooner I could return the manuscript to Merrick and tell him it wasn't my thing.

Later that evening, after Merrick had gone to bed, I went out to sit by the pool. No bets on whether he'd stay there or get up for a snack or whatever, but for now he was doing whatever he did to prepare for bed. So I took a glass of iced tea with lemon out to the poolside table and propped up my feet. I would take only a few sheets at a time out of the envelope for fear I'd drop them or the breeze would snatch them and carry them into the pool, or they would fly all the way out to the beach itself. Besides, I'd only need a very few pages to form an opinion. I didn't read for entertainment. Reading was simply too much of a grind.

I looked at the first sheet. I rather liked the title. *The Book of Lost Loves.* There was no "by" line, so I still didn't know Davis's last name. That little mystery was beginning to have an amusing aspect.

The Book of Lost Loves

Part One: Lost and Found

He met Danielle at The Point on the day she crossed his line, and they ended up tangled in each other's lives.

Most things—good or bad—just couldn't be planned for. Mike Johanson had figured that out long ago. And what couldn't be counted on to happen also couldn't be counted on to stay. His mom had always told him to enjoy the good while you had it, outlast the bad, and don't sweat the in-between. Another thing he knew was that whatever happened, the operative word was "happened." Fortune, for good or ill, rarely had anything to do with planning or with being deserved. He'd figured that out for himself after a series of business and personal failures that had nearly broken him, but ultimately had ended in the sale of his last venture. A sale that had enabled him to retire five years ago at the age of forty-three. But since everything was random, nothing could be counted on.

When he'd signed off on the sale and the noncompete clause, Jeff had asked him, "What are you going to do with yourself now?"

Mike hadn't had an answer. But he'd had an answer at four o'clock this morning when Jeff had asked why they had to go out to The Point to fish.

"Because it's what I do on Mondays."

"You can fish any day of the week."

"Stay here if you want to." Mike was loading drinks and bait into the cooler. "That'd be fine by me." He grabbed a lightweight nylon jacket. "In fact, why don't you go home to your wife?"

"It's just fishing, man," Jeff said. "Don't make it complex."

"Not me. Complex is on you. How's Suze doing, anyway?"

Jeff Hanscom, Mike's childhood buddy and old school chum, had a knack for inflicting small, ankle-biting, Chihuahua annoyances without even trying, but Mike had always given him extra leeway for what they called "friendship longevity." Not Jeff's fault that he was an idiot. Just born that way, mostly. He was the kind of guy who often brought trouble along with him, or created it out of boredom, if necessary.

And Suze had married him—no one had made her do that—so Mike had little sympathy for her when she complained. He had to listen, though, and make the right noises, because she was his little sister. But he'd warned her—way back when she'd met Jeff and gushed that he was "awful cute"—that Jeff wasn't husband material. She'd insisted any man worth fixing was fixable. But Jeff was Jeff. He wasn't a good bet as anyone's reclamation project. So Mike considered that Suze's poor choices were all on her—as were his on him. Jeff was the king of bad choices, and when he wanted to lay low and avoid his wife, he usually showed up at Mike's place at The Point. And Suze said that was all on Mike. That Mike had invited himself into their troubled marriage by allowing his good old buddy Jeff to avoid facing up to his poor choices and mistakes.

And wasn't that how it went? Everybody blaming everybody else? That's why he went fishing on Monday mornings. Most mornings, in fact. It was quiet, and no one was blaming anyone.

A BAREFOOT TIDE

The landscape was silent and unoccupied—the lighting of the world before the official rise of the sun. Catching fish was a lesser reason to be present on that shore. He didn't know what the primary reason was, but one day he might. What he didn't need was the griping.

He said, "Go or not, Jeff. But shut up."

This morning Jeff was agitated. Mike had had his say and meant it, so now he picked up the cooler to carry it out to the truck.

"Hold on. Wait up," Jeff said. And as he tried to shove his foot into a boot, he lost his balance and hit the bookcase. He fell into it hard enough that it knocked stuff off the shelves, including a shoebox that landed facedown. "Sorry, man," he said as he knelt to pick things up. As he reached for the shoebox, Mike was ahead of him, but even so, the photos spilled out.

Jeff laughed, picking one up. "What's this? Is this Shelley? Seriously? And this one is Becky?" He waved the photo in Mike's face. "You've kept all these?"

Mike took the photos from him and returned them to the box. He put the lid back on. The box would go back in the closet—which was where they'd been until he'd taken them out and then Jeff had arrived.

Irony or serendipity? When he thought of it, it seemed like Jeff was always around somewhere when things like that went wrong.

Mike stood slowly, in that deliberate movement reminding Jeff that he was taller, broader, and not in the mood to be messed with. He set the box back up on the shelf, put on his jacket, grabbed his keys, and walked out the door.

Jeff was right behind him. "Wait up. I'm

111

coming."

As they drove along the roads, nearly empty at this hour, Jeff apologized. "Sorry, Mike. But why? I mean, pictures of the girls you've dated, broken up with . . . Why?"

"It's just a box of photos. Of people and moments that mattered to me through the years. You didn't see them all. Mom. Suze when she was a kid. You saw the surface, but not what mattered. That's your problem, Jeff." He slowed as they drove along the residential street approaching The Point, slower still when the tires hit the sand. "Try using your brain sometime. Give the rest of the world a break."

They parked the truck away from the other early-morning fishermen and set up their own lines. The sun was just rising, breaking through the leftover ocean fog that had yet to dissipate, when he saw the woman walking toward them. Mike noted she was wearing those stretchy pants—the ones the gals called exercise tights—hiked halfway up her calves to avoid them getting splashed as she walked near the water. She was also wearing a dark, bulky sweatshirt with the hood pulled up and was sort of turned away, as if trying to avoid being seen. He couldn't tell if she was sixteen or sixty. She was just someone out for a predawn walk or to see the sunrise. If she wanted privacy, she'd get it from him, no problem. He turned away to find his coffee cup.

The fishing lines were thin and hard to spot, but their chairs were easily visible, plus he and Jeff were standing beside the fishing poles and impossible to miss—in their world, anyway. He turned back and saw the woman was evidently somewhere else, and wherever she was, two middle-aged guys in baggy sweatpants and T-shirts were either invisible or not there at all, because she wasn't angling up the beach to avoid the lines.

Mike saw a tangle coming. He started to yell a warning but was too slow. Jeff cursed as she snagged in the lines and her stumble changed to a twisting flail, and the pole flew forward. He went after the pole, but Mike rushed to help the woman as her struggles ramped up and were quickly on the way to becoming frantic.

As she fell backward, Mike grabbed her. "Hold still," he said, and eased her to a sitting position. "Stay put. I'll cut the line."

She was breathing fast, like a deer trapped in a wire fence. Her eyes were big. A color like deep water. He knew, without checking, that her pulse was racing and her next actions would be unpredictable. He raised his hands to show they were empty of threat.

"Easy. It's all good," he said. He was still holding the swiss knife between his thumb and forefinger, but she got the idea. She released her defensive grip on his arm and took a deep, almost painful-seeming breath. He saw when she understood he was her rescuer. She reached up— her hand delicate and long-fingered—to her face to brush the strands of black hair away.

And he swore that in that moment he lost his heart. Again.

As he held the line, grasping it for tension to cut it, he told himself that this was yet one more weak-minded moment that might lead to an interlude—yes, he might very well be open to testing a relationship. Her eyes alone drew him— and a hint of a smile . . .

He felt the response—then threw on the

brakes.

Whoa. Hold on, Mike, he told himself. *Cut the fishing line and move on.*

"Got it," he said, snapping the knife closed. He offered her a hand. She accepted it and rose to her feet lightly, gracefully, coming only as high as his shoulder. He told himself he was releasing her hand right away, but then he saw he was still holding on and tightened his grip instead, asking, "You all right?"

"Danielle. My name, I mean."

He grinned. "I'm Mike. Pleased to meet you."

She laughed with a sheepish look. "Sorry about your fishing line."

"There's more."

She nodded. "Thank you." Impulsively, she reached up and touched his cheek.

For one moment there was no sound between them but that of the waves and the seabirds flying by in the search for breakfast. It was just the two of them, her hand still in his. In the dim light her face was pale, but showing the beginning of a smile. And then Jeff was there, coming toward them, muttering curses as he gathered up the broken line.

Some guys—true lifelong friends—might've noticed something with potential was happening and would've made themselves scarce without a big deal, but not Jeff. He made a show of waving the pole and the line that was now severed. "Hey, Mike!"

She glanced at him, that uneasiness back in her manner and in her unusual eyes. "Sorry for the interruption."

Before he could say a word more, she was hurrying on. Almost running.

I could chase after her . . .

The thought surprised him. And he would've looked a fool. And yet . . . He laughed out loud. Wouldn't be the first time he'd been played for a fool. And it hadn't killed him yet.

She disappeared into the mist. He was almost thankful, until Jeff came up behind him sounding somewhere between half-interested and half-amused.

"You can thank me another time, buddy. When you come back to your senses, you'll realize you owe me one. Another one, in fact. I just saved you from yet one more big fall." He laughed. "From one more photo going into that box."

It had been daylight when I'd started reading. At some point, the light had fled. I was amazed I'd been reading for so long—and oblivious to the passing time. I took the pages with me into the adjacent screened porch, turned on the small table lamp, and sat in the wicker chair. I resumed reading in the full dark. The ocean and the wind combined to provide low background music.

"Lilliane?"

I jumped. "Merrick?"

"Sorry for startling you. And I'm sorry I asked you to read that partial. It was unfair of me. I apologize."

He was wearing his matching jammies, robe, and slippers. Deep green tonight. Well dressed, even for bed. He looked fine but sounded regretful. Concerned.

I was confused. "What are you talking about?"

"It was an imposition. It was thoughtless of me to put you in that position, asking you to pass judgment on someone's work. I'll take the manuscript back."

"You didn't ask me to pass judgment. Only to offer feedback. No worries."

"I'll take it from you." He extended his hands, palms up. "Again, I apologize."

"It's not a problem, truly." My grip tightened on the pages. "Now that I'm reading it, I'd like to continue." I felt a frown forming on my face.

"But . . . it was only three chapters. You have a lot of pages left yet."

"I'm slow. You know that."

There was a long silent pause as he leveled his gaze on me, as if decoding my frown, and stated, "You are enjoying it."

"I am. Very much." I hurried to add, "Please don't be offended." He must be hurt that I hadn't liked his book but was enjoying this one written by Davis. I stood, holding the pages against my body. "Perhaps it truly was a thriller thing. Not your writing, but the genre, as you said. This is . . . very different reading."

"What do you like about it?" He sounded almost eager, then hurried to excuse that eagerness. "It would be wonderful if I could give Davis good news."

I opened my mouth to speak.

He held up his hand and said, "No, wait. Don't tell me. Continue reading. We'll discuss it when you're done. But remember, don't say a word to anyone about it. Most especially not to Davis."

"Okay. Sure. Whatever you want. I understand." In fact, it was likely Davis would be very angry that his trust had been betrayed, so from my point of view, it was all the more important for me to finish the story before he found out and took these pages back.

Merrick stared. I couldn't read his expression, so I waited. But instead of speaking, he turned and went back into the house.

I decided to do the same. I could read in bed—and likely with less interruption from my wandering charge—until I fell asleep. It was okay if I was slow, because I could read tomorrow too, if that's how it worked out. There was plenty of time for reading on this job. Pleasure reading, in fact. Even if it meant reading some of the paragraphs twice, or stopping to think about the setting or the characters and how the words were being used. That was okay. For people like me, it could simply be part of the experience.

I'd never thought I—Lilliane Moore of Cub Creek—would ever be in the position to think such crazy words like *pleasure reading* could apply to me, but this one time, at least, it was true.

CRSO

When I realized I was nearing the last pages, I looked at the bedside clock and saw it was two a.m.

Two a.m.

How had that happened?

The Book of Lost Loves. Thinking of the title and knowing what had followed immediately—with that man fishing with his annoying friend and meeting that mysterious woman. A guy whose heart had clearly been broken before, many times. Enough to fill a book? Too many times, anyway. He'd sounded disappointed, bored. Or maybe dissatisfied and heartsore. About loneliness.

I knew about heartache and regrets.

These three chapters had ended with the woman returning a few mornings later and meeting up with him again, clearly expecting—perhaps hoping—that he'd be there. He had drinks and food in a cooler—and no Jeff. So maybe he was hoping for company too. They shared an impromptu meal sitting on the tailgate at sunrise. No actual fishing happened. The chemistry between them was undeniable. And then—last page.

I flipped it over to see if more might be written on the other side. No.

Not fair.

I sat on the edge of the bed and tidied the sheets of paper

so I could slide them neatly back into the envelope.

In fact, while reading I'd noticed that the paper seemed old. Not dirty or crumpled, but just old. Maybe Davis had been trying to use up leftover reams. More unimportant, silly details that meant nothing to anyone.

So now I'd run out of story. As the pages had grown fewer, I'd tried to read even slower than usual, but still the last page had been reached and read.

The irony was that I could continue this story in my imagination—take it in any direction I wanted. But for now, I wanted the *real* thing—*this* story. Which, ironically, was totally made up, right? Not real at all. Nothing more than a representation, right? Of the human experience and condition.

The human mind was a crazy thing. Sometimes I wondered if we were just living in one big, elastic imagination, making up rules as we went along and throwing everyone else's reality into constant upheaval. And the people who liked how things were? Who were comfortable in their lives and not hurting a soul? Always the losers. Change could be cruel. Devastating, in fact, for many.

I empathized. It squeezed my heart. So the reality wasn't in the story's details, but in the shared experiences represented in the story. Hadn't everyone experienced unwanted change? Or a love that had ended too soon? Or perhaps had begun too soon.

Many years ago, in my first year in high school, a boy had decided he loved me. He sent me little notes, tight scribbles on scraps of paper that he'd folded and refolded until they looked like tiny squares of nothing. Finally, he got up the nerve to ask me out. I told my parents. Dad didn't have much to say, but I knew he wasn't happy about it. My father tended to shut down when presented with the unexpected. Momma was more relaxed. She smoothed my hair, placed a light kiss on my forehead, and said, "I'll talk to Daddy."

I was fifteen, so I knew what the outcome would be.

Ultimately, my parents' answer was no. One more year before dating, they said. But when the next year arrived, the boy had found someone else. It was okay. I didn't mind all that much, really. *But . . .*

There was always a *but*—a *what-if*—wasn't there?

And all these years later, I was still living in my childhood home. No close friends. Just keeping my eyes focused on the ground ahead of me and never moving off the path or beyond the path's end. I wasn't a fool. I knew that wasn't . . . right. It wasn't normal or healthy to hold on to the life I knew, clinging to it like a safety vest. I should've tried other things, instead of voluntarily staying in place and waiting for life to happen.

I'd always known that. Yet, I'd stayed. There were concerns and responsibilities bigger than the basic *me*. As Dad had said when I was a child—we were blessed to be where we were, there in Cub Creek. We had our loved ones and special memories to treasure and protect. And he'd been right. But there was more. In my heart, I'd always known there were things to be seen. To be experienced. And I'd never followed that knowing, that yearning, to see where it might lead.

I put the manila envelope on the desk. It was after two a.m. I felt restless. Not ready for sleep.

My brain was busy thinking of the story I'd read, and about my life. Merrick must've been right about that genre thing. Maybe my teachers had been too, telling me to work on my comprehension, insisting that persistence and practice would make a difference.

Or as Merrick had said, practice didn't make *perfect*, but it made *better*.

I'd tell him he'd gotten it right. He'd like hearing that.

And then there was Davis.

By now, my feet were moving. Clad in my pajamas, and with my robe over my shoulders, I left the room and headed down the stairs.

That Davis could write such an emotional story . . . The characters felt so real to me. As did their troubles. Mike's big heart. The hurts he admitted to and laughed off. Danielle's secret hurt. There was not one bomb or flying shard of glass on the pages. No wonder Merrick, who'd devoted his writing career to action-oriented thrillers, wanted another opinion before giving Davis feedback.

By now I was sitting on the edge of the pool, my pajama pants hiked up over my knees and my feet soaking in the sun-warmed water.

What about the rest of the story?

I wanted it. Merrick could get it for me.

What else might Davis have written? Would it be like this? No, as I recalled, he'd written the one thriller. Like Merrick, right? Still, if he could write *The Book of Lost Loves*, maybe his thriller style was cozier than Merrick's?

Needing to move again, I dried my feet on the hem of my robe and went back inside. I stopped in the study doorway and listened. No sound was coming from Merrick's room. No light showed around the edges of the closed bedroom door.

I turned on Merrick's desk lamp and walked along the bookcases that occupied almost every wall. The books were a mix of old and new. Some were fabric covered. Others wore bright, glossy jackets. Merrick's books were arranged together on several shelves in one section, but I couldn't tell how the rest were ordered. Not alphabetically. Not by topic, or by fiction or nonfiction. At least, not as far as I could see. I saw nothing written by Davis . . . though my search was hampered by me not even knowing his full name.

Tomorrow, first thing, I'd fix that.

Chapter Ten

The next morning, Merrick's voice came out of nowhere, saying, "Lilliane, I'm up."

I jumped, startled, nearly knocking the plate I was preparing with his breakfast off the kitchen counter.

The monitor, of course.

He added, "I'm up and *on the move.*"

I pressed the Speak button. "Meet you in the study."

Shortly thereafter, I was in his study, manila envelope in hand. I'd already put his breakfast of fresh fruit, hard-boiled egg, and toast with cherry jelly on his desk. When he emerged from the bedroom, he was dressed for the day, but his hair was all awry, as if he hadn't bothered to comb it or perhaps had been running his fingers through the length of it all night.

"Did you sleep well?"

"Well enough." He shook out the napkin and put it in his lap.

"I brought coffee. If you'd like tea or something else, I can fetch it."

"This is fine for now." He looked up and noticed the envelope on his desk. He stopped and stared at it, but like it was a snake or such, something with teeth that might lunge at him. Might bite.

Putting it down to morning crankiness, I ignored his behavior and said, "It's a wonderful story. Thank you for suggesting I read it. You called it right. Thrillers are just not my thing. This was entirely different."

No response from him. Had I said something wrong? I hastened to add, "If there's more to the story, I'd be delighted to continue with it."

Still no answer. He stared at me and then at the envelope and back at me again.

"Is everything okay, Merrick?"

"Yes, of course. It's all good. Quite."

"Dreams again?" I asked. "Would you like to discuss it? Or maybe get my feedback about the story?"

He tapped the envelope with his finger and made that grunty noise he was prone to, then said, "Too early. Not yet. Later." He added, "I appreciate you reading this. We'll talk over lunch, if that's okay."

"My pleasure, and of course, over lunch will be fine." I added, "Do you think you could ask Davis for more of the story? I'd love to see what happens next."

Another odd look briefly flitted across his face. He recovered quickly as I assured him, "He won't know that I read it. I did promise not to tell him, and I meant it."

"Yes," he said. "Yes . . . I can ask him. Better to ask in person, though. I expect him to drop by in a day or so."

"Oh."

He frowned, and his voice got a little grumbly. "I could call him, of course, but if I seem too eager, he'll get an inflated opinion. Could lead to . . ."

Lead to what? None of this rang true to me. Merrick had said other things about the issue of confidence with writers, and he should know, right? But I felt like some of these things might be being doled out to . . . to direct me. Manipulate me? Maybe. But why bother when it was so much easier to just ask me outright?

"Well, let me know." I changed the tone and subject. "I'll get out of your way. You've barely touched your breakfast."

"Why don't you stay for a moment. I'll eat."

I was surprised. "Sure. By the way, Ms. Bertie left meatloaf and mashed potatoes in a casserole dish for supper today. I admit I'm pretty excited about it. I haven't had meatloaf in years."

"Turkey loaf," he said, making a face.

"Probably. I'll bet it's good anyway."

"Dr. Barnes says I have the arteries of an eighteen-year-old. Beef worked fine for me for seventy-five years. Now, here I am, at the mercy of . . . well-meaning, but . . ." He shook his head. "Never mind. I know I'm fortunate to have someone as reliable and accommodating as Ms. B." His voice dropped lower. Maybe he was hoping I wouldn't hear him. "Don't get old, Lilliane. The things you loved are either lost forever or substituted for. It's not the same."

Nothing ever stayed the same. Except for the things that did. I didn't say the words aloud because we both already understood the obvious.

Suddenly feeling deflated, I sat abruptly in the chair I'd left beside his desk. It had been here since I'd carried it over a couple of days before.

"You okay?" he asked.

"About the same as you, probably. Maudlin."

He raised his bushy eyebrows. "Maudlin," he repeated after me as he pushed the fruit around on his plate. "*Maudlin*. That's a fine word."

"It is indeed. My aunt used it. She had to tell me what it meant, of course, but it stuck with me."

"And? Who was she using *maudlin* in reference to?"

"A friend of hers who'd spent more time grieving over what she'd lost than enjoying what she had. Foolish, sentimental melancholy. And totally human."

"*Melancholy*. Another good word."

"Autumnal."

"Yes." He nodded and took a bite of his toast.

"My mother liked the big words. Instead of *fall*, she always said *autumn*. When it was fall weather, she'd call it *autumnal*."

The shadow seemed to be lifting from Merrick. From me too.

"I'm going to throw some clothing in the wash. Do you need anything?"

"I'm good. I'll be on the computer for a while, catching up with some old friends, doing email, all that stuff. Nothing special. No need to disturb me until lunch."

Surprised and slightly amused at being dismissed—phrased nicely, but still a dismissal—I agreed.

He added, "If Davis calls or drops by, I'll see what I can do about getting you more chapters of that book."

"Thank you." I paused before asking, "Would you like a cup of tea? A glass of water? Anything?" I stood. "I'll have my phone. My number is programmed into yours. Call me if you need me."

CRSO

I did my little bit of laundry, including my shorts and khakis, wishing I had a better wardrobe. Today, I was wearing jeans. The denim was old, and oft-washed. Hard to beat the feel of soft denim. I cleaned the kitchen, washing up surfaces that didn't really need it, perhaps pretending just a little that it was *my* kitchen. Having a kitchen like this might inspire me to cook with more enthusiasm. As I was finishing up, I had a brief moment of alarm seeing a man out by the pool, but then I realized he was the man Merrick was paying to maintain it.

A pool boy—except this one wasn't anything like the ones in the movies. He was an older guy who did his job and then vanished as silently as he'd arrived.

Merrick had made a point of asking not to be disturbed, so I took a walk down along the beach. I rolled up the legs of my jeans as best I could and donned my flip-flops. As I neared the end of the crossover, I saw Miranda Wardlaw's canopy and below it her bare feet poking out from between the chair legs. From this distance and angle, the colorful canopy hid her body and face from me. Impulsively, I switched on the camera, hoping to capture the color and shapes in the bright sunlight with the blue sky all around, and that striped canopy in the middle of it.

Thank you, Gwen.

I approached Miranda cautiously, not wanting to startle her if she was dozing. She wasn't, but she was deep into a book. I thought of Davis's manuscript and felt a kinship with her that I hadn't before.

"Good morning," I said. "Soon to be afternoon, in fact."

She looked up and pushed her hat up out of her way a bit. "Well, and good morning to you too. How are you doing over there?"

She meant with the ornery Merrick, of course.

"I'm having a lovely time."

She squinted at me. "Seriously? Well, maybe his manners have improved."

I didn't want to discuss Merrick with her, so I let that remark pass.

"Won't you join me here? You're welcome to share my shade."

"Thank you, but no. I only have a few minutes before I have to be back for lunch." I gestured with the camera. "I want to try some photos."

"You're a photographer?"

I laughed. "Goodness, no. I wish. A friend loaned me this when she heard I was coming to the beach. Said I had to give it a try. I'd never been to the beach before."

She squinted again, and I moved closer, realizing that the sun's glare behind me was causing the problem.

"Never, huh? Where are you from? Inland somewhere?"

I almost laughed again at the way she said it, as if *inland* was a dig. "Definitely inland. Virginia, near the mountains."

"Whereabouts? I grew up in that direction. Bumpass."

"Seriously? I'm from Cub Creek."

She slapped her book. "Well, small world. Small, small world. Practically neighbors. But I haven't been there in many years. My father got a new job elsewhere, and we moved away while I was still a child. But I remember it well."

"It is a small world." I was a little relieved that she hadn't been there in many years. Stories get around and are seldom forgotten. I was glad that wasn't a potential problem with her. I said, "We'll have to chat about it sometime, but for now, I'll leave you to get back to your book, and I'll give this camera a workout."

Gwen had mentioned the memory card in the camera would hold a ton of pictures, and I hoped she was right because I found myself letting go and just having fun with it.

⚜

Over lunch, Merrick seemed almost like a different man. The stunned man who hadn't had much to say was again full of questions, but this time about the manuscript I'd read.

"I should've asked you more specific questions before, but frankly, you surprised me. You were so . . . enthusiastic in your approval for the chapters you read. I'd like to know what caused you to feel so engaged with the story?"

"I don't know. I wasn't thinking about that while I was reading."

"Yet you lost yourself in the story."

"I did." I thought about it. "Yes, the story was told by a man—from how he saw things. His perspective, right? But very relatable. The woman was much less open than the man and clearly a gal with secrets. It reminded me of myself—or rather, of how I felt about choices I've made and not made." I closed my eyes to think. "There was a different rhythm to the story. Slower, with more time to see and taste and feel than with a thriller. Does that make sense?" I shook my head and leaned forward. "To be honest, I did have to reread certain passages. Pages, even. Reading—reading comprehension—especially when there's lots of text, has always been difficult for me. But after a while last night, when I was being carried away by the story, I found the experience . . . less difficult. I almost forgot I *was* reading." I focused on him. "Are you going to ask Davis for more?"

He coughed a little and then sipped on his drink. "I called him. Left him a message to call me. I'll keep you posted." He added, "Meanwhile, you should go amuse yourself. I'm going to lie down for a little nap. "You should go somewhere."

"Maybe you're right. I might take a short run to the store. I passed a clothing store on the way here, and I could use a few things. Are you sure?"

"I'm not a baby. I'll be fine."

"Excellent. You have my number in your phone. Call me if—"

He interrupted, "If I need you. Yes, ma'am."

CRED

It was fun to get out of the house and see a bit of the world. I bought some toiletries at the grocery store and found a discount clothing store that had what I needed—just some shorts and a couple of T-shirts—to stretch my clothing options. Beachy wear. I checked my phone from time to time, just in case Merrick might've called and I'd missed it, but no call. He'd looked tired, so maybe he really did just want an uninterrupted nap.

But when I returned and took the elevator up from the garage (just because I could), I heard him yelling as the doors parted.

"Lilliane, is that you? Are you back?"

Though only a few feet away from the study doors, I hollered as if I was calling across a valley, "I am. It's me. I'm back!" I went to the open study door, grinning.

He said, "I'm not deaf."

I smiled. "Neither am I."

He squinted. "You should be nicer to me."

"Oh? Give me a good reason."

He pointed to the corner table. The manila envelope was there.

I switched my gaze right back to him. "Seriously? He brought more? This morning?"

He looked away, as if it were no big thing. "He dropped it off while you were out." He shrugged. "Three more chapters. Don't rush through them too fast. I don't know when there'll be more."

My heart rate increased. I put my hand to my chest, finding the key pendant, resting my hand on it, but thinking of the manuscript. Merrick truly did not understand how novel, how ironic it was for me to be cautioned not to read through something too quickly. Reading, and enjoying it, was something so familiar to him that he took it for granted. To me, it was truly a wonderment.

CR80

I resisted jumping right into it. I set the envelope on the kitchen counter, close to me, but didn't open it. I could've. I could've pulled it out of that envelope and started reading right away.

But suppose it wasn't the same this time? Suppose that first flush of reading and finding pleasure in it was a fluke? Or suppose the story took a turn that let me down?

Also, I preferred to wait until I could be reasonably sure of not being interrupted.

At supper, Merrick seemed disappointed, almost personally offended that I hadn't already read it.

He frowned and sounded put out. "You seemed in a big hurry. Apparently, you've lost enthusiasm for the story."

"No. In fact, it's the opposite. Is it possible to enjoy a story so much that you can't take the chance that it—the enjoyment—won't continue?"

He moved his jaw. He scratched his cheek. He blinked several times. His Adam's apple moved up and down. He asked, "You liked it that much?"

I nodded.

"Then you must trust the author."

"Pardon?"

"Just what I said. Think about it."

"Okay." I nodded.

"And eat the meatloaf. It's surprisingly good. Ms. B can do wonders with ground turkey."

As per Merrick's advice, I put my attention to the food. It was good. I was midchew when the doorbell rang.

Merrick started to rise. I waved him back and went to the desk where the window gave a view of the front porch.

I turned to Merrick, surprised since the visitor had already been here today while I was out. "It's Davis."

"Remember our secret," he said. "Don't mention any of this."

I pressed the napkin to my lips and went to the door.

CHAPTER ELEVEN

"Hello, Lilliane. Good afternoon."

Davis seemed genuinely pleased to see me. All I could think of was the book—*Don't mention it to him*—and that he'd dropped that second installment off earlier today. *Don't mention that either*.

"Hello," I said.

He smiled, and his eyes lit up. "Is Merrick available?"

No longer thinking of the book, I noted that the hint of topaz in his eyes was a slightly different shade today and seemed to match his shirt. This shirt wasn't tropical or floral, but a geometric pattern. Didn't recall ever seeing a shirt like that back home. And his dark hair . . . looked like he'd gotten a trim.

What was wrong with me? I shook it off.

"He's having supper," I said. "In the study." I gestured for him to precede me into the room. When he did, I veered away and went directly to the half bath off the kitchen to check my teeth for food. By the time I returned to the study, Davis had pulled up a chair, and he and Merrick looked comfortable together. As if time had moved on.

And so must I.

Besides, relaxing there, getting comfortable with them, was too risky. I'd say something for sure about the book Davis was writing. That I was reading. Secretly.

I picked up my plate and utensils from the table.

Merrick waved at me, saying, "Sit, Lilliane. Finish your meal."

"Oh, I'm done. No worries. I'll take these dishes back to the kitchen." Which I did, and as soon as I got there I stood at the counter and finished eating. When I returned to the study it was only to tell Merrick that if he was done, I'd clear the table and clean up the kitchen now.

"You should join us."

"Thanks, but I'll get this taken care of."

He accepted that, and I did as I'd said. A meal for two, and one that had been prepared in advance, didn't generate much mess, so it was a quick job. But doing the dishes had provided me with an easy excuse to make myself scarce.

Why did I feel so reluctant to sit next to Davis at that table? Because I couldn't be trusted not to blurt out about the book? Yes. Especially if Davis decided to discuss it with Merrick right there in front of me. I was quite certain I'd jump in and share my thoughts.

Merrick might not mind playing the conspirator, but to me it felt like lying, and Davis—whose manuscript it was—was the only one not in on the game.

Felt wrong.

But I'd promised.

And I was helping, right? Helping Merrick give Davis feedback that would encourage him?

Besides, what was the deal with him coming over every day? I supposed it was good for Merrick, having a regular visitor and a guy to hang out with. But it bothered me.

I snagged my flip-flops, rolled my jeans as far up my shins as the cut would allow, and set off for the sand and sea.

If Merrick needed me, he had my number.

And I fled the scene.

CR80

I hadn't planned to return to the beach. I was going to read by the pool after supper. It was true irony that the person's manuscript I was so eager to read had shown up unexpectedly and was the very reason I couldn't read at the moment and whose presence had caused me to flee. Not to mention my guilt over not being truthful with Davis or betraying my promise to Merrick. *Ugh.*

As I walked along the crossover, I called Gwen. Why not? In a way, she was responsible for all this—the good and the bad.

"Gwen, it's me. Lilliane."

"Do you need a rescue?"

I laughed. I'd mostly forgotten that I'd told her she was on the hook to rescue me if I needed it. "No, actually, I wanted to thank you. I am having fun."

"It's going well?"

"So far as I can tell. Merrick can be moody, but we manage together quite well."

"Merrick?"

"Sure. He's not formal."

"I knew you'd have fun. From what Susan said about Mr. Dahl—plain spoken and at times contrary—I thought you'd get along."

"I guess that's the nice way to say I'm rude?"

"No, I'm not saying you are rude, but you are honest and don't put up with drama or machinations."

Machinations? Good word. I stored that word away to share with Merrick. "At any rate, I'm having a good time, and I appreciate the camera too."

"What do you think about him being an author?"

Oh. Dangerous territory. Of course, she wasn't asking about Davis—didn't even know about Davis—but once I got started on a story, I didn't always stop when I was supposed to. Not telling Merrick's and my secret would have to include anyone other than Merrick, and that meant Gwen.

I settled for, "Really interesting."

"I'll bet. People get funny about fame and money and all that stuff. Susan was concerned about not allowing someone who might take advantage of Mr. Dahl to have such close contact while she was out of the area. I gather it's been a problem before. That and people who wanted to glom on to his status in the industry. It's wrong for folks to be pestering ninety-year-olds, isn't it? An old man who hasn't written a word in twenty years."

"Twenty-five," I said, sort of mindlessly because I was thinking of Davis. Maybe I shouldn't be so quick to reverse my initial opinion. *Oops*—Gwen was still talking. "What did you say?"

"Nothing important. I'm just so glad and relieved it's going well. I was sure it would. Otherwise, I wouldn't have suggested you do this, but knowing it is such a relief."

We disconnected soon after that. Gwen had a meeting to attend. She was a wonderful person. Hard to imagine her and Susan Biggs as best buddies in college. They were so different, at least on the surface. Sometimes it seemed that made for a better relationship than with those who were just alike. That thought took me back to Davis's book. And to Davis himself. I needed to give him another chance—a fresh start—and not be so quick to judge this time.

I sat there awhile, thinking and not thinking—sometimes just enjoying the ocean show, the hypnotic rhythm and movement of the waves, and digging my feet into the sand. I held on to my phone, feeling that as long as I didn't let it go, home and Gwen—the representation of the folks I knew and cared for back there—were close to me. And yet, I wasn't in a hurry to go back. Despite the weird homesickness that had rolled over me the day before. Today I didn't feel it at all. Maybe I was adjusting. Maybe it was okay to love two places—forested hills and beaches. Too soon to say I loved the beach, I supposed. People did. Or said they did. Some people used the term *love* pretty easily.

"Excuse me."

No. Not again.

"May I join you?"

"Suit yourself. It's a public beach."

"Kind and generous as always," he said as he sank to the sand next to me. Not too close. He kept some distance

133

between us.

If he'd intended his words to sting, he'd misjudged. I was doing a job. I had a client and a charge, and my responsibility was to him, not to Davis. I kept my response neutral. "Maybe I deserved that. Maybe not."

"Look, I'll leave if you prefer. I only wanted to chat with you away from Merrick. Just for a minute."

There it was, what I'd suspected—ulterior motives.

Behind Merrick's back. Intrigue. Taking advantage of . . . What Susan Biggs, and even Merrick, had warned me about. And how on earth was I going to break the news to him that his friend, Davis, was conniving behind his back?

Davis said, "I always know where to find you." He nodded back in the direction of the house, then swept an arm in a grand gesture encompassing the ocean and the beach strand. "Either back there or over here."

I almost replied sharply but pulled it back. This was the time to listen and discover. But I couldn't help my guarded tone as I responded, "Both places are pretty good, as far as I'm concerned. I'm feeling pretty fortunate."

He asked, "You and Merrick are getting along okay?"

"Fine."

"I know he can be difficult at times."

"Aren't you his friend?"

"I am," Davis said. "At least, I *think* we're friends. For his part, I may be more of a convenience." He grimaced. "Not exactly what I meant. What I'm trying to say is that if I wasn't in his life, he wouldn't miss me for long. I fill up an empty space for him, but I think he does enjoy our friendship when he's in the mood for it."

"Sounds one-sided."

"Maybe one-sided for both of us. I'm company when he's in the mood. For me, he talks about writing. We chat. He reads my stuff and offers feedback. I get a kick out of hanging with a legend, I guess."

"A legend?"

"To the writing world. At least in the thriller world." He added, "Forty books. Five of them turned into movies. Translations in I don't know how many countries around the world."

His bare feet were only inches from mine. I was mesmerized, but only for a moment before I shifted my gaze to the horizon.

He had nice feet. Not like shoe feet, the way feet get sort of pale and bony when they're shut away all the time. In fact, his feet and toenails looked better than mine. I suspected he'd treated his tootsies to a pedicure. Casually, unobtrusively, I eased my feet deeper into the sand, allowing the warm grains to cover my toes and sandpaper heels.

"How many books have you written?" I was getting the sense that maybe he wasn't finagling a way to use Merrick. Maybe I'd misread that.

"One. I came late to it. I was one of those folks who talked about wanting to write. Went to college, then went to work every day. Tried to write here and there. I thought I was supposed to wait for the muse. That if the book was worth writing, it would come pouring out. That didn't happen. And in total honesty, my life has always been easy. Didn't really see how I'd earned it. So when I did finally complete a book, I didn't have the confidence to send it out anywhere. Then I met Merrick."

"And?"

"With Merrick, you either exist or you don't. Know what I mean?"

"I'm not sure."

"Well, you'll know soon." He laughed briefly. "So, when I met Merrick several years ago, it was by chance. He got out more often then. Was still driving, in fact. One day I happened to be at a writers' conference. A group of us had gathered in the foyer of the hotel, and we were talking about writing and markets and all that. I said something flippant about how long it had taken me to write a three-hundred-page doorstop, and this stranger turned toward me and went off on me. Set me straight. Told me it was up to me to do something with it—or not. Not to waste other people's time with self-pity and my own choice of inaction."

"Harsh."

"Nope, he was right. And it turned out well. I'm working on a new book now. Merrick is reading the first draft. That's what I brought over to him."

I squeezed my fingers so hard I almost yelped. I bit down on my lip. Anything to hold the words in. To keep my promise to Merrick not to tell Davis that I'd read his opening chapters—*and that I'd loved them.* I may have groaned with the effort of keeping the words unsaid.

Davis looked at me oddly. "Is something wrong?"

With a show of shrugging and stretching, I said, "No, just sitting too long, I guess." I sought to change the subject. "So what's the deal with your name? *Davis.* Merrick calls you that. Is it your first name or last name? Is it a secret? I asked Merrick, and he sidestepped the question."

"Oh? You asked Merrick about me?"

"Please. We aren't thirteen. I asked because it just seemed odd to have one name. Some music or movie stars do. But generally, being a one-name person isn't normal. You should have at least two."

He scratched his head and smiled. "Lilliane Moore, correct?"

I frowned. "Yes."

He extended his hand for a shake, and after a short hesitation, I accepted it. He said, "I am pleased to officially meet you, Lilliane Moore. My name is Davis McMahon."

"Pleased to meet you, Mr. McMahon."

"I insist you call me Davis."

"Indeed." An impulse prompted me to add, "And I insist that you *never* call me Lillie."

Surprise showed in his raised eyebrows and amusement in the twinkle in his eyes. "You have my promise."

We shook hands slowly and thoroughly. When the introduction was over, I reclaimed mine. I was amused, too, despite myself.

"So," he said, "the reason I disturbed you . . ."

Uh-oh. "You mentioned you wanted to say something about Merrick. I thought you'd already said it." He'd gotten me all warm and fuzzy to disarm me. I saw his intent in a heartbeat of understanding.

"Actually, what I wanted to say was that you are good for him. He almost glowed when he talked about writing stuff today. I was telling him about someone he used to work with who just went to another agency. He talked about knowing the guy when he first came into the industry, and there wasn't a single snarky, cynical moment in it."

"Oh."

"None of the other aides had this effect on him."

"Oh." I didn't know what to say. "Actually, I see myself as more of a companion. I'm not really trained as a proper aide." How stupid did that sound?

"Well, whatever magic you're working, keep it up. He's had a few down years. I presume you know about his former wife?"

"She's been mentioned."

He nodded. "Marie. I didn't know him then, but from what I've heard, and seen, he took it hard. For a long time. I'm glad to see the change you've brought in his life."

"Thank you, but I can't take credit for it. Maybe we're just two cranky people and it's a relief for us not having to tame it—to give it free rein."

And he laughed. He laughed like laughter was free and the healthiest thing in the world and he was on an extreme health kick. Locks of hair fell in his face. He leaned backward onto one elbow, half reclining, and with his free hand, he unselfconsciously raked the hair back with his fingers.

Gravity pulled at me. It was all I could do not to fall

backward myself, following his lead.

He left soon after—might even still have been laughing a little—as he waved goodbye.

Somehow it felt like a narrow escape. Not for Merrick's faith in Davis, but for my heart.

CR&O

After Davis left me there on the beach, I felt changed somehow. I stood and brushed the sand from my jeans.

I'd had crushes before and knew the signs. It was important to recognize what was happening and acknowledge it to take its power away. These two weeks at the beach were going to pass quicker than I'd ever suspected. No need to add more angst to the leaving. No complications welcome, thank you very much.

I returned to the house as I'd come—via the crossover and the gazebo gate. The hallway was quiet. I went directly to the study. It was empty, but the door to his bedroom was cracked open.

"Merrick?"

"One moment."

He must've been near the door because he was there quickly, and already dressed for bed.

"Would you like a snack or tea?" I asked.

"No, I overate at supper. I'm just going to bed a little early. I'll put on the TV and will likely fall asleep, so don't worry if you hear noise."

That felt off. But why? Lots of people fell asleep to a TV lullaby.

I said, "That's fine. You're feeling well?"

He attempted to smile. "Perfectly fine. Just tired."

"Well, good night, then. Unless I see you up and about on your midnight stroll." I said it in jest with a bit of a smile. "Otherwise, I'll be reading by the pool for a while."

He nodded, a pleased look in his eyes. "I hope you'll

enjoy it."

"I'm sure I will."

I left, and he closed the door. But I paused in the study as something caught my eye. His desk. His computer was gone. I hadn't noticed him taking it into the bedroom before, which was what I assumed he must've done now. But then again, I reminded myself, I'd only known him for three days.

Only three days? Gosh.

In some ways, it felt like a lifetime.

I made my usual hot tea brew and set it aside to cool while I went upstairs and donned my swimsuit. When I came back down, I poured the tea into a glass and plopped a few ice cubes in. Tea was very versatile. And this time, I took not only my tea but the robe *and* a towel with me. I was getting the hang of this pool and beach life.

I propped my feet up and sat back with the envelope on my lap.

Was I delaying on purpose? Almost like I was teasing myself, or perhaps protecting myself because of the "what isn't started can't end in disappointment" premise.

Nonsense.

Davis, I thought, *you need to live up to the expectations you set with those opening chapters.* And then, since I was thinking about Davis, I remembered how he'd laughed just before leaving the beach, and I remembered the handshake—our official intro—firm but not tight, warm but not sweaty.

I opened the envelope and pulled out the papers.

CRITO

As with the first chapters, there was no header at the top of the page. The book's title was again in large type in the middle of the page: *The Book of Lost Loves*. Below that was the title of this section: "Part Two: A Heart Given and a Heart Stolen."

This section followed the relationship of Mike and

Danielle, growing bit by bit, with occasional interruptions by his friend Jeff and a growing mystery about Danielle—she was obviously trying to hide something.

Mike and Danielle had gone out to dinner. Over dessert, Mike took a small gift box from his pocket.

> Danielle frowned at the box he was holding, then she smiled. He'd been surprised by her frown. Was that first instinctive response the truer one? Was she hoping to mask her initial response with the smile? Mike shook the doubt off. At best it was a guess on his part either way, so he dismissed the attempt to read her mind and moved forward. He laughed pleasantly, saying, "It's a gift."
>
> "A gift?"
>
> Did she think it was an engagement ring? Not to say that something more permanent hadn't crossed his mind . . . "No worries, Dani. It won't bite."
>
> The jeweler had wrapped the box. Dani had the paper off in two neat moves by sliding her fingernails under the tape. Mike took the paper from her and held it while she lifted the lid from the box.
>
> Was that a sigh he heard? Was it one of relief or disappointment?
>
> "It's a bracelet," she said.
>
> "Yes, ma'am."
>
> Two heart-shaped silver shells hung from the bracelet like charms. She touched each with the tip of her fingernail. "It's lovely."
>
> "There are two."
>
> She laughed. "I can see that."
>
> "Two shell hearts to mark the two months since we met."
>
> "Mike . . ."

"Or, if you prefer, consider one shell heart to represent me and one to represent you, but"—he grinned—"that analogy might be an awkward fit next month when the third shell heart joins them."

"Please, Mike, listen to me."

He waved her words away. "I know you like to take things slow. This gift is only to remind you that I'm here and you can count on me."

"Of course, but . . ."

"Seriously, Dani. I want you to have it. To wear it."

She allowed him to put the bracelet around her wrist and close the clasp, but his fingers felt clumsy. When she raised her hand so that the bracelet and charms could catch the light, the clasp failed, and the bracelet fell to the floor.

Mike leaned over and reached toward the floor, saying, "No worries. I've got it."

But when he righted himself and held the bracelet out to her, she said, "Mike . . ."

"No," he said. "Don't." He shook his head, but she wasn't offering her hand. "It's just the clasp." He showed her. "It works fine. I didn't close it completely, that's all."

Danielle finally accepted the bracelet. I was a little miffed about the crap she was putting Mike through. It was just a gift. *Thank you* or *no thank you* would do the job just fine. If she was having doubts about their relationship, then she should say so. This hot-and-cold business was unfair to both of them. Unless it had something to do with her secret . . .

That evening Mike was sitting at home—no

Dani, no Jeff—when he noticed he'd never returned that shoebox to the closet.

It was one of those things—the things people plan to do but never get around to. They say they have no time or have lost interest, but there's usually a reason. It applied to him too. When he was younger, he'd planned to make a photo album. A book about the people and events that were important in his life—their arrivals and departures equally random and unaccountable. The book was a way to keep them. To remember them.

Tonight he picked up the box and tossed the lid aside. He sifted through the photos. *In a book? Nah.* It wasn't going to happen. Maybe it was time to toss the works. Let the past be the past.

For several minutes, he stood beside the trash can, the box almost tipped far enough forward to empty it, but in the end, the box, the photos, and the past won. He all but threw it back onto the shelf.

By now the sun had set. I was sitting in the dark and about halfway through this batch of pages. Deliberately, I put the manuscript aside, fixed another cup of tea, and while it cooled, I went into the pool, down the steps as before, but with more confidence this time.

Danielle had secrets. Mike did too, though his seemed more like past baggage. What about Jeff? I knew he'd be back in the story sooner or later. I didn't trust him one little bit. Maybe he had secrets too.

Secrets . . . I had some of my own.

As I waded in the water, it struck me that the characters

had a different feel—the whole tone of the book did—of being slightly old-fashioned. I tried to put my finger on it but failed. Had Davis done that on purpose, as a technique, maybe?

As for this secret that Merrick and I shared, maybe one day it would become unnecessary and I'd get the chance to ask the author himself.

Chapter Twelve

In the morning, Merrick looked tired again. The dark circles and swollen bags beneath his eyes seemed more pronounced. The study doors were open.

I stood there quietly observing him at his desk, concerned. His laptop was open in front of him, but he was staring past it, and his shoulders were sagging.

"Merrick," I said softly.

His head jerked up.

"Are you sleeping? Did you sleep last night?"

"You snuck up on me. Just to see me jump, right?" But his grumpiness seemed half-hearted.

"You look exhausted. More so every day."

"I'm old. In fact, growing older every day, as you noted."

"Maybe you need to get out for some sunshine, fresh air and exercise."

He nodded, but it was like a whole-body nod where he just kind of rocked forward and back again. He said, "Davis wants to take me out to lunch."

"Excellent idea."

"Told him I was too busy."

"Too busy? With what?"

"I have things to do before I die."

"Lovely, charming sentiment for a beautiful, sunny day at the beach. Much better to act on it and get out and enjoy the day while you can."

"All right. Whatever."

"Good. Do we need to call him?"

"No, he's coming anyway. He wants to go to lunch and

to the barbershop."

"Excellent. Fresh air, exercise and a haircut. Hard to beat that." I was glad. It would be good for him to get out with the guys, so to speak. "If at any point you don't feel well, or just want to come home, I expect you to inform Davis so he can call me."

"Yes, Mother."

"Ha. Very funny. Just remember."

"By the way, Susan called." He added, "I just got off the phone with her a short while ago."

I waited.

"She wanted to know how we're doing together."

"Why?"

He gave me a funny look. "Because she works for me?"

"What's her story, anyway? Her card says she's a business manager. She hires me to work for you and then takes off. Literally. Where was she flying off to?"

"She manages my business. She does it well."

"She was rather . . . Well, let's say she wasn't exactly friendly."

"I don't pay her to be friendly. I, along with other clients, pay her for her skills. And she's good."

"Fair enough. So where was she in such a hurry to fly away to?"

"Personal."

"Vacation?"

"Just personal. Not my information to tell."

Names and tales—still didn't go together. "You are right, Merrick. And on that note, I'll get out of your way. Do you need anything?"

"Aren't you interested in what I told her?"

"Susan?"

"About how we're doing."

I smiled. "I already know. We get along fabulously. At least, in my opinion, so if you told her anything else, I don't want to know."

He looked at me blankly.

"It would hurt my feelings. I'm only here for another week. I'd like to remember this visit as a time of firsts. Good firsts that I never would've experienced if Susan—cozy or not—hadn't hired me." I paused. "Fair enough?"

He nodded but didn't speak.

I smiled. "Yell if you need me."

⊙⃝

When Merrick and Davis returned, the afternoon was nearly done. I expected to see an exhausted ninety-year-old man leaning on his cane, struggling to stay upright as he dragged himself home before zooming right out into a nap. Davis had called using Merrick's phone to let me know they were minutes away. I got the tea ready as a restorative. Merrick was going to need it.

But he didn't. He returned talking and doing that grunty thing—the grunt that sounded satisfied—and his cane was hitting the floor with extra gusto. His hair had been trimmed, and he was closely shaved.

I smiled at him, and at Davis too. I told them to stop and stay where they were. I'd be right back. My camera was just in the kitchen.

When I returned, they were still standing in the foyer, near the doorway to the study. The light was definitely better here in the foyer. Merrick protested a teeny bit when he saw the camera, but it wasn't a sincere protest, and he and Davis posed together. When I said, "Smile," Davis did, but Merrick gave a glorious mock pouty frown. I snapped it.

"Now, let's do it with a smile." And this time he did.

I took the camera away from my eye and thanked them.

"Not so fast," Merrick said.

Davis said, "Your turn."

I protested.

"No," Merrick said, and he tapped his cane against the

floor tiles, hard.

I touched my hair, thinking I should brush it or something first.

Davis said, "You look perfect."

Perfect. I was without words and simply handed him the camera and joined Merrick.

I was embarrassed. Embarrassed to be having my photo taken with Merrick? No. But suddenly, somehow, I felt exposed. Me, grinning beside Merrick, Davis snapping photos of us. Up close, far away.

Finally, I said, "No more. I only have the one memory card. You're going to fill it up."

Davis gave me a curious look. "You'll download the card and clear it."

I reached for the camera. "I can't do that until I get home. My friend is going to do it for me on her computer."

The curiosity had changed to something else. I didn't want to read it. I looked away and reclaimed Gwen's camera.

"Thank you both." I turned to Merrick. "I'll bring your tea to your desk." I asked Davis, "Would you like some?"

"Tea?"

"Hot tea. Merrick enjoys it."

"Yes, then. Thank you."

He didn't seem to be in a hurry to leave.

When I returned with the tea, Davis said, "Aren't you going to join us?"

Merrick was at his desk, and Davis was sitting at the end—in my spot. "I don't—"

"I'm certain Merrick is bored with just my wit." He laughed. "He's been stuck with me for hours. He'll be kicking me out any moment now."

Merrick grunted. He was already nibbling on a cookie.

"I'll be back." I went to fetch my tea.

When I returned, Davis had vacated the chair he'd been sitting in and pulled up another. His courtesy at recognizing that spot as mine touched me.

Davis sipped the tea and frowned.

It was my turn to laugh, but I held it in. "Dandelion tea. Excellent for this and that. I add honey spice tea for a little extra flavor."

"And a cookie."

I said, "*Always* a cookie. Two, in fact."

Merrick was watching us. I would have to disabuse him of whatever imaginings he was conjuring up in his mind later. I admit, though, that it amused me. Which was always risky for me because I very much liked being amused.

Davis said, "You're leaving in a week?"

Wasn't expecting that. "Yes."

"Going home? I know you love the beach. Have you considered staying in the area?"

My heart responded. I forced myself to complete my sip of tea and casually set the cup back onto the saucer as if I were unaffected by his interest in where I might go.

I cleared my throat. "Well, I'll be going home, of course. I have responsibilities there." My brain whispered, *You're the unencumbered one.*

I reached for another cookie to hide the oddness I felt.

Oddness? Yes, but it was the truth. Oh, there were people who might miss me a little and would hopefully remember me fondly if they happened to think of me, but would they miss me for more than a passing thought?

Not really.

So, Davis was interested.

That bothered me. It didn't take much for a guy to be *interested.* I knew that for a fact. A warm body was sufficient temptation for some guys. And I'd sworn off those kinds of distractions and stumbling blocks a long time ago. I knew nothing about Davis's personal life or history. For all I knew, he was a serial seducer.

Nope. I wasn't in the market for that.

I stood. "This has been lovely, but you made a full day of it, didn't you, Merrick?"

Davis looked at the windows, still bright with sunlight, and then back at me.

"Mr. Dahl retires early," I said, then turned to Merrick. "I think you might like some supper?"

Merrick frowned. "No. We ate late. As for early or late, I'll call it a day when I choose."

"Of course," I said.

"This evening I'll be taking care of some business here in my study. I don't need companionship for that. You two go on about your own business and leave me to mine."

"No, but—"

"Yes, I insist. Shut the door behind you when you go." When I delayed, Merrick said, "I have your number, but I promise I won't need you."

Somehow the force of his glare, his certainty, had moved me toward the study door. Davis too. I went the rest of the way, and Davis closed the door carefully behind us.

We moved a few yards away.

Davis said, "What was that about?"

"I don't know." I shook my head. "I truly do not know. One minute we're having our tea, and the next he's too busy to have us hanging around."

"Well." Davis shrugged with a bit of a smile on his face. "He's the boss, right?"

"Guess so."

"He has your number, right?"

"He does."

"Well, then, I suggest we follow orders." He looked at me. "What do you usually do this time of the evening?"

"Hang around while he prepares for bed."

"He goes to bed early."

"He takes a while, and he doesn't stay. I think he watches TV or reads or does stuff on his computer. Maybe dozes. But then he gets up again for a snack before truly going to bed for the night."

"So he really is okay. Maybe he just wants to be alone."

"But . . ."

"We won't go far."

I frowned. "We?"

"You like to walk on the beach in the evening, right?"

Yes. "Sometimes."

"Have you ever walked to the sunset?"

Bemused, I said, "I've seen the sun both set and rise from the beach."

"Not what I asked."

"Then I don't understand your question."

"Let's go."

"Where?"

"I already told you. Let the rest be a surprise."

I sighed, but inwardly, and hoped he hadn't heard.

※

We left by the beach door and passed the pool as we headed for the gazebo and the crossover. I was uneasy—not because Davis was doing anything wrong, but because I was worried for myself.

The sun was lower in the sky but still above the horizon. Sunset happened at the end of the island, at the westernmost edge of Emerald Isle. When I'd looked at it on the map back before this trip, I'd seen how the land ended there, and I'd assumed it was empty and marshy. But in reading Davis's manuscript, I came to understand that the land's end was called The Point. That some folks drove their vehicles out along the shore down there, and some did fish. For whatever reason, I hadn't walked down the beach in that direction.

Strange to think that I was walking down there now with Davis, relatively fresh from reading a story he was writing, of which a goodly amount was set here, at The Point.

Life was too weird sometimes.

And when it got that weird, you had to pay extra-close attention.

CHAPTER THIRTEEN

I walked next to the water with my jeans rolled up to my knees and my hands in my pockets. Davis was wearing khaki shorts. Both of us were barefoot. I felt awkward because the relaxed, companionable feel of strolling the beach together could easily fool us into a friendlier interaction. One that might take me where I wasn't ready to go.

Davis's dark hair, longer on top, wanted to fall forward across his forehead, and from time to time he'd use his fingers to sweep it back out of the way. He laughed easily, and he chatted nicely about inconsequential things like weather and beaches and so on, and I was pretty sure his manner was intended to disarm and charm me.

I looked away, first down at the water and sand beneath my feet and then around us as we left the oceanfront homes behind and the view widened to show a landscape of low, rolling sand hills topped with a variety of dune grasses. I wished I knew the names of the grasses and the correct names for the geography around me.

Davis was saying, "And this is where the White Oak River meets the Atlantic. That dark landmass hanging just above the horizon is Bear Island. No one lives there except waterfowl and other birds."

Bear Island. Was it named that because in the waning light it looked black and crouching? The hulking landmass was growing darker as the sky above grew orange and the sun dipped ever closer to it. Birds of some sort, large enough for me to see them clearly, soared and flew in singles and in groups of two or three. There were pickup trucks and a few SUVs parked in the sand near the water's edge. A couple of men were fishing. Two women were sitting on the dropped gate of a truck and chatting quietly as the sun descended. It was amazingly quiet, as if the world held its breath, watching the last light of day vanish.

My hand was no longer in my pocket, as I realized when it brushed against his inadvertently. Davis responded with a light touch of his fingers along mine—deliberately, I thought—but he didn't try to take my hand in his.

"Wait," he said.

"What?" I asked. Was I alarmed or eager?

"Don't leave yet. The moon is full tonight. It'll be coming up soon." He pointed back up the strand but out over the water. "In that direction. We can watch it from here or as we walk back." He added, "Your choice."

It was all I could do not to turn directly into his arms. I'd been too long alone. One might think that managing on your own made you tough, but no—it made you vulnerable. A person's greatest weakness was always what they believed they were most immune to.

Momma had told me that *too*.

Suddenly we were too close to each other. And then a wave we weren't expecting rolled in and slapped us. Davis was wearing shorts, but the wave soaked my rolled-up jeans. I squealed and stumbled. He caught and steadied me as my semi-scream was quickly doused by laughter, but the important thing as far as I was concerned was that the spell was broken. I moved away, plucking at the clinging denim and laughing at my surprise.

Together, but well apart this time, we walked back toward the house as the moon broke free of the clouds cloaking the horizon. When Davis tried to bring up my plans and that my stay was almost halfway over and everyone had options . . . Well, I just ignored him and changed the subject. One of those subject changes occurred as the moon lit a cloud beneath it and looked like it was sitting on a thin golden shelf suspended in a deep-blue sky.

A BAREFOOT TIDE

Out of nowhere, I asked, "What are you writing now?" And I nearly tripped and fell into the ocean as I heard myself speak those words.

He took a deep breath. "Well, good question. I'm working on two different projects. One similar to the first book—a thriller—the other . . . something different."

"Oh?" That seemed the safest response. I almost bit my tongue trying to stop any other uncontrolled questions. He was surely referencing the one I was reading.

"Yeah. Hope you understand, but I don't like to discuss my specific projects while I'm working on them."

"Sure. Of course."

"Seems to sort of take away their magic."

Magic.

Was I stealing his magic by reading his manuscript?

If so, it was too late, but I didn't think that was it. After all, we weren't discussing the story itself. But the magic? Maybe the magic hadn't been taken, but had been shared unaware, thankfully without diminishing the source. Because I'd been touched by that magic. Even if I was never able to finish reading this specific book, I'd still learned I could enjoy reading. This book wouldn't be the last I'd read for enjoyment.

Honesty was needed here, but I'd promised Merrick. Plus, discussing it with Davis would likely trigger the exact loss of writing magic he wanted to avoid.

As we approached the gazebo entrance, not only the moonlight guided us but also the soft lamplight extending out from the houses nearby. Davis paused, and I stopped beside him.

He said, "Please listen."

"Okay."

"I think we almost had a moment back there on The Point."

I may have tensed or made a noise, because he quickly assured me, "Don't worry, it won't happen again. I thought

153

it—that something was happening between us. That it was mutual. I'm generally pretty good at reading people, but you made your feelings clear. I apologize for making you uncomfortable."

Stunned, I said, "Of course." And I was deeply grateful that the words came out sounding normal. A little sad, too, though. I'd have to save that feeling for later and think about it. This was not the time. But I couldn't deny that a moment of promise may have been missed.

"Thank you, Davis. I appreciate that."

He nodded. "Did you enjoy the walk? Seeing The Point?"

"It was beautiful. Thank you."

He smiled. "Great." There was an odd little pause, during which only the sound of the waves could be heard, before he said, "Let's go see what Merrick is up to."

CRSO

The light was off in his study, and his bedroom door was closed.

In the foyer, I said, "Looks like he's done for the day."

"I guess the same is true for you and me."

I smiled. "Yes. In fact, I think I may find myself a book to read. The one I was reading—" I broke off in the nick of time.

"You finished." He nodded, smiling. "That happens. And I have a book I need to resume work on. I have a new scene in mind. I'll get some words down for that tonight while the idea is fresh."

I walked with him out the front door to his car. "You write at night?"

"I write whenever I can. Sometimes it's a grind, but other times I can hardly wait to get the words on paper. Tonight has become the latter."

"Thank you for the walk," I said. "For showing me The

Point."

"My pleasure."

There was that pause again. More electric this time but with a less awkward feeling.

"Good night," I said.

He nodded, got into his car, and drove away.

I waved as he went out of sight. Then, alone, I gave a last, smaller wave. And felt lonely. That lonely feeling followed me back inside as I walked out to sit by the pool and watch the small lights and the moonlight play across the surface of the water.

I sat there, not really thinking much at all. Pure feeling. I hadn't felt this restless in years. A restlessness born of dissatisfaction. Not dissatisfaction with being here or with accepting this job. But with decisions and choices I'd made over the years. The thing was, how did you know if you'd made—or were making at any given time—the right or best choice? It wasn't like you were conducting an experiment with a control group where you could compare and judge actual outcomes. There was no undo button.

This was a maudlin mood. A restless state of being where it was hard to tell the difference between regret and eagerness.

"There you are," Merrick said. The slight squeak of the door and the tap of his cane on the tile confirmed his presence. "Give me a hand, will you?"

છ૬૭

He was struggling to juggle his cane and a cup of tea. He was wearing a plaid robe, this time with burgundy-red pajama pants. But no slippers.

"Merrick," I exclaimed as I rose to assist him. "I thought you were in bed asleep." I took the cup and saucer from him and set it on the table. "Where are your shoes?"

He sat with a sigh, saying, "If I'd known you were out

here in the dark alone, I would've prepared a cup for you too." He made his grumpy noise. "Couldn't find the darn cookies."

A little bubble tickled in my chest. Amusement. "I'll go fetch some for you. And your slippers too."

"Don't need 'em," he called after me. "Barefoot's good enough for everyone else. Thought to give it a try myself."

I didn't wait to hear more. I needed a moment to breathe before I was ready to have a reasonable conversation with him.

The cookies were right there beside the tea in the cupboard. *For heaven's sake.* But then he'd managed pretty well with the tea, so I gave him credit for that. I skipped the slippers for now since he wanted the barefoot experience. I poured a glass of cold water for myself and took it and the cookies back out to the table.

"What's up?" I asked him.

He ignored me.

"Not ill, are you?"

He snorted. "I'm fine. I'm always fine. Fine for ninety years."

"Good to know. It'd be nice if you could bottle that. I'd like to be fine."

I swear that his ears literally perked up.

"What's wrong with you?" he asked.

"Nothing. Everything. I don't know. It's that kind of evening."

"You took a walk with Davis."

"I did. That has nothing to do with my mood, though."

"Sunset, moonrise, at The Point. I remember when Marie and I . . . Hard to beat that view."

"True. But it's a good illustration. Moonrise. Sunset. You can't have them both at the same time. We make choices. We all do. We must. If you have to choose one and lose one, or lose both . . ." I stopped to breathe, alarmed that I'd sounded almost manic.

"I don't get it. Sorry."

I sighed. "No, *I'm* sorry. I guess it's about choices and regrets."

"I never minded making choices, or decisions, but I do have regrets."

"Big ones?"

He looked at me with a somber stare, then shrugged. "Maybe it's the night. Maybe Mercury is in retrograde or something else along those lines, but if you repeat this, I'll deny it. Got it?"

"Yeah."

"I regret my marriage. Not marrying late, though that's what I tell the world. I regret not fighting to keep it. For letting Marie leave so easily. Was it pride? Maybe. But if I could do it over again . . . I might not be able to change the outcome, but I would toss pride right out the door and beg her to stay."

I didn't know the right words to offer.

He said, "My first marriage was early in life. Short. Tempestuous. When we ended it, I was so self-absorbed and busy building my career that I hardly gave it a second thought. But that second marriage? I regret letting it go so easily. So quietly. As if it didn't matter. It *did* matter, and it deserved more effort than that."

I said, "I have regrets too, though I tell myself I shouldn't. But I'll never know. Maybe that's the harshest fact of all. No do-overs. And what-ifs can drive you crazy. They bind you to the past."

"You're speaking of your marriage? The one to the getaway driver?"

I shook my head.

Was it the dark? The false mask of privacy it offered? Maybe it was the moon playing hide-and-seek among the clouds—the clouds themselves so dark that you could see their forms only when lit up from behind with some sort of silent lightning. Heat lightning? I didn't know, but the effect was eerie, beautiful, and hypnotic. It was a night for mysteries and secrets. And I felt a story coming on. One I didn't want to tell.

"No, not about my marriage. Regrets, I mean. But about my parents?" I nodded. "Yes."

I expected him to say something. To ask, to prompt me to continue. He didn't. Now he'd fallen silent. But I'd cracked the door—had opened that gate—and the words wanted out.

"They died together." Words were such pitiful tools when it came to big truths, and I was a poor craftsman. "It was always the three of us. Always. Except . . ."

I cleared my throat. "When Dad wasn't working other jobs—paying jobs—he spent his time in his workshop building or tinkering." I ran out of words again. In a weak effort to fill the gap, I tacked on, "They were wonderful parents."

All I could do was stare ahead. The most important thing seemed to be tracing the shape of the gazebo against the night view with my eyes. When that cloud lightning lit up, it reflected in the weathervane atop the roof.

Merrick put his hand on mine. It was a sizable hand, but gaunt. The fingers were thin between the large joints. Arthritis. Reminded me of Aunt Molly.

"They were excellent parents," I repeated. "Dad had been spending more time in his workshop as summer ended and fall began. I told you it was nice, right? The workshop? Snug even in winter. On cold nights, Dad would shut that door and get the space heater going, especially when Momma joined him out there. I told you they'd been sweethearts since they were toddlers." I smiled. "I have a photo of them when they were hardly more than babies, each seated on a swing, but not swinging because they were clasping hands, pulling the two swings together. Their little feet were stuck straight out in front because their toddler legs were so short." I sighed. "Anyway, he liked it when she joined him wherever he was and whatever he was doing. She'd bring a book or needlework along and sit nearby while he worked on his projects. Lately, though, he'd been out in the shed a lot and wasn't saying much. Sometimes he got that way, especially as the days grew shorter." I looked at Merrick. "Some people just like to be alone, right? Solitary. Some people are just quiet. Sad, sometimes. It happens. It's natural." That weathervane lit up again. "Everyone has down times."

After a short pause to breathe, I continued, "It was just short of Thanksgiving. A cold snap. That night I was curled up on the sofa filling out a job application. I'd just turned eighteen—was going to graduate in June—but that was months away, and I wanted to pick up some part-time work to help with the cash flow at home." I groaned. "That job application? It was awful. I don't write any more easily than I read. But I was working on it after supper when Momma came over to me, smoothed my hair, and told me she was going out to sit with Daddy. She was wearing her coat and carrying a warm blanket. 'I'll be a while,' she said. Sometime after that I fell asleep.

"I woke hours later. The house felt wrong. I knew immediately that Momma hadn't come in to go to bed. I looked out the kitchen window, and the exterior pole light was still burning out by the workshop. It cut the dark, but the door to the shed was closed, as it should be, so I couldn't tell what was up by looking through a window.

"Momma would not have stayed out until the wee hours of the morning, no matter how engaged Daddy was with his project." I paused and rubbed my arms. Shivering. The goosebumps popping out. Not from cold.

"Something felt wrong. So wrong that instead of going out to the workshop, I went to their bedroom. The late-November moonlight was coming in stark and strong through the windows. That cold light touched their bed and showed the bedspread was still smoothly in place and the pillows were perfectly fluffed."

I went silent, remembering the pain in my knees when I'd fallen to the floor, overwhelmed. But by what? How could I know anything for sure? I imagined myself going out to the workshop, steeling my nerves, my heart, and throwing open those doors. The cold air would rush in, and Momma would say, "What on earth, Lilliane? Close those doors, honey." And Daddy would look up from tightening a screw or adjusting a panel and ask, "What's wrong, sweet girl? You look like you've seen a ghost." He'd smile and tell me to join them. They'd laugh at how they'd lost track of time. They'd apologize for alarming me.

Merrick's hand was gone now, and he was silent. My hands were over my eyes, refusing them the ability to see what should not be seen, nor be relived by remembering.

"Daddy had weather-stripped that workshop with batting and plastic to a fine point. For Momma, he'd always said. So she'd be cozy. He vented the space heater through a large hole he'd cut in the wall and made a little door that would close it up when it wasn't needed, to keep out small critters. Even with the vent, he made sure to open those wide front doors from time to time to freshen the air. He was careful with Momma and me." I sipped my water. "He always put our family first."

"When I opened those doors—" I broke off for a deeper drink of water. "I didn't see him. I saw Momma on the floor. She was stretched out. Her arm . . . She was reaching over and had a hand on Daddy's. He was mostly behind the hulk of that airplane."

I stopped to shiver again and crossed my arms tightly. "The air was thick with exhaust, and I coughed, pushing both doors wide before going over to Momma. I knew already. You see, I knew. The heater had stopped running, so it must've used up the last of the kerosene, and the cold air rushing in with me helped clear the inside air and my head too."

Merrick coughed. A long, deep cough. As if he'd been in there with me, struggling to breathe. He cleared his throat several times before he said, "She must've found him out there and was overcome herself before she could get help."

I looked sidelong at him and then back at the wavering pool lights and the gazebo, and at the clouds overhead, before saying, "No. Oh, I think she found him overcome, but believed it was too late. I think she decided to go with him. She shut those doors tight behind her. She made a choice. To go with him rather than live without him."

"An accident, Lilliane."

"No. Someone had blocked the ventilation. That wasn't Momma. Daddy must've made that first choice, before Momma found out what he'd done and made hers." I shook my head. "Nobody checked with me before destroying our family. They just left me behind. Left me to find them gone."

"How do you know for sure that your mother did that? How can you possibly know?"

"Because I found her book—the one she'd taken out to read while keeping company with Dad. She'd dropped it just inside the doorway, likely when she saw him. It lay there while she figured out what Dad had done. Then she went and slid those doors closed behind her. She left the necklace he'd made for her on top of the book for me to find, then folded the blanket into a pillow and lay down beside him."

I stood and left Merrick at the table. I walked to the gazebo and sat on the bench, hugging myself tightly.

That night, barely eighteen, I'd been left behind. First thing, I'd checked that vent and found the ventilation panel in the wall was closed—had been shut. I pushed it up and checked the latch, which seemed tight, so I fixed that, wiggling the nail, working at it until it was loose enough to raise the question in people's minds. I let it fall closed again. Next, I retrieved the blanket, which was the part that nearly did me in. Then I called the sheriff.

I'd never discussed any of that with anyone ever again

after I'd told the sheriff and coroner the parts they needed to know—which was that Momma had gone out to keep Daddy company, as was their habit, and must have been overcome when the faulty latch had caused the vent to be blocked. The sheriff knew my father well. He asked about his mood. Had Daddy been depressed lately? I pretended not to understand what he was hinting at and said that the latch on the vent panel had failed and the little door had fallen closed with them unaware. On such a cold night, with the heater running full-on, they could've been overcome pretty quickly. I told him that Daddy and Momma were making plans to take a little road trip to see the fall color along the Skyline Drive that weekend and were looking forward to going. We were going to take a picnic lunch. I told them he'd even showed me on the map where we'd be driving.

I told them everything they needed to know. And it was the best, most convincing story I would ever tell—I was sure of that.

Looking back toward the house, I saw Merrick was still at the table. He hadn't moved. I couldn't just leave him, plus I needed to put some sort of end on this story for him.

Returning to the table, I sat slowly—I felt old—and said, "In the end, the deaths were ruled accidental. Not . . . the other." I shook my head. "I don't discuss this, Merrick. Ever. I don't know why I told you about it."

"I do." He asked, "Did it help? To unpack it after all these years? To air it out?"

"No." But I found a small grin still left inside me. I said, "That sounded perilously like a cliché."

"Someone smart told me that clichés are often the most efficient way to communicate something tricky or difficult."

"You added a little onto it."

He said, "It's called editing."

I put my hand on his. "I don't know how I feel about saying it aloud. Thinking of it again after twenty years. I don't want to discuss it anymore, though. I'm sure of that.

Feels like it's had enough fresh air for now."

"I understand." He tapped the table. "One more question?"

"Okay." Not welcoming, but he wouldn't expect me to be.

"What did you do then?"

"Stayed put." I shrugged. "You already know that."

"After . . . Did you go on to college?"

"Oh." I drew in a deep breath and released it in a long sigh. "I never went back to school. Didn't graduate high school. That's my big regret. I wish I'd pulled myself together and graduated, and maybe then I would've taken some classes at the community college. Who knows?" I laughed with a tinge of bitterness. "I wouldn't have. It's just one of those things people say. *I would've . . . I might've . . . if only.* But, no, it's my failure, and I own it."

"Thank you for sharing."

"Are you ready to try sleeping again?"

"I think so. By the way, you didn't mention the book to Davis, did you?"

Given what we'd been sharing, his question jolted me as if it were coming from a different, alternate reality. I answered, "No, of course not. I promised."

"Excellent. I think he's about to give me another chunk of it, if you're still interested in reading more. If not, no matter."

At the moment, no, I wasn't interested, but I knew everything would be better in the morning, in the daylight. "Yes," I lied. "I am very much interested." I *would* be.

"If you change your mind and want to talk some more, just let me know."

"Thank you, Merrick. I think, however, I'm ready for bed myself."

I wasn't, though. After he went back into his room and closed the door, I walked down to the beach. Away from the houses, it was especially dark. The cloud-lightning show had ended. The stars were showing now. Their reflection on the water and white sand gave light. The whitecaps riding the waves to shore also gave the impression of light. A darkling glow.

I sat on the dry sand near where the ocean had reached before beginning its journey back out with the tide. The rhythm of it, the constant, recurring motion of the waves, maybe the energy of the churning water infusing the air around me, consoled me as if nature had the power to touch me, to hug me. I cried. I sat beneath the sky—beneath the stars that filled it from horizon to horizon. An infinite family of light. Or one little family multiplied by infinity.

And one member left down here on earth. Alone.

CHAPTER FOURTEEN

On Saturday morning, the bags under his eyes were fuller than ever, and his eyes themselves looked dark. This seemed to be an everyday thing now.

Concerned, I said, "You're going to lie down, Merrick. I'm calling the doctor to come check you out."

"Hah. No, you most certainly are not. One night with less rest than usual isn't going to kill me."

"You're ninety. Your candle stopped burning at both ends a long time ago."

He gaped at me, then said, "All right then. No doctor. I'll have a bite of breakfast, and then I'll lie down again. That will fix me up right."

"I still think I should talk to the doctor."

"Why?"

"Instinct, maybe. Merrick, I'm serious. If I'm not convinced by lunchtime that you're okay, then I'm calling the doc, regardless." I sat in the chair beside his desk, crossed my legs, and leaned to the side, my elbow on the arm, telegraphing that I wasn't going away.

"Okay, okay." He ate his breakfast.

As I waited for him to finish, I noticed a few sheets of paper on the floor near his printer. I got up to retrieve them.

He snapped, "What's that?"

"Blank pages. Must've fallen from your printer. Shall I put them on your desk?"

"Blank? That's fine. Put them on top of the printer."

"Must be a quiet printer. I haven't heard it at all. The one at the Fuel Up Fast makes so much noise that you can't hear yourself on the phone."

"Is that a real name? Seriously?"

"Fuel Up Fast? It is indeed. Been in operation since 1972."

He grunted. Asked, "Is that all? Any interesting or curious details about it that you'd care to share? Perhaps quirky characters?"

Was that a sneer on his face? He was definitely in a mood this morning. I said, "Mockery will get you nowhere with me. Are you suggesting I run on too long at times? If so, I'll remember that. Might even cut you off from the stories."

"Nope. No mockery. Just wanted the tale if there was a good one to go with a name like that." He went back to chewing.

"Well, actually, there might be a tale concerning the man who originally owned it." I smiled. "We'll save it for later. Rest first."

⊗≫⊂

He went to lie down. I made sure the blinds were closed and he had a glass of water beside the bed. But I didn't go far. Something wasn't right about Merrick. Was this an actual health decline? Or something else? At his age, things could change quickly. So I stayed nearby without aggravating him. I tidied up the kitchen. I put a load of laundry in to wash. I checked what Ms. B had left us for our prepared meals. Funny how she so easily faded into the background. Her efficiency, of course, was part of that. But also her professionalism—the same professionalism that made her exceptional at her job also kept her slightly apart from the rest of us who came and went around the Dahl house.

Kind of like me. Trusted, but not quite a member of the family.

I was less professional than Ms. B, true. Also, I felt like

Merrick and I had a relationship. An affinity. Something very much like a friendship, despite his being my employer and the difference in our status and ages.

So I stayed nearby or passed and paused near his bedroom door quite often, until the monitor buzzed in the kitchen. It had happened so seldom that I jumped, not sure what it was at first. I rushed back to check on it.

"Merrick? On my way."

"No." His voice came through the speaker as cranky as ever. "Go do something. All that puttering and listening at the door is making rest impossible. How can I get any peace? Go out. Go somewhere."

I smiled. Maybe he truly was okay. "All right, then. I'll go for a walk. Not far. You have your phone nearby, right? I'll have mine with me."

That seemed safe enough.

CRESO

Instead of going down to the beach, I took a walk through the neighborhood. Some of the houses were bold and big. Some were smaller, at least from the angle of the street, and tucked away from easy view. Some were grand, like mini-estates. And woven in and around the houses and fences were shrubby bushes and low, twisted trees.

I hadn't been away from the house for more than thirty minutes or so when the phone rang.

Susan. I took the call. I hardly got "Hello" said before Susan cut me off. "Lilliane, is everything going well?"

"Yes? As far as I know."

"Excellent," she said, as if not interested in my answer to her question. "I have a request, if you don't mind helping me out?"

"Sure. What is it?"

"I need a package picked up."

"At the post office?"

"No, at a gallery in Beaufort."

"Beaufort?" I'd seen the town on the map.

"I would ask Ms. B, but her schedule is always so tight. Thought you might have more time to play with. Plus, it's a nice place to visit."

"Okay."

She rushed on. "Just pick it up sometime this week. Whenever it's a good time to get away. It's a gift for Mr. Dahl, so please don't let him know. Maybe you could let him think you're out shopping or such. You'll figure that out, I'm sure. Ask Ms. B where best to stash it when you have it. Probably in one of the upstairs bedrooms."

"Okay."

"It's a painting from a local artist he admires. It should come wrapped up. Please don't disturb the wrappings."

I almost said something rude, but she didn't pause long enough, adding, "At any rate, the point is, it's a surprise for him."

"Okay. I'll keep it secret." Secrets, or what they hid, always made me uneasy, but it was different with presents.

"Excellent. Go sometime this week. Did I already say that? Anyway, Maia is holding it in her office there until we can pick it up. It's the Front Street Gallery, located on Front Street, facing the waterfront. Talk to Maia. While you're there, have lunch at one of the restaurants on the boardwalk on me. Totally worth the time, and we'll cover the cost. Just keep the receipt and give it to Ms. B."

"I'll plan to go on Tuesday when Ms. B is here."

The conversation ended soon after.

I'd been like a good parrot, repeating, *Okay, okay, okay.* Where was my cracker?

Humph. Don't disturb the wrappings. Seriously?

She was so annoying. Just her way, I reminded myself. She probably found me just as aggravating.

Beaufort. I'd better double-check my map.

CRSO

His study door was closed. Working at his desk wasn't part of our deal, so I eased the door open to check. Empty. His bedroom door was closed. Maybe I *had* been making too much noise. Creeping around and trying to be extra quiet could be more disturbing with its stealthier noise than just normal activity. I closed the study door again and went upstairs to change into shorts and a T-shirt. I was getting better at this beach life thing.

I wandered out to the pool and settled in the shady gazebo. I put my phone on the seat next to me and double-checked that Merrick's medical alert pendant was still hanging against my key pendant—and against my heart.

He might or might not have chosen to wear his, but in case he did, I would be prepared to respond if the alert came.

The days were passing. The first week had flown, and I knew this next week—the last week—would speed by even faster. I felt the tug of home—I loved Cub Creek and missed it—but I would miss this place and these people too.

CRSO

After his rest, the under-eye bags were still there, but much less noticeable because his color was better, his posture was straighter, and the twinkle in his eyes was as close to charming as Merrick Dahl generally got.

He smiled. Big. And pointed over at the table.

An envelope. The manila envelope with more of Davis's book.

"Did he come by while I was out by the pool? Weren't you napping?"

"Indeed," he said. "That's for you."

I picked it up. Same envelope. And showing wear. Maybe Davis needed to restock his office supplies? I'd better be careful with this one before it wore completely out.

He asked, "Well, are you going to thank me?"

"For sharing? Yes. For the manuscript, I should thank Davis."

He frowned. "You promised."

"I did. And I'll keep my promise. But it's harder now—because I know him better."

"Then do him a favor and don't tell him. He appreciates feedback, and I give that to him. More than that would make him feel awkward, at the very least, and he might choose not to share any more of his writing."

I nodded. I said, "I understand," but inwardly, I disagreed. Knowing Davis better now . . . but then I remembered what he'd said about sharing too much too soon. So maybe Merrick was right. I held the envelope closer. "I appreciate your trust. Thank you. Even though I resisted at first, my reading is actually improving. Truly. Something I never thought I'd be saying."

He made a super-grumpy noise. I saw the emotion in his face and that he wanted to hide it. "How about some tea?" he said.

"I could go ahead and fix our lunch."

"Not yet. Tea and a cookie. For both of us. There's something I want to discuss with you."

Was it good or ominous?

"Sure. I'll be right back."

CRSO

He sipped his tea maddeningly slowly. To draw out the suspense? He was a thriller writer, after all. I hid my annoyance and sipped my tea too, and then I upped the ante by delicately biting a corner off my cookie.

He leaned back in his chair and pressed his fingertips together.

"I talked to Susan while you were out. I told her what a wonderful job you've done here."

Done. Past tense. Were they letting me go early? I felt a little sad, but said, "Is that how you rest? Did you nap?"

He ignored my questions. "Susan said she was having difficulty finding someone to replace you—someone who would be available at the end of next week. They are in current jobs, which makes sense." He shrugged. "Plus, most people have family at home and other obligations. Live-in jobs are problematical for most competent in-home health professionals."

But apparently not for me. Ouch.

"They don't want to move in with an ancient has-been who does nothing but complain."

Where was this going?

"Face it, Lilliane—this job is far from stimulating for a young person like you."

"Get it said, Merrick. Please. Enough suspense. Cut the dramatic buildup."

He grinned. "Could you stay a little longer? Two weeks more?"

At first I was confused. "I'm still here for another week."

"Yes, but for planning purposes—no need to be last-minute—two weeks in addition to the two you'd already committed to."

The excitement, the eagerness that rose in me scared me a little. I started to speak, but he held up his hand.

"I'd like to say that I know you have another life. A perfectly fine life. And that this . . . interlude . . . doesn't replace that life. Susan said the best candidate won't be available until after the fourth. She was going to call and ask you herself, but I told her I wanted to tell you—to speak to you directly about it."

⊂⊰⊱⊃

The smile felt permanently attached to my face, and I

felt light, as if I had little wings on my feet like Mercury. Hermes? Yeah, that guy. My boundaries had expanded, and at the same time they were shrinking again as I was getting better at the beach life. Now I was going to have a chance to use what I'd learned and enjoy it.

I made some quick calls to Gwen and to my neighbor to let them know I'd be here a while longer.

After lunch, Merrick said he was going to rest again. He was behaving sensibly, and I was pleased. After cleaning up the kitchen, I took the manuscript out by the pool. The envelope might be the same one, but as I discovered when I pulled the top pages out, the paper was different. Newer. As if Davis had finally used up the old stock. The text looked crisper too. Maybe he'd upgraded his printer? I smiled, glad to have these new pages in my hands, regardless of the age or condition of the paper.

They were back where they'd met—geographically, at least. Emotionally, it was a different matter. The Point. The truck. But no fishing poles or lines to trip anyone up. He might've been grateful for the distraction because it was obvious that whatever had been bothering Danielle hadn't gone away. He'd had too many breakups not to recognize it and to guess that something he didn't want to hear was in the offing. The small arguments, the growing chill from her—it was all a dead giveaway. But he felt a deep resistance to hearing goodbye this time.

Whatever was troubling her, he could help. Together they could resolve it. If she'd let him in. Confide in him.

He'd already run down the list of failed relationships in his head, like a litany of the lost opportunities for love. Some were well gone, but others he might've fought harder for. Should've, maybe.

Mike closed the tailgate. Danielle was standing down beside the water, no more than a shadowed figure, almost anonymous, with the sun dropping behind Bear Island painting the sky orange and voiding all other color everywhere else, possibly in the whole wide world. Mike suspected that would be true for his world after Danielle had her say.

It was almost as if she were already gone. Her dark form fading into night seemed already no more than a memory.

He called to her, "Danielle, honey, come on back."

She did. She stopped a few feet away, saying, "I have to leave for a while."

"Leave? How long?"

She shook her head. "I don't really know. A while."

"I'll go with you."

"No."

"You aren't coming back."

"Maybe. I don't know."

It was all wrong. He couldn't reconcile the memory of her laughter—her joy when something delighted her—with her present state. Where had that gone? He couldn't make it work in his head.

"Marry me. Whatever is wrong, we'll figure it out together."

It was all said in her eyes. He was the burden she feared. Having him with her was what she wanted to avoid? It hit him in the gut.

"Trust me, Mike," she said, still at a distance. "I'm doing what's best for both of us."

> He turned back toward the truck and
> tried to breathe. He was glad it was dark
> because it meant no one could see him cry.

My heart squeezed. My eyes burned. Mike was losing the love of his life after having already endured so much heartache. The person he'd put his dreams of a different future into had gone. Gone before she'd even left. And I knew, just reading the hopelessness in the words, that he was doomed to more heartache.

I reminded myself that these were fictional characters.

But their stories weren't *totally* fictional, right? They played out with variations across all sorts of lives. Loss. Grief. Love.

Sigh.

I was astounded that I'd already read through this entire section.

And I was out of pages. But this time I was okay with that. I needed some time to grieve with two wonderful characters. I empathized with Mike. I wanted Danielle to open up to him. To . . .

How silly was I?

C ⁊ ℥ つ

Susan called after supper.

Before she could ask, I said, "I don't have the package yet. I plan to get it on Tuesday when Ms. Bertie is here."

"Yes, thanks so much for doing that. I appreciate it. What I called to say was that Merrick is very happy with you being there. Usually he complains about having an aide or companion, but you two get along very well. I want to thank you for that. My assistant has been having some difficulty finding your replacement, so I'm doubly grateful. I'll be back at work as soon as possible and hope to be able to take the reins on that myself. Merrick said you'd agreed to stay an extra two weeks. I'll see that your check for the first two weeks arrives at the house by Friday. Merrick insisted you receive a bonus in addition to the pay for the second two weeks."

"Wow. Great." I didn't know what to say. But I was confused. Not quite the story I'd heard from Merrick. In what way? I tried to recall exactly what he'd said.

Susan said, "I'll be in touch. Thanks again." And she was gone.

Any discrepancy in their stories was minor and didn't matter. The important part was that Merrick wanted me to stay. Well, I wasn't surprised about that, but apparently it hadn't been Susan who'd proposed that I stay longer because she had no replacement. That had been Merrick's idea.

It made me feel wanted. Appreciated. Like maybe I was in the right place at the right time for a change. In fact, that hadn't happened in more than twenty years.

Additionally, it hadn't gone unnoticed by me that suddenly Susan was calling him *Merrick* to me, instead of the formal, businesslike references to *Mr. Dahl*. Had I passed some sort of test?

Maybe I'd become more than just the help. Still not family, but perhaps a member of the trusted circle around Merrick Dahl?

I wiggled my feet and stretched my toes. I couldn't see those tiny wings on my heels, but I could feel them in my light step when I walked.

CHAPTER FIFTEEN

On Monday morning, Merrick said, "Davis is taking me out to lunch today. If you're interested in joining us, I'm *sure* you'd be welcome."

I couldn't miss the slight emphasis he'd put on the last part of the invitation.

"No thanks. You two go along and paint the town."

"Just lunch."

"Wild times," I said. "Thanks, but I'll hang out here."

Merrick gave me a sidelong glance. "Davis usually drops by about once a week. Or used to. Never seen as much of him as I do now."

And? Nothing to do with me. Nope. Not a thing.

When Davis arrived to pick up Merrick, he was as friendly as ever. "You're welcome to join us."

I smiled. "Thanks, but I'm good."

"Do you have plans?"

"I do, but don't ask what because I'm not sharing."

As soon as they were gone, I went upstairs and changed. Thus far, I'd put on the swimsuit a few times to wade in the pool after dark when no one would see me. This time, I put my flip-flops on my feet and tucked a towel under my arm. I decided resorting to a T-shirt or bathrobe would be too pitiful. Time to walk out into the world and own it like I meant it.

CR80

A family was on the beach. No one I'd met. They ignored me. To them, I was a woman at the beach for a swim.

Pretty ordinary.

I spread the sunblock from the Fuel Up Fast on those parts of my body that hadn't seen the sun in decades. I laid out my towel on the sand and put my phone near the corner, flipped the corner over to hide it, and then left my sandals and the lotion on top to show my stuff was mine.

I wouldn't go in too deep. I was swimming alone with no one, except maybe that family up the beach a ways, to call to for help or to attempt a rescue.

The feeling of being able to overcome, to do anything, to take a risk, was strong in me. I waded out to my knees. I'd been out this far before. The water was warm due to the Gulf Stream and how it brushed past the ocean side of Bogue Banks while bringing the more tropical water up from the south. The sand beneath my feet was soft and clean. The waves weren't too rough, and I felt steady, so I moved a few steps farther out. The waves hit my waist and then reached up around my chest. I found myself taking a little jump, rising with the swell. It was like free-floating, almost flying, for those few seconds of lift. I was delighted.

Each successive wave gently picked me up. With my arms held out to the side, I rose with the water and then touched back down to earth. But then the ground almost eluded me. The swells had been gradually taking me out. My toes stretched to find the sand, and when the next wave hit, I wasn't ready. It sloshed up against my chest, and drops sprayed into my eyes, stinging them. I reacted instinctively, closing my eyes and flinching—then the next wave hit, taking my feet out from under me and rushing over my head.

I couldn't swim, but it didn't matter. This was crashing water breaking on an incoming tide, not swimming water suitable for a novice like me. I sank below the waves deliberately, trying to get closer to the bottom. I needed a foothold to push up against, to reach the surface for a breath. A badly needed breath. I pushed against the sand, and the current seemed to help me move, but it wasn't enough. As I broke through and gasped for air, the next wave hit, filling my nose and mouth.

I was in trouble.

Back under the water and feeling the pull of the undertow, I grabbed at the sand, my fingers trying to dig in, but it was too soft. And in that moment between hope and final panic, I noted the gentle tan color of the sandy bottom. I felt the graininess of it beneath my knees. I saw the impossibility of it, and calm filled me. Such calm, like an assurance I'd be okay. That time and danger, and even the need for fresh air in my lungs, had been briefly suspended for my convenience. As I waited in that weightless state, I noticed it was dark behind me in the deeper reaches of the ocean, and light lay before me. That the sun's rays streamed through the water, illuminating it, giving a soft green tone. I saw that the sandy bottom sloped up toward the greater light, toward the more inviting water.

It seemed impossible to me, yet perfectly natural, that I crawled, following the upslope until I felt the change in the water—rougher now as it grew shallower and the waves broke just over me, then against me, and crashed the calm. Suddenly feeling earthbound again, I pushed up with great effort and fell forward, and somewhere in that graceless movement, I found oxygen and gasped in air.

I lay there, air and sun on my face, the waves breaking just behind me and swirling up around my body. I was exhausted and scoured by the sand and salt. But not beaten. I was alive and breathing. I pulled myself farther up the beach, away from the water until I was mostly beyond it, then rolled over onto my back and simply breathed, still hardly believing I was alive. Not drowned. I'd survived my own inexperience and foolhardiness.

And I wasn't afraid.

I'd been plenty scared when I'd realized I was in trouble, but I'd become amazingly calm under that water—calm enough to think. How had that happened?

I hadn't felt alone.

It was probably why I hadn't drowned.

I should be thinking, *Never again.*

I laughed and then coughed. I raised up on my elbow to clear the salt water from my mouth and throat, then wiped my flowing nose with my forearm.

Alive.

And I'd go back. But next time, I'd be smarter. Maybe take someone with me who'd been in the ocean before.

But not today. Today, I'd just be grateful.

I'd never felt so alive as I did at that moment.

So . . . euphoric.

A nearby voice said, "That was a swim that almost went way wrong, if I'm any judge."

I rolled over and pushed to a seated position. "Miranda. It's a pleasure to see you."

"Well, now, it's a pleasure to see you too—alive, that is. I'm past the age of lifeguarding. Mind you, I was a fine swimmer in my time, but now I live for the good days when I can walk reasonably well."

I looked around. She was here alone.

"Today must be one of those days. You crossed the sand without any help."

"I saw you come out of those waves as you did, like you were being shot from a water cannon, and figured I could at least whop you on the back with my cane if you needed resuscitation."

Was she joking? I didn't test it. I took her remark as kindly meant.

I stood, grateful my legs held me up. I wasn't even shaky.

"I'm okay. Got in over my head." I laughed. "That truly was unintentional."

"Getting in over your head? Or the pun?"

"Both." I looked across the beach. "Where's your canopy and chair? In fact, there was a family here when I went into the water. I guess they left?"

"Didn't see no one when I arrived. I didn't plan to stay today. Just felt an urge to see the ocean on a day when I could manage the walk." She gave me a look. "Have you ever actually been full-out in the ocean before?"

I shrugged.

"Didn't think so." She shook her head. "Some folks aren't savvy enough to know when to be scared."

"Seriously?"

"You know what I'm saying. No need to act offended. Also, missy, you better be more careful about slathering on the lotion too. You're getting burned."

"Yes, ma'am. I guess it washed off."

"Want to take my arm and escort me back to the road?"

"My pleasure." I picked up my towel, flip-flops, and phone, then took her arm.

"How's it going with Merrick?"

"Quite well, actually."

Miranda said, "Come to think of it, despite you being half-drowned, you look pert." She eyed me. "Something must be agreeing with you. Can't be Merrick, so maybe you've found a nice man? A sweetheart?"

I thought of Davis. But no, I wasn't in the market for a long-distance relationship, even if I might otherwise be interested.

"I think that what you're seeing is my delight that I'm still walking, talking, and breathing."

"Ah, a risk-taker."

"I never was before."

"Then it's past time, apparently. Risky behavior isn't for everyone. But it's good for some. Gets that heart rate up. So long as you don't get yourself killed."

"Were you a risk-taker?" I asked as I located her shoes. "Wow, you really kicked those shoes off pretty hard. They traveled."

She steadied herself with a hand on my back as I knelt

to slip her shoes onto her swollen feet.

"I was in a hurry. Saw a mermaid flopping around in the foam." She laughed. "Yes, Lilliane, I was a risk-taker in my time. One day, if you stay around here long enough, I'll tell you some tales. For now, for today, I've done enough traveling."

Fatigue gave her voice a low, heavy sound. I took her arm again. "I'll walk you the rest of the way home."

"Much obliged, Lilliane. Much obliged."

"No, I am. I don't believe anyone has ever gone to so much effort to rescue me. Frankly, though, I'm glad you didn't have to strike me with that cane."

"As am I, dear. But one does what one must."

Chapter Sixteen

When Ms. B came on Tuesday, she pulled me aside, whispering at me in the kitchen as if the house were bugged.

"What's up? What's wrong?"

"Nothing. Not . . . just, he don't look good. Those bags under his eyes, you know. The way he holds himself. His color. He's not sleeping, looks like."

"I noticed that too, but I think he's okay. Not sleeping well, maybe."

She looked doubtful, almost disappointed by my reaction.

"As I said, I did notice, but if you're noticing too, and you've known him for a long time, then I'll let Susan know and talk to his doctor."

She nodded, her expression moving from concerned to agreement. "Hope you don't mind me speaking up."

"He's more than an employer. He's someone you care about, and I know how highly he values your being here with him. Speak up anytime." Impulsively, I gave her a hug, but I kept it super short and sweet because I wasn't sure how she'd respond. She looked pleased.

"I'm supposed to go pick up a package in Beaufort for Ms. Biggs. I was about to call her and tell her I wasn't comfortable leaving Mr. Dahl today after all, but with you here, maybe I will."

"Sure. Okay."

"Susan also suggested I ask you where best to hide it? Maybe upstairs?"

"Put it in the bedroom across from yours."

"Seems a big deal about a gift for someone she's worked

for over so many years. Or is that just me being curious and looking for a mystery?"

Ms. B's eyes got big. Her cheeks pinked up, and she almost laughed. "Not curious. He's got a birthday coming up. Not for a while yet, but that Ms. Biggs—she always runs ahead of the future."

Runs ahead of the future? I had to think about that one. In fact, I might try it out myself if the right moment presented itself. "No doubt."

She added, "Gruff people like him need surprise presents all the more."

I smiled. "You are likely right about that. So when is his birthday?"

Her eyes widened, and she seemed almost alarmed, but then she recovered her composure, saying, "Almost three weeks from now. July. End of. Almost August."

"Good to know. I'll be gone by then. Too bad." I added, especially for her, "I'll bet you make an astounding birthday cake, Ms. B."

"No mystery there, Lil-li. I make the best cakes ever."

"I don't doubt it. I'll call Ms. Biggs and inform her of our concerns, and then I'll go on my errand to Beaufort." I touched her arm. "You still have my phone number?"

"Yes."

"It's a relief to have a good team, isn't it?"

"Good team," she echoed, and nodded. "I'll call you if there's a problem. Take time to see Beaufort. It's a pretty town. Maybe a walking tour. See the boardwalk."

"That's what Ms. Biggs suggested. I may stay for lunch, but only if that won't be a problem for you?"

"Me? Oh, my. No indeed. I'll stay right here until you're back."

"I'll keep my phone close."

I called Susan and left a voice mail. I told her that Ms. B and I had both noticed Merrick was looking particularly tired. I told her I was keeping a close eye on him, that he was out with Davis, which had seemed to invigorate him before, so it might be what he needed. I just wanted to give her a heads-up that there was some concern and that I was on my way to Beaufort.

⊂≈⊅

I was back in Atlantic Beach, driving along the main drag and crossing the bridge I'd arrived on. But for this trip, as I reached Morehead City, I took a right onto another bridge to reach Beaufort.

Amazing view. The water stretched away into infinity as I tried to catch a glimpse without sailing the car off the bridge.

Beaufort was lovely. The old homes, the sparkling waterfront with pristine boats at the docks—altogether like a picture postcard, complete with baskets of flowers on the boardwalk railing. I strolled through the tree-shaded square, past the benches. Inviting. I could imagine sitting on one of those shady benches enjoying the breeze. Nearby someone was doing exactly that, sitting on a bench and pulling a sandwich from their lunch bag. I looked away. Directly across the street from the water, but with a direct view of the sound, was a house-turned-gallery named after the street where it was located.

Front Street Gallery.

The closest I'd ever been to entering an art gallery was visiting Biltmore. But that was far different than an actual art gallery business. More like a museum. Plus, my interests were in storytelling as opposed to art. When I considered art, I knew almost nothing about it.

Speak to Maia, Susan had said.

How could she be sure that Maia would be here? Well, I'd find out. Susan seemed to know a lot more than she divulged. This was a bit of an adventure within a larger adventure.

I climbed the front steps up to the porch and the main door. There was a plate-glass window fronting on the porch. I snuck a peek through it. Many pictures hung on the walls. Round tables were situated in the center of the room, with small objects—little knickknacks and shell things—arrayed on them. I caught a glimpse of a glass-topped counter toward the back of the room.

Customer service/cashier counters—I knew those. You might say they were a specialty of mine.

Laughing at myself, I pushed open the door, and a bell tinkled overhead.

Now that I was inside, I could see a woman talking to a man. The woman must be Maia. She was pointing up at a seascape on the wall, and he was asking questions. The woman spared me a quick glance with a smile that acknowledged me as she held up one finger indicating that I should wait and she'd be with me shortly. I smiled and nodded back. Yes, I spoke the customer service/cashier sign language.

Looking around, I spied a heron right next to me. He was thigh high and carved out of driftwood. Soft colors, paint of some kind, had been rubbed lightly into the wood such that you almost didn't realize the coloration had been added.

I knew a guy named Liam who lived on Elk Ridge just on the other side of Cooper's Hollow who was a fabulous woodworker. He made everything—from carving sculptures out of massive logs to crafting furniture from scratch. I made a mental note to tell him about this. About how the subtle color, and the suggestion of touchable texture, caught the eye. Surreptitiously, I brushed my fingers along the smooth wood of the heron's head and neck. Silky.

On a shelf nearby, several clay works were arranged. I guessed they were abstract representations of sea life of some kind, and they were gorgeous. That led me to think of Hannah, in Cooper's Hollow, who was well known regionally for her pottery. In fact, some of her pieces were on display at the university in Charlottesville.

Frankly, the idea of the connections between home and here kind of blew my mind. I was oblivious, absorbed in considering it, when the bell over the door jingled as the other customer departed. It gave me a split second of warning that it was my turn.

"Hello, I'm Maia. Welcome to the gallery. Have you visited us before?"

Perky, but pleasant. Nothing fake here. I saw it in her eyes and in her body language. Nothing stuffy about her either. Not in her petite height, the attractive but simple dress she wore, or in her dimples. I couldn't help but return her smile and greeting.

"I'm Lilliane Moore. I'm here on a mission."

She laughed. "Oh my goodness. Do tell me about it."

I shrugged. "*Mission* sounds a lot more interesting than saying I'm here on an errand. For Susan Biggs? She said to talk to you."

"Of course. I have the artwork she purchased. Are you here to collect it?"

"I am."

"Super. I saw your interest in the heron."

I glanced down at the bird. "It's beautiful."

"Are you looking for anything for yourself?"

I put my hand to my chest. "For me? Oh, I wish, but no. I work for her."

Maia gave me an odd look. "Doesn't mean you can't enjoy art too."

"Just means I can't afford it."

She smiled kindly. "I see. Well, if you ever decide to splurge, you let me know. I'll give you a good deal." She paused, then added, "Come over to the counter and I'll grab the paperwork for Susan's purchase."

She pulled out the receipt and made a note on it, and as I signed it as the person picking it up, she asked, "Where are you parked? Out front?"

"Yes."

"Excellent. It's a good-sized piece. Also, it's packaged, and I'm leaving it that way for Susan per her instructions, but it adds to the bulk." Abruptly, she turned and stopped at the door in the back wall—a breakroom–kitchen area from the glimpse I caught. She said, "Brian, come give us a hand."

She turned back to me. "My brother, Brian. He's here eating his lunch with me today."

"Oh, I'm sorry for interrupting."

"Not at all. It's the business. I don't complain. I'm glad to see folks walk in. My sandwich will wait, and my brother doesn't mind either."

The man named Brian came out of the breakroom. He was sandy-haired, where his sister had dark hair. He was tall, and she was short. They both seemed very nice.

"What's up?" he asked.

"That piece for Susan Biggs? Can you get it from the office and carry it out to Lilliane's car for her?"

I said, "Oh, I can manage."

"Nope. Not on those stairs. Brian will give us a hand."

"Yes, ma'am," he said with a smile. "Be right out."

I didn't know this guy Brian at all, and I'd seen the wedding band on his hand right away, but instinctively I did like the two of them, Maia and Brian, very much. If they'd lived back in Cub Creek, I knew we'd have been friends.

Brian settled the artwork on the back seat, laying it down so that the edge was against the back of the front seats to keep it from sliding. Brian shut the car door, but then he stood there looking at the car. My face grew warm.

The words popped out: "It's old."

"Oh, sure. A great car, though."

"It's an old Escort."

"And still runs."

"It does."

"I had one," he said. "Probably the same year. First car. Dad bought it for me used."

I relaxed. "My aunt gave me this one a couple of years ago. I do my best to keep it working."

"Nice. You've got a good mechanic."

"Yes, I do."

He glanced at Junior's graffiti, and noted the effort Tammy and I had made to disguise the marks. "You can get that buffed out, you know." He ran his fingers over the scratched surface. "It probably won't come all the way out, but I know a guy. He does good work."

"Thank you. I appreciate that. But it's an old car. I don't think it's worth it to get body work done. Plus, I'm only here for a short time."

"Let Maia know if you change your mind." He patted the roof of the car. "All set?"

"Yes, thank you, and please thank your sister for me."

"Will do."

He walked back up the steps. I wasn't ready to leave. I wandered across to the shady park and sat on one of the benches.

It wasn't any one thing. Not the nice brother and sister I'd just met or the feeling of being someone who could do whatever—because the world was open to me. It wasn't the friendship that was growing with Merrick, or even Davis. Not any one thing that made me wish I could stay.

Stay longer, I meant. Indefinitely. Not forever.

And it wasn't any one thing that would prevent me from staying indefinitely.

Job? Not really. I could find a job around here. Family? No. Friends? They might miss me, but they'd probably be happy for me—breaking out of my own self-imposed mold.

In the end, it was fun to think about the idea of staying in the area, but thinking didn't cost—living did. And I did have obligations back home. Things I couldn't just walk away from.

I took Susan up on the offer of lunch. I even snagged a table at a window looking out on the boardwalk and the sound. I tucked the receipt in my purse, and with a last look up at the Front Street Gallery through my windshield, I started my car and headed back to Emerald Isle.

On the long drive from Atlantic Beach back to Emerald Isle, I considered whether I should ask Ms. B why she'd fibbed about Merrick's birthday being in late July. Right after I'd asked her when his birthday was, I'd remembered that Merrick had already told me that the gate code was set with his birth date. I was curious, but I'd chosen not to contradict her.

No reason to put her on the spot. Seemed like everybody had secrets, not just me.

CHAPTER SEVENTEEN

Mid-morning on Wednesday, I heard shouting. I was just leaving the kitchen when I heard the raised voices funneling up the hallway and I ran to the foyer.

Tense voices—no longer raised but gruff and tense—were coming from the other side of the closed study doors. The voices had dropped in volume, and I couldn't make out what was being said. It was Davis and Merrick, obviously. But what was going on?

Unashamedly, I put my ear to the door. One more exchange like before, and I was going in. I might go in regardless. My hand was on the doorknob, at the ready. When the door opened with sudden force, I was thrown back, my feet scrambling against the smooth tile and failing to stop my motion. My butt took the hit, so it could have been worse. I might have worried about my dignity, too, except that I couldn't believe what had just happened.

Davis rushed to my side to help me up. "Are you okay?"

In a flurry of anger and concern, I pushed his arm away and made it to my feet on my own. I yelled, "What is going on? Is Merrick okay?" I hissed at Davis, "What were you thinking of? Never mind me. He's the one you should be worrying about."

I pushed past him and dashed into the study. Merrick was sitting at his desk. I stopped when I reached the rug. His color was heightened, redder than usual, but pale would've scared me more than high color. His eyes looked brighter.

He said, "Calm down. Davis and I had a difference of opinion. That's all." There was finality in his voice, cutting off any questions.

"Excuse me," I said. "I have an interest in this too."

He leaned forward. "What do you mean?"

I heard concern this time. I said, "I don't care whether it's my business or not. I want to know what was going on. What were you arguing about?"

Merrick slapped his desk. "I may be old, but I still have a private life."

"Don't even think about manipulating me with remarks about being old. In fact, there's no excuse for not being smarter and better at discussing differences at your age— with your vast years of experience."

He looked aside. Gave a tiny puff of a sigh. In a sad voice, he said, "People never get so old that they don't make mistakes or bad choices, Lilliane. Human frailty is baggage we carry with us for the length of our lives. The baggage gets fuller and heavier as the years pass."

I felt his . . . discouragement? Sorrow? Regret? What *was* he feeling? Whatever it was, I felt it too, and I went to sit in the chair, my chair, beside his desk.

"Anything you want to talk about?" I asked.

He looked away.

Davis said from behind me, "Are you okay, Lilliane? That was quite a fall."

"I'm fine."

"I wasn't aware you were there. You know that."

I kept my back to him. "I do know that. And I don't generally eavesdrop, but I heard angry voices and was deciding whether to interrupt when . . . Well, I'm fine."

"I'll let myself out. Merrick? Give it some thought." And he was gone. The front door clicked quietly shut behind him.

"Merrick?"

"Yes? What?"

"Would you like a cup of tea? Maybe lie down for a short rest?"

"Tea, I think. And then I'd like to be alone for a while."

"You should rest."

"It will be more restful if I'm doing what relaxes me. What I want to do."

I heard the stubborn *I won't be told what to do* loud and clear in his voice.

"Okay, then. I'll be back shortly. I'll bring you a small sandwich too, in case you get hungry while you're . . . by yourself."

While the water heated, I assembled a sandwich with the chicken salad Ms. B had left, and I added a little fruit on the side of the plate. I put it on a tray, along with a glass of ice water as well as the tea.

"Where would you like this? Desk or table?"

"Desk, thank you." His laptop was on the desk blotter in front of him with the lid raised. I felt as though I'd interrupted his thoughts. Important thoughts.

I said softly, "Call me if you need me."

∞

With what had happened, I didn't feel free to leave the house, so no beach or anything. I tidied the kitchen, then poured a glass of iced lemon water and took it, along with several biscuit cookies, out beside the pool.

And found Davis.

I stopped abruptly, and the water sloshed over the lip of the glass. The scent of lemon surrounded me.

His chair squeaked as he stood. "How's Merrick?"

Now what? I shook my head. "He seems fine."

"Is he in his study?"

"You can't go in there. Leave him alone."

He shook his head. "I wasn't going to. He's opinionated and hot-tempered, but he's also ninety." He shrugged. "I just wanted to make sure he'd settled down."

"He has." I set my drink and cookies on the table. "I took him a snack, and now he's relaxing."

192

"I'm glad."

"Why were you two arguing? It sounded awful."

"Did he say anything?"

"About the disagreement? No."

"Well, it's something he'll have to tell you about, if he chooses to."

The secret that Merrick and I shared nibbled at my conscience. Fair or not to Davis, I'd promised Merrick, and if anyone was going to confess to Davis, it would have to be Merrick. Had he? Perhaps?

I felt a shock. But it rapidly passed. If Davis knew I'd been reading his work-in-progress, he would surely say so or show it in some way.

"Then I'll leave it to him to do that, if, as you say, he chooses." It was warm, even in the shade of the umbrella. "Have you been out here this whole time?"

"I left but didn't get far. I had to know that all was well." He offered a small, embarrassed-looking grin. "You too. That was quite a fall."

"Not your fault. No apology needed."

"Even so."

I gave him a small smile back. "I'm fine." I didn't know what to do now. I tried courtesy. "May I offer you a drink of water or lemonade?"

"Thanks, but no. I do need to move on. Have an appointment this afternoon."

"I don't think Merrick will stay angry."

He actually laughed, though it came out as more of a rueful chuckle. "No, he won't. He has a temper, but he doesn't hold on to anger. That's the advantage to being a person who can throw it all out there and not worry about collateral damage." He shook his head. "No, Merrick, insofar as his conscience, is fine already." With deliberate intent, he caught my eyes with his. "Lilliane, please don't disappear without being in touch."

"I'm here for a while yet."

"I just mean . . . if your plans change. That's life, right? Just when we think we have everything lined up to suit us, chaos takes a spin at the wheel. It pays to be flexible in life."

"I know this job will end. Can even end unexpectedly. But I intend to enjoy it while I have it, before I go back to real life."

"Sounds like a great attitude." With a nod and a wave, he turned and left.

My legs felt odd. Almost shaky. I sipped the water and then sat at the table. I was still clutching my book. And now I saw a scrap of paper on the glass tabletop. The edges were ragged, having been torn from a larger piece, and a corner was tucked under the plastic trim around the umbrella opening in the glass to prevent it from blowing away.

I slipped it out. No notations except for his name and phone number.

I held it for a long minute. What did I feel? Confusion. I put the paper in my pocket. I'd have to see what came along. I wasn't in a position to make any decisions right now anyway.

Daggone secrets.

I would've liked to have been able to ask for the remainder of the story. Seemed like now I'd have to rely on my own imagination to supply an ending.

⚭

By the next day it was clear that Merrick would have no ill effects from the blowup with Davis. In fact, he brought up Davis, referring to what had happened the day before. He said, "Not his fault." He focused on me. "Not that I owe anyone an explanation"—he paused for effect—"but I don't wish for him to be blamed for my temper."

"Okay." I waited, standing there with my arms crossed. I wanted more than that.

He stared at me, expecting me to leave.

I asked, "Does this mean that he is forgiven? All is well? Shall we let him know he is welcome again? Or might he be needing an apology? I don't know who was at fault. I don't really care. But, Merrick, you scared me. You pushed yourself too far. If you are going to resume your friendship with Davis, is this going to happen again?"

I felt like a parent and was annoyed to be put in this position. "Because next time you can forget about privacy. I'm going to barge in right away."

The smile grew on his face. "You were worried about me."

I frowned. "Of course. I thought I made that clear yesterday."

"Would you have kicked Davis out? To protect me?"

I uncrossed my arms and put my hands on my hips. "You're the guy funding my paycheck."

He laughed out loud—that same laugh I'd heard early in my stay. Hard to believe it could come out of such a frail body.

In a kinder voice, I said, "I'm glad you are better. But I don't want that happening on my watch ever again."

"Hard to cage a tiger, Lilliane. Even an old, grizzled one." He nodded. "I'll try, but I can't promise."

He added, "Don't hold it against Davis. The disagreement was justified on his part." He shook his head slowly. He massaged his left temple with his gnarled fingers. "And it was private. I may tell you about it one day, but not on *this* day."

CHAPTER EIGHTEEN

No Davis. It had been a week and a day since the argument. I accepted that I would probably never have the chance to read the ending of *The Book of Lost Loves*.

Maybe he'd publish it one day? If he did, I might call the phone number he'd left and ask for an autographed copy. Did I have the audacity that such an act would require? Yes, I did.

The manuscript might be out of my reach, but I refused to accept that I'd let the ocean best me. I was into my third week now. The next week and a half would fly by. I wasn't about to miss my chance to engage more with the ocean, to walk into the waves, enjoy myself, and be able to leave the water gracefully on my own terms—more like a sea nymph than a grounded walrus.

Miranda saw me coming. She lifted her sunglasses and showed me a frown. "I don't see a book in your hands, and you're in that suit—looks good on you, by the way. Too bad there's no fella out here to appreciate it. But my point is to say that I hope you aren't going back in the water again without a buddy. The *buddy* system." She laid her book in her lap and leaned forward. "Mind you, I have my cane with me, but I'm not as fleet of foot today. Don't know that you can count on me to rescue you."

"I'll be fine." Impulsively, I gave her shoulder a gentle pat. "I'm glad to see you here."

"How is Merrick?"

Her question threw me off balance. "He's fine."

"He's ninety, and he's been grieving over Marie for twenty-plus years. That doesn't sound fine to me."

Hearing her say that concerned me. I tried to straddle the privacy line without being rude. "He's in amazing shape, given his age. He's active, and his brain is sharp."

"Like his tongue, I'm sure." She laughed. "Oh, I see your face, your expression. I admire your loyalty to him. And your kindness to me. But in my opinion, he's wasted too many good years wanting her back."

"Isn't that his choice to make?"

"*Ah, she's judgmental,* you're thinking. Just an old woman who can't keep her nose out of other people's business. But you're wrong. It's my business too, whether he likes it or not."

A light sheen of sweat had appeared on her face. The flesh around her eyes and mouth looked pale.

"Miranda, please relax." I picked up her drink. "Have a sip."

She did.

I said, "Let Merrick make all the bad choices he wants. If it's a waste, then it's his days and years that he's wasting. Actually, though, I think he has come to terms with losing her."

She looked doubtful, or maybe regretful. "I've spouted off too much. Guess I *am* an old foolish woman. Don't know when to shut up." She picked up her cane and shook it at me. "Don't you go drowning in front of me. I insist on that. I couldn't bear it."

"It'd be tough on me too." She didn't take my invite to laugh off that odd conversation, so I added, "I'll be fine. Thank you for caring, but please don't worry."

"Just you be careful."

I moved closer to the water and spread my towel on the sand. I put my shoes and phone on the towel as I'd done before, but I couldn't shake the lingering oddness of what Miranda had said. Not about me being careless and drowning, but about Merrick. When I thought of it, she was younger than Merrick, but old enough to have been an adult and living here when Merrick and Marie did. Hadn't Merrick said he'd bought the house when he and his Marie had married? So, maybe thirty years ago?

Merrick would've been sixty. Miranda might've been in her fifties or perhaps her late forties. That was a guess, of course.

That sixth sense—the one that hummed a little when you were close to something previously unknown or unseen—made itself known, tickling the back of my neck up near my brain stem.

Which was foolish. Their history, both Merrick's and Miranda's, was none of my business. I was a traveler. Hopefully, a kind one. But merely passing through these other lives.

I cast a glance back at Miranda. She was looking down at her book and so deeply in shadow beneath that canopy and her hat that I could hardly make out her face. I hoped she was okay. She didn't seem herself today. I'd check on her again before I left the beach.

Poised at the water's edge, I affirmed to the world that I wasn't going to get into trouble again. Forewarned was forearmed. I wouldn't forget where I was and what I was doing. This was about focus.

I walked forward, feeling the ocean, observing the swell of the waves farther out, rising, and then the breaking and the rush, dying out as it neared me. By now I was out to my knees. Now just over my thighs. Watching the horizon. Watching the swells. Shifting as the sand was pulled out from around my feet.

"Lilliane!"

I spun around and saw Davis. In that instant, a monster wave rolled up and hit me from behind, throwing me forward, my knees buckling under the force of it, and I went down flat, with the wave moving me forward like a boogie board. My arms splayed, and my face ended up planted in the sand as the ocean withdrew, pulling the earth around me back out to sea with it.

He was there in an instant. He grabbed my arm and helped me stand. By then the next wave arrived, hitting the backs of my knees, but he didn't abandon me or even lessen his grip. He simply allowed the ocean to soak him and his slacks and dress shirt, until I was steady. With his arm still around me, we moved away from the water's reach.

At least he was barefoot, so no ruined dress shoes.

Davis said, "You okay? I did it again, didn't I?" He pushed the wet strands of sand-and-sea-coated hair out of my face. "I distracted you at exactly the wrong moment."

"You're wet," I said.

He gave me a funny look. "So are you."

"I was in the ocean and wearing a swimsuit. You're dressed for . . . What are you dressed for?"

"A meeting."

"Oh, Davis, oh . . ."

"No, the meeting already happened. I came by to tell Merrick. He said he thought you were down here."

"Is he okay?"

He smirked. "As well as ever."

"So you two are good now?"

"We are." He released me. "We continue to disagree for the time being. I hope that one day we can talk about it."

We. I didn't press him, but I presumed "we" meant Davis and Merrick. Could he mean Davis and me?

There was sand in my swimsuit. Uncomfortable sand. I pretended it wasn't there. I shifted position.

My name was being called. Miranda.

I waved, hoping to shut her up. I asked Davis, "So you came looking for me? Why?"

"To tell you that I have a new contract. A contract for my second book. There was no way I couldn't thank Merrick for his help." His tone softened. "And I wanted to tell you too."

I tried to dim the glow I felt. Had my feedback helped?

I wanted to jump up and down and cheer him. Instead, I tried a happy but slightly sedate congratulations. "That's so great, Davis. So wonderful." And I gave a happy little hop anyway because it simply couldn't be contained. When I did, Davis reached out and touched my cheek, my neck. And as his face moved close to mine, I held my breath.

"Davis. The timing is wrong. The place is wrong."

He shook his head. "It feels absolutely right."

I wasn't afraid of the ocean. But I was afraid of him.

I didn't need another disappointing relationship. Wasn't sure I could survive another. And we were so different. Davis lived in a different world altogether. I didn't need . . . It all played through my head in a whiplash second. In the end, he touched his lips to mine gently, lightly. I saw the depth of something serious in his eyes and felt the tingles running the length of my body. And I wanted more. I repeated my list of "why nots" in my head, and Davis backed off. I hoped he understood my actions weren't meant against him. But as protection for me.

How could he understand? He knew nothing of my life. My history.

He didn't smile to soften his words. He spoke with great seriousness. "I won't apologize this time. I don't understand the barrier between us, and I'd like to say we can be friends, but I don't think that's going to work for me. Think about it, Lilliane, please." He touched my face again. "Give me a chance."

He dropped his hand. "And be careful. The ocean is beautiful but can be dangerous."

"I'll be fine. Thank you."

He nodded. "I have to go, but anytime you'd like someone to swim with, you let me know. I'm a strong swimmer."

I tried hard to fight the grin, but it forced its way onto my face.

Davis saw my reaction to his silly offer and his eyes lit

up.

"We'll talk," I said, my hand on his chest. "But not here."

Apparently, he decided to push the point. He undid some shirt buttons. "In fact, we can go in now. I'm an excellent swimmer. You'll be in good hands with me. I promise."

I touched his hands. "We'll talk, I promise."

Now he was full-out grinning. "This is kind of fun."

I put my hands on his arms and made a show of looking around him. Miranda saw me and waved again.

"You will shock Miranda."

He glanced back. "Miranda?"

"Miranda Wardlaw. One of Merrick's neighbors. She already has some kind of grudge . . . Correction: she has a poor opinion of Merrick. She's very sweet, despite the outspokenness, but I don't want to fuel any rumors."

"Miranda Wardlaw? You may have been right the first time. Grudge. Maybe she has a right to that."

"What are you talking about?"

I saw him thinking. The words he'd been ready to speak were being reconsidered. He decided to speak them anyway.

"I don't want to engage in rumors and old news, but I think you should know. Merrick's second wife, Marie, left him twenty-five years ago." He added, "That's when he stopped writing."

"I know that."

He grimaced. "But when she left, it was with someone else's husband. The neighbors . . . the Wardlaws. Miranda's husband. I think his name was Brandt."

I shook my head, refusing the idea. "No, Miranda hasn't said a word to indicate that . . . that . . ." She'd started to say something this very day when I'd arrived on the beach and we'd been chatting. What had she said?

Later, I told myself.

I said, "If that's true, if Merrick's wife left him for

Miranda's husband, and if they've continued to live in houses across the street from each other . . . Then every day must be a reminder." My eyes stung. I brushed at them and felt the sand still on my face. "It's just sad, that's all. Too sad." Grief? Was that what I felt rising within me? I felt like flat-out crying.

"Lilliane?" His hands were now on my arms. "Are you okay?"

"It's just so many years—unresolved heartache, grief, regret."

"Lilliane." He put his arms around me, pulled me close, and said, "Listen to me. They made their choices, then and now. And I assure you that what happened so long ago has not been on their minds every day for the past two decades. They've lived their lives and had their joys and disappointments, just like everyone. If for some reason it's uppermost in their minds again, then maybe that's good. Maybe they'll come to terms with it and each other, if that's even the desired outcome. Maybe it isn't. But it's about them. Not you. And you can't let it upset you like this."

I pushed away. "You're right. We all make our choices, don't we?" Was that it? Had my choices—and the choices of my parents—hit too close to home? Pretending to have a reasonable life but not living fully?

"I'm okay now. Thank you." I forced a smile on my face. "Go now. Change and whatever. I'm heading back too, after I speak with Miranda. Almost time to get supper together."

"Okay. We'll talk."

"We'll talk."

He left. I turned my back to the world and stood looking at the ocean. My brain felt disarranged. I needed to reset it, to go back to before.

I knew loss.

My hands shook. I crossed my arms and tucked my hands underneath to hold them still.

Still living in my parents' home.

It was the sensible thing to do. Even had I wanted to move, I couldn't afford to do so.

I could've gotten a GED. I could've found a better way. Opportunities—maybe made some, instead of waiting and hoping.

That water . . . that dark water underneath the waves. The dark water that led away from the shallow end where the sun could penetrate with its rays and give light—I'd seen that. The dark water hadn't held any allure for me that day. It didn't now, did it? Maybe a little. Like the power of forgetting. Of putting painful things aside. A rescue of sorts from having to face reality. Not ideal, of course. But still a solution.

I rubbed my face. What was happening? Such morose thoughts out of nowhere. On a day I *didn't* almost drown. Shame on me.

A voice came to me from a distance. It seemed eerie, almost borne on the wind. Which it was. I'd forgotten about Miranda. I rubbed my face again.

I wrapped my towel around my waist and carried my phone and shoes with me. When I reached her canopy, I saw she was smiling.

"A young man after all. I see I was right." She turned her book upside down on her lap. "I believe I've seen that particular fella coming and going from Merrick's house for quite a while. Is that how y'all met?"

"Miranda, you said something earlier about Merrick and his wife and getting over things. It got stuck in my mind. Will you tell me more?"

Her smile vanished.

"Marie. You knew her?"

"Yes."

"Why did she leave Merrick?"

Would she answer? Was it wrong for me to ask? "Please," I said.

"You should ask *him*."

"I'd appreciate it if you would tell me." I added, softly, "You know you want to. I think you've wanted to almost since the beginning when you first found out I was working for Merrick." Yes, I'd slipped and said *working*, but I let it go.

She caught what I'd said but didn't dispute it. She'd known all along I wasn't a relative. Now she looked away. "In part, you're right. But it's also Merrick's business, not just mine. I will tell you this—neither Merrick nor I were at fault. I suppose you could say we were the injured parties. But I think we blamed each other. Because that's what you do when the ones who should take the blame have absconded."

I dropped to my knees so I could see her eyes. I touched her hand.

"Thank you, Miranda. I appreciate you telling me that. I hope you are still my friend. I'll be leaving here week after next, but I want you to know I won't forget you. I've enjoyed knowing you. And I'll never forget that you wanted to save me when I came close to drowning."

She said with more energy, "Which you almost did again today. Or did you do it on purpose so that handsome man would have to rescue you?"

She was teasing. The glint in her eye was obvious. She'd moved on.

I patted her hand, saying, "I need to head back. Do you want me to walk you home?"

"You're sweet and thoughtful, but no, I'll stay yet awhile. My granddaughter will be over soon to collect me."

"If you're sure . . ."

"I am." She held up her hand to stop me. "Would you, if you don't mind, please give Merrick my regards? Please tell him how much I've enjoyed having his cousin around. That maybe one day he and I should get together for a cup of coffee."

I paused, taking in her words. I said, "Tea. He likes dandelion tea and biscuits." I leaned toward her. "They are actually cookies, but I call them biscuits. Makes them sound more elegant."

She chuckled. "Then please amend that to getting together for tea and biscuits."

"I'll tell him. Thank you for being my friend." I leaned close enough to give her a swift hug. "I'll see you later."

As I entered the house and reached the foyer, I called out, Merrick?"

The study doors were open. He was at his desk.

"Merrick?" I repeated, more softly. "I'm going to clean up and change, then fix our supper. Do you want a snack while you wait?"

"No, I'm fine. In fact, I believe I'll close my eyes for a few minutes."

"Want to lie down?"

"No, I'll rest here. I'll just put my head back. Let me know when the meal is ready."

"Will do."

I took a quick shower and brushed out my hair and dressed in shorts and a shirt. I felt invigorated with my swim, Davis distracting me and then rescuing me. Not to mention perhaps a small beginning of healing the breach between Merrick and Miranda. Those wings were suddenly back on my heels, and I practically danced down the stairs and made a quick turn down the hallway to the kitchen. I'd caught a quick glimpse of Merrick napping, so I tried to be quiet as I pulled out the plates and utensils and heated the casserole.

When I returned to the study with the plates, I said, "Merrick?"

He made a noise and closed his eyes tighter.

"Food's almost ready. What would you like to drink? I made some iced tea for a change. Any interest?"

His eyes opened halfway, and he reached up with one hand and massaged his left temple and jaw. I moved closer.

"Groggy?" I asked. "You must've gone off into a deep sleep."

His eyes, his expression, seemed a little too unfocused to me. Then again, naps could do that.

"Don't get up until you're fully awake. Stay here while I fetch that tea. I'll be right back." He made another noise, those grumpy noises he seemed to favor, and I took his response to mean he'd do as I'd asked.

I poured some iced tea into a glass and went straight back. He accepted the glass and drank several swallows of it before making a face.

"Not sweetened," he said.

Relieved that he seemed perkier, I smiled. "Unsweet."

"Well, it does work to wake you up."

"Were you wakeful again last night?"

He grimaced and pushed the glass away. He moved his hand in a *so-so* gesture. "I had some ideas I wanted to get down on paper, so to speak."

"Ideas on paper?" I sat in my chair. "Are you writing again?"

CHAPTER NINETEEN

"Seriously, Merrick, that's exciting."

He looked rather alarmed. Perhaps I'd overdone my enthusiasm.

"Have fun with it. There's no commitment outside of what you choose to do, right? It's for yourself."

He mumbled, "Maybe. Not sure."

I backed off. Was he still feeling the effects of the spell he'd had? I tried to take it down a notch.

"Just do what you enjoy. Please sit here and relax while I finish getting supper ready."

"You have any of those cookies?"

"I do. I'll bring you one." I made a mental note to call Susan to mention the possibility of low blood sugar and ask if I should contact his doctor. This was not an emergency. In an emergency, I would've gone straight to the doc, no question. I'd give Susan a ring this evening after Merrick had gone to bed.

Food was heating in the microwave. Meanwhile, I ran the plates and utensils back to the study to sneak another peek at him. What I saw reassured me. He was at work on his computer. For having such knobby, skinny fingers, he could type pretty well. I went back to the kitchen to finish up.

∞

We didn't chat much over our meal. His attention and focus were elsewhere. He didn't ask me about my life in Cub Creek or what I thought about Davis's book or any of that. I

toyed with the idea of bringing up what Miranda had said—
not about their spouses, but about their own relationship and
the wasted years—but again, he wasn't fully with me.
Distracted, perhaps. He ate, not with his usual gusto, but he
did eat. His movements were steady, and his color was good.
It seemed like his mind was somewhere else.

But as we finished up, I gave it a try.

"Merrick, guess what?"

A quick glance up. "What?"

"I saw Miranda at the beach today. She said to please
give you her regards—to say hello—and thought you two
might get together for coffee or tea one day soon."

He looked up again and this time kept his focus. "And?"

"That was all she said."

"Oh, I see." He grimaced. "Please say hello back to her."

Humph. I'd expected more than that. "I will. You've
been neighbors for a long, long time, haven't you?"

"What? Oh, neighbors. Yes. We moved here about the
same time." He laid his fork and knife on his plate. "That's
it for me."

"There's more."

"No. I'm getting back to . . . a project."

"A writing project?"

"A . . . I'm not ready to discuss it yet. Soon, I think."

"Anything I can do to assist?"

"No. It's all on me." He grimaced. "I'm sorry about the
delay in getting more of that manuscript."

"Davis's?"

"Yes. Definitely a delay. I believe he's been distracted
by another project he has prioritized."

"I see." And that made no sense. I could understand a
new project, and that getting a new contract might cause
Davis to reprioritize what he was working on, but all the bits
and pieces of it didn't match up for me.

Really, this was stupid. I should just be honest with
Davis. I would have to tell Merrick my intentions first,

though, and that deterred me.

Merrick said, "Thank you for supper. Excuse me."

He seemed in a hurry to get rid of me. I almost laughed out loud about it, but his manner didn't invite joking or sparring. No lingering. No small talk. I gathered the plates and stuff, and he remarked, "I'll be in here for a while, and then I'll be going to bed. Maybe watch a little TV while I go to sleep."

"It's so early, Merrick. Are you sure?"

He rose from his chair and walked over to the desk. "I'm sure. If I get up once or twice during the evening . . . Well, as you know, that's what I do. And as you say yourself"—he picked up his cell phone from the desktop—"I know how to reach you."

"Okay, then. I'll probably be out by the pool after I clean the kitchen. I'll keep the phone close."

He gave me a rude expression but didn't prolong the exchange. He settled in his chair, opened his laptop, and proceeded to ignore me.

Should I be reassured or concerned?

After cleaning the kitchen, I checked on him again and he was fine, but still preoccupied. I took my phone out by the pool and dialed Susan's number.

I got her voice mail. "Susan, this is Lilliane. Merrick's fine, but he had a spell earlier today that made me think he may have had a low blood sugar episode. I don't know that for sure, of course, and he seems fine now, but I think it should be discussed when next he sees his doctor. If you'd like me to contact his doctor now, please let me know. Merrick said he was fine, and he probably is, but he doesn't seem quite himself. Call me when you have the opportunity."

Was that adequate? I hung up. Was I an alarmist? Didn't matter. I had a responsibility.

I walked back to the foyer again, unable to dismiss my concern for Merrick. I felt drawn. The study doors were open, but he wasn't there. His bedroom door was closed. I put my ear to the door and heard small noises—what I'd expect to hear if he was getting ready for bed as usual. *Okay, then.*

As I turned away, I noted his computer was missing from his desktop.

He'd all but admitted he was writing again. *So . . .* But the sense that he was up to something was so strong that I nearly knocked on his bedroom door to demand he give an explanation. But I didn't. He wasn't a child. I told that little inner voice to shut up and leave me alone, and I'd leave Merrick in peace.

He was fine.

⋘⋙

It was a warm, breezy evening. Sunset was still a way off, but the light in the sky was gentling, and the few errant clouds were changing hue—a soft gold tint. I leaned my head back and closed my eyes, listening to the easy sound of the water in the pool backed by the low roar of the ocean.

My phone rang. Either Merrick or Susan. I was on my feet before I'd even answered it. "Hello."

"Lilliane? It's Davis."

"Oh. I thought it might be Susan."

"Susan? Biggs, you mean? Is something wrong?"

"No. Yes . . . no. I don't know. Merrick had a spell today, nothing serious, I don't think, but when you're ninety . . ."

"What kind of spell?"

"A little woozy. Because of the timing, I'm thinking low blood sugar. He seemed fine after a snack, but he wasn't the usual chatty, grumpy old man I'm used to."

"How so?"

"Distracted. He seems to be . . . elsewhere. He speaks, he eats, he responds when I prompt him, but . . . it almost seems like he's in another world. And secretive."

"You're probably smart to mention it to Susan, but I think it's because he's writing again."

"Did he tell you that?"

"Yes and no."

"You're as bad as he is." I made a rude noise. "If he is, could that account for the distraction?"

"The more engaged the writer is with the new story, the more . . . removed he or she can be from the real world. Just like a reader, right? Sometimes readers can get so engaged in the world of the book that they forget to eat or sleep. Has that happened to you?"

"Not quite to that degree, but I understand what you're saying."

"So if he's functioning well otherwise, that's probably all it is. Ask him. He might fuss at being interrupted, but if you ask, he'll likely tell you." There was a pause, and he added with a change of tone, "In fact, you should ask him what he's writing about. He might *want* to tell you."

Odd. That sounded odd. I was about to tell Davis to just spell it out—get it said because I wasn't in the mood to read between anyone's lines—when an incoming call showed up on the phone screen.

"I have to go. It's Susan." I disconnected and grabbed her call.

CRSO

"Got your message. How is he?"

Had I overdone it? "He seems okay now. I was worried because I hadn't seen him out of it like that before. He seems tired but then recovers pretty well after he eats. He seems to be spending more time in his bedroom—napping, I presume, or possibly watching TV. And over the last few days he's been asking for time alone. I don't think it's me or anything that's gone wrong between us. He seems distracted."

"Oh. He's probably fine, then. He's had low blood sugar

before, so I'll talk to his doctor about checking him. If he's distracted, then don't worry too much about it. When he asked me if you could stay longer, he also hinted that he was writing again." I heard background noises. "Honestly, it's been so long since he tried. I've just been managing his backlist. And Lilliane, this is very important—do not mention this to anyone. Anyone. A comeback by a nonagenarian, after a quarter of a century, could be dismissed, could be mocked. Who knows? He doesn't need any of that. Nor does he need to be barraged by opportunists when I'm not there to field them. Just let him do as he wishes. Believing he's got another book in him isn't a bad way for him to spend his nineties. But we'll keep it between us. Promise?"

I promised. But if Davis also knew, then . . . I heard noises again in the background again. "What is that?"

"What? Oh, the squealing. The grandkids. The grand-toddler twins, I call them. I'm working from my daughter's house. She's having a difficult pregnancy and put out a call for help." I heard her speaking low, and now I understood it was to a child. I heard the love in that soft, talking-to-the-baby voice. She came back to me, saying, "I've always put business first. All my life. But I've gotten smarter in recent years. When the call came, I went. That's why I was so desperate and in such a hurry when I hired you."

Oh. Wow. Not at all what I'd imagined.

"If you continue to be concerned, go ahead and reach out to the doctor directly. Better safe than sorry. But one thing I've learned is that at some point quality of life trumps quantity."

We ended our call soon after. I'd heard a toddler giggling in the background and another whining, which sounded like he or she was gearing up to full tantrum mode. I'd wished Susan well before we'd disconnected. She'd laughed. She'd sounded harried and happy.

I wished I'd asked about her daughter and the new

grandchild. Next time. Meanwhile, it seemed like I was worrying needlessly about Merrick. I smiled and put my phone on the table. Done.

No sunset stroll on the beach tonight. I wanted to stay nearby. I went upstairs and put on my swimsuit. This time, I remembered to bring a towel and left it, with my phone, on the table.

I moved with much more confidence down the steps and into the pool. I still couldn't swim properly, but anyone could hold their nose and go under. Even me. I'd done it unintentionally, hadn't I? Probably a good idea to practice managing underwater.

And I did. The first attempt I only went to my chin, but then I took a deep breath, held it, closed my eyes, and picked up my legs. Under I went. Over my head. My body bobbed over. I let it happen and kept holding my breath. The water picked up my hair, enough for me to feel it being tugged at by the water and floating around my face. And then I was up and wiping the water from my face with my hands, taking a breath, and blinking my eyes. I repeated it a few times until it lost its novelty, and the sunset began to grow. I wished I could float on my back and watch the show that way. People made it look easy, but it wasn't. I kept folding in the middle and finally gave it up. I waded out of the water, dried my face and hair with the towel, then wrapped myself up in it.

Now what? For the first time since I'd been here, I felt adrift. No, that was too close to a pun. I felt . . . without. Without a task or goal. In about ten days I'd be heading home. I wanted to use these days fully. I should focus on *now* instead of thinking ahead.

But maybe I was also ready to return home.

Not to the Fuel Up Fast, and not to a position at Ethel's Home for Adults. The folks there had offered me a job a while back. But I didn't have whatever it took to deliver that kind of care with patience and grace.

Some of the money I was earning here would cover the

cost of taking a class at the community college. Maybe learn computers. If Merrick could manage a laptop, then surely I could learn. There was more to life. I felt it in me like a real thing for the first time. Maybe it had taken seeing that Merrick had wasted more than twenty years tied to a loss that couldn't be remedied. Yes, I'd done the same. But I wasn't forty yet. I had a lot of good years ahead of me.

Maybe Davis could visit me in Cub Creek? No. I'd be embarrassed. My life there was tied to my old house, with no pretense of gracious living, and a scraped-up car and accepting almost any kind of job that would hire me. My face warmed as I thought of it.

I didn't want Davis to see that person. I didn't want to be that person—the person who felt defined by shoddiness and lack of ambition.

That was up to me to change too. I had no idea how, but if others could change their lives, then I could.

I could change and still honor my parents. Still treasure their memory. And forgive them for leaving me as they did.

Give up the past. Make it possible for my future to be better.

It seemed to me that these minutes of floating, of facing head-on the feelings of being useless and adrift in a wasted life, might be the most valuable time I'd spent in years. Real thinking.

Like light dawning.

Wow. And it had taken leaving home for me to figure it out.

Double wow.

CRED

I went inside, still clutching my towel. Before going upstairs, I paused in the foyer. The study doors were still open. Merrick was not in sight, so I presumed he was behind that closed bedroom door—and hopefully, he was sleeping well.

Despite myself, I moved into the study and listened at the bedroom door. No light was visible around the door. No sound. I started to move away and then heard . . . what? Maybe nothing. I twisted the knob and eased the door open.

A nightlight burned faintly in the bathroom. I stood, staring, as my eyes adjusted, but I couldn't make out his form in the bed. In fact, I realized the covers were thrown back. Could he be in the bathroom? I opened the door wider. As I did, the foyer light making its way through the study spilled in an arc across the bedroom floor, highlighting a lone slipper on the rug near the foot of the bed.

And near the slipper, I saw pajama-clad legs sprawled on the floor, unmoving.

CHAPTER TWENTY

"Merrick, Merrick," I repeated softly as I felt for a pulse with one hand and pressed my other hand to his chest, checking for a rise and fall. His pulse was slow but steady. He was breathing. I said his name again, but louder, shivering. The AC was hitting my wet swimsuit and I shivered. My hair dripped onto Merrick's pajama shirt. I focused on the phone in my hand. I'd programmed the doctor's number into my phone. Susan had said it was a direct number. Some sort of concierge service.

"Hello."

"Dr. Barnes?"

"Yes?"

"I'm Merrick Dahl's companion. He's unconscious but breathing. His pulse is slow but steady. His eyelids are flickering, so he may be coming around."

"Are you at his home?"

"Yes, he's on the floor."

"Leave him there. If he wakes, tell him to stay put. Cover him to keep him warm. I'll notify EMS on my way."

"Good. Thanks."

We disconnected.

Now what? I reached over to the bed and dragged a blanket onto the floor with us.

"Merrick," I whispered.

"Lil . . ." His eyes were partway open. "Wha—"

"I don't know what happened. I found you here on the floor."

His arms moved.

"Stay still. Dr. Barnes is on his way."

"Oh, no, I'm—"

"No, you're not fine. He'll be here soon. Are you chilly? Do you need another blanket?"

"A cloth. A cool cloth for my forehead."

"Okay, I can do that."

I started to rise. He turned his head toward me and frowned. "Where are your clothes?"

I looked down and remembered. "My clothing is *on* me. It's called a swimsuit."

"Is that appro—priate . . . given the . . ."

He was a little breathless.

"Stop talking and breathe. I didn't choose the circumstances, you know. But I'm glad to see your sense of humor is returning."

"I'm okay."

"We'll see."

Vehicles were arriving. One of them had flashing lights. I ran to the door, wrapping the towel around my waist as I went. Yeah, no one would notice me in a swimsuit. *Gee whiz.*

CRBO

The doctor pronounced his vitals good. No signs of stroke or heart attack. The emergency responders helped get him back into his bed, and I explained to them and the doctor and anyone who'd listen that I was concerned about a low blood sugar episode earlier in the day. The doctor performed a finger prick to check his blood. By then, Merrick was ornery and demanding food and coffee.

"Your heart sounds better than mine," he told Merrick. "Your blood sugar is low, but not bad. What have you been up to? Anything energetic? Are you sleeping well?"

Merrick said, "Lilliane takes excellent care of me, but she worries too much."

"She isn't the one who was passed out cold on the floor. Lucky you didn't hit your head or break anything."

"I don't want to go anywhere. I'm fine. I could get up right now."

"If you do, then I'll insist you go with the EMTs to the hospital."

"Lilliane," Merrick said, "why don't you go change while the doc and I chat. I'm sure you'll feel more comfortable."

Well, that was certainly true. I suspected what Merrick really wanted was a private conversation with the doc.

I said to the doctor, "Sounds like a good idea, if you can spare me?"

He smiled. "Certainly."

"I'll be right back."

"We'll be here," Dr. Barnes said.

⚬⚬⚬

After the hubbub, after the adrenaline surges, the anxiety, the action, the arrival and departure of the doctor, fighting with Merrick to make him get into bed and stay there—nothing was more important than him giving his body a rest after what he'd put it through—I closed the bedroom door, but not all the way. I wanted to be able to hear him. To peek in on him should I feel the need. I'd taken the opportunity as suggested to put on real clothing while Merrick and the doctor were quietly talking. Now I fetched a blanket from upstairs and looked for a spot in the study where I could settle in for the night.

The chairs were padded but upright with rigid frames. Comfortable for sitting, but not cozy. That left his desk chair. It was plenty big and would rock back a little. It felt like trespassing for me to use his desk chair, but it was necessary.

His laptop was back on the desk. I hadn't noticed before, but Merrick must've brought it back out here before he collapsed. The lid was up, but the screen was dark. In the course of arranging myself and the blanket in the chair, I probably jostled it because the screen lit up.

I didn't know much about computers, just what I'd seen as others had used them, but it didn't open to a password screen. This was a page with words on it. A writing program.

Had Merrick saved his work? I knew it was important because I'd heard someone freaking out in the library one day about not having saved their work before their computer had shut down unexpectedly.

I was afraid to touch the machine. Fearful I'd mess something up. But as I was trying to figure out how to save the work and close it down, the actual words on the screen caught my eye.

Mike said, "Did I hear what I thought I heard? Is that true, Jeff?" I wanted him to confirm exactly that—that I'd heard him wrong. I wasn't sure I'd believe him if he took back his words, but I was willing to try. When Suze had called that morning, she'd said Jeff was out. On his own. For good and forever. She'd said she didn't want him back, that she'd kicked him out two weeks before. "I'm sorry I didn't tell you then, Mike. Truly, I think he's up to no good again."

She'd laughed ruefully, but the laugh turned into a sob.

And now Mike felt his anger surging. Dangerous anger. The kind that could cost more than hurt feelings and tears.

Was this from *The Book of Lost Loves?*

My first instinct was to read a little more, to see this part of the book that I hadn't seen before.

"Sorry, man," Jeff said, backing up a step. "It wasn't intended. Danielle and I . . . I didn't mean for it to happen. We just clicked."

The words came out of Jeff's mouth likes sleazy, oily bits of cast-off refuse. Nausea that came from disgust and rising anger wanted to overwhelm Mike. He clenched his fists—holding it back.

"Soon after we all met on the beach that day. She kept trying to tell you . . ."

Jeff stopped talking as Mike grabbed him—his fingers fitting around Jeff's throat, his thumb pressing against the hollow in his throat against his larynx, feeling the glands themselves tucked inside, round and soft like grapes ready to be split open—

Jeff rasped, "Mike."

"Where is she?"

"Waiting." He made a sound like sandpaper on concrete. "Please."

Mike eased his grip just enough for Jeff to speak.

"For me. She was afraid. Didn't want to face you. Begged me to tell you."

Jeff needed to shut up. When Mike slammed him in the face, Jeff did exactly that, falling to the sand, his hands touching, clutching at his throat where Mike's fingers had been.

This didn't feel finished with Jeff. Mike wanted to hurt him more, but he sensed that time was running out somehow. He'd done enough, though, to slow Jeff down.

He wasn't taking Jeff's word for anything, except for when he'd said that Danielle was waiting.

And Mike needed to find her first.

My brain was growing increasingly insistent that I pay attention. Not to the words, but to the fact that I was reading them—material I hadn't read before—and they were on Merrick's laptop.

This was the last thing Merrick had viewed before he'd collapsed.

Jolted by the idea of it, my finger spun the wheel on the mouse, and pages flew by. It took a moment to realize I was the one causing the pages to pass. When I did, I let go of the mouse and squeezed my hands together.

I willed my heart to slow. When I felt less agitated, I tried again. My brain said, "Don't." But I did because I had to. Like when you pass a traffic accident and you try to reconstruct what happened by the evidence by the evidence of the broken tail lights and busted fenders.

Scrolling down the page, skimming as I went, the writing seemed to be less polished. There were references to Mike driving like a madman to Danielle's home on the sound side of the island. He was frantic and rushing. There were more misspellings and disjointed sentences here, but then it came together again, as if his focus had firmed up and had been poured into this scene:

Her car wasn't parked out front, so Mike drove around back. He saw her SUV back near the old boathouse, the small one-room building she'd redone into a hideaway. The vehicle was almost camouflaged within the shade of the tall pines and at eye level by the massive thick shrubs. On purpose, maybe?

Wanting to avoid him, maybe?

But she'd brought him here many times, back

when their relationship had swept them from picnics on the truck tailgate to hours and hours entwined together here. Before she'd started talking about leaving.

An ugly voice whispered in his ear: Had she done the same with Jeff? And here? It was as if Mike could hear her laughter mixing with Jeff's bigmouthed big talk. It rang in Mike's ears as he jumped from the truck, moving without slowing as he raced toward the small one-room retreat, and nearly stumbled over a book left on the front step. That stopped him. He knelt to pick it up. The poetry book he'd given her.

And more.

Across the cover of the book glittered the silver ~~bracelet~~ chain of the necklace with its amethyst pendant. For a long moment, Mike paused, as if time itself had been suspended. The delicacy of the chain glinting against his rough, tanned hands almost hypnotized him.

How long before Jeff got here?

Mike looked away from the necklace and stared at the small front window. Was she standing inside, looking out?

No, he didn't think so.

But she would've heard his truck. She should've—even if she wanted to avoid him— she should've come out to face him even if she only wanted to scream at him to go away and leave her alone.

Jeff's words wouldn't quit echoing in his head. Life might be random, but when something didn't make any sense, it didn't make sense—that simple. There must be more. A reason. An explanation he could understand. He reached up to rub his temple—where the headache had lodged that morning when Suze had called, and now it wouldn't quite go away. The chain of the necklace scratched his skin. Had tangled itself around his fingers. He tried to pull free of it, and the links snapped.

How long had she been involved with Jeff? Almost from the beginning, as Jeff had said? No, Mike didn't believe that.

He dropped the necklace into his shirt pocket and left the book back on the step.

Though he didn't know what was wrong, every instinct he had insisted that something was. Something was dreadfully wrong. Something more than cheating, or simply falling for someone else.

In that moment, he heard her car idling, but so softly he hardly noticed it over the pounding in his ears. He now saw the tubing attached to the back of the vehicle and running up the side of the house to fit in over the . . .

My stomach seized. The supper I'd eaten hours earlier tried to come up. I grabbed my midsection, closed my eyes, breathed, and counted to ten. Then to twenty.

Merrick. How could you?

I'd been used. Mocked, apparently. Absolutely lied to. *The Book of Lost Loves* had never been Davis's manuscript.

Davis had urged me to ask Merrick what he was writing. Davis had known.

Lies and secrets—*against* me.

My personal details used against me.

The nausea had switched to heat—heat in my face and body and my brain—now dropped in temperature to a cold, so cold, anger and resolve. A wish for revenge. I gripped my blanket with one hand and the arm of the chair with my other.

His bedroom door was partly open. I wanted to scream at him. Demand an explanation. And it might kill him.

I couldn't do that. I couldn't live with that.

But I wasn't required to accept betrayal, or to put up with it either.

Standing, walking, pacing—I crossed the foyer and went to the pool. But still I moved. I tried sitting in the gazebo, but there was no peace. Not anywhere. I punched the keycode on the gazebo gate and stumbled down the steps to the sand. The beach. People might've seen a shadowed woman in the night, stumbling in the sand, running along the water's edge, perhaps even falling and lying there, but if they did, no one interfered or called for help. It was just me. For which I was grateful.

Finally, I found myself sitting on the sand near the water at The Point. The moon above was accompanied by the stars and planets. Same as ever. Beautiful as ever. Going on regardless of whatever I'd done or hadn't done. I was less than a speck of this sand in terms of importance.

It was time for me to go home. Past time.

Thinking of how I'd been embarrassed at the thought of Davis seeing where and how I lived, I laughed, but not pleasantly.

He'd never see it. Not my home. Not Cub Creek. Not even the Fuel Up Fast. We were done. Had Davis actually meant any of the things he'd said? About not leaving without talking to him? And so much else that had been implied in his manner, his touch?

Some people were so good with words that they were careless with them. Careless of their effect on the hearts and hopes of others who didn't know that it was just their manner. And meant nothing.

☙❧

When I returned to the house, I peeked in on Merrick,

almost afraid of finding him awake. I wasn't sure I could control myself. But he was sleeping soundly.

I understood now what had kept him up nights. Working who knew how late. Writing in secret, so I wouldn't know the truth.

It was a lie. It was also pathetic. I could pity him, but I wouldn't bother. He was going to be someone else's charge as of tomorrow.

I dialed Susan as I walked back out to the pool area.

"Sorry it's late. Merrick passed out. The doctor came and pronounced him okay, just overtired. Probably a result of the late-night writing sessions and complicated by the low blood sugar."

"Is he in the hospital?"

"No. He didn't want to go, and Dr. Barnes didn't judge it necessary. Merrick's resting now. Sleeping soundly."

She gave a long sigh. "Thank goodness. I'm so glad."

"I'm leaving tomorrow. First thing."

There was a long silence. I thought I might have to repeat myself, but finally she said, "Why?"

"I prefer not to talk about it."

Another long silence, during which I could hear only the sound of her breathing.

I added, "Ms. Bertie will be here tomorrow, so Merrick won't be alone."

"Lilliane. I don't understand."

"Nothing to understand. It's time for me to go home."

"Okay. Okay, I'll try to find someone tomorrow. Obviously, I can't tonight. I'll ask them to start ASAP."

"I'm going home tomorrow."

"Lilliane. Please. If my daughter doesn't deliver tonight, she is scheduled for a C-section tomorrow. I . . . I can't really deal with both situations at this moment."

I heard the plea in her voice.

"I'll stay tomorrow. But that's it. I'm gone the next day."

"I'll figure something out. Thank you."

Could I hold it together that long? I'd been through worse, right?

One more day.

Chapter Twenty-One

Merrick had a quiet night. Friday morning was almost as usual—for him. For me? Not so much.

He was rested and hungry. I was burdened by betrayal, anger, resentment, and a lousy night's sleep. I'd abandoned the chair partway through the night and stretched out with my blanket and pillow on the cushiony rug. Ironic, sort of, that the rug that had stunned me when my bare feet had first stepped upon it, was now, shortly before my departure, serving as my bed.

I brought Merrick his breakfast. I tried not to pout or scowl, but it was hard. Harsh words and accusations wanted to pour out of me. But that wasn't my job. I was a companion. Nothing more. I'd forgotten that this was a job, and I was not really a friend.

Ms. Bertie had arrived at seven a.m. and found me sleeping on the rug. I'd given her a rundown of the night before. I gave her a moment to get past her shock at Merrick's passing out and to understand that he'd had a good night's rest and was doing fine, before adding, "By the way, today is my last day. I'm leaving tomorrow morning. Mr. Dahl doesn't know yet, so please don't say anything. I'll tell him later today. Ms. Biggs is working to find a replacement to start tomorrow." And then I walked out, leaving her with her mouth gaping. There were no questions she could possibly ask that I wanted to answer.

Soon after, Susan called. I was surprised. But it was what I wanted, right? She said she had someone who'd come by the house later in the afternoon. "Could you please introduce her to Merrick and give her the information I left with you?"

"Of course."

"I thought an introduction would be helpful. She won't officially start until tomorrow morning."

"I'll take care of it."

"From everything I've heard, you've done a wonderful job, Lilliane, and Merrick would be delighted if you'd stay indefinitely. I don't know what happened with you, or between you two. I haven't spoken to him. Frankly, I'm reluctant to break the news over the phone."

"I'll tell him personally. I wouldn't just disappear on him, anyway."

"If this is what you want . . ."

"Thank you, Susan. It's been a pleasure. Or was. Thanks again."

"Is there anything I can do to convince you to reconsider?"

"No, Susan. I'm sorry it ended this way. Best wishes to your daughter, and I hope the delivery goes smoothly."

CREO

After breakfast had been cleared away and Merrick had taken his pills, I'd left him in his study alone because I told myself I needed to pack. But packing for me was easily done in a few minutes, so the real reason was that Merrick knew something was wrong and had asked a few times, then apparently decided that it was my worry over him that was weighing on me. I knew I should take the opportunity to sit down with him and explain that a new aide was arriving to meet him today. That I was leaving.

I hadn't yet because I'd have to tell him why—but coolly and without rancor—and I couldn't find the right words. Procrastination whispered in my head that I needed to pack. So that's where I went. Upstairs. And that's where I was an hour later, sitting on my bed and staring at nothing, when the front doorbell rang. It echoed throughout. No one with any level of hearing could miss the doorbell in this house.

My heart flipped, and an electrical charge seemed to surge through me and brought me to my feet.

She—the new me—wasn't due yet.

Ms. B beat me to the door. From the top of the stairs, I saw her in the foyer with her hand on the doorknob and almost called out for her to stop. I didn't, of course. But it was just one more example of how things never went as planned. *Maybe it's for the best. Maybe . . .*

Miranda Wardlaw was on the doorstep.

I flew down the stairs, saying, "Miranda? Are you okay?" I reached for her arm, asking, "Is something wrong?"

"Wrong?" She leaned on me as she stepped over the threshold. "What could be wrong? Oh, I see. I haven't darkened this doorway in twenty years or more. But last night there were flashing lights bathing the neighborhood in red. No one, especially old people or parents of teenagers, wants to see that."

She looked at me. "How is he?"

I hugged her. She reached around and patted me on the back.

From behind me, Merrick said, "Why are you here? There's nothing wrong with me, as you can see. It was a big fuss over nothing."

"Well, ain't you just as disagreeable as you were twenty years gone. Land sakes. Shut up and invite me in."

He said, "That makes no sense."

"Just do it. I need a cup of coffee, or even tea. Be a gentleman and offer me a chair." She gripped my arm while she shook her cane at him.

He tapped his own cane against the tile floor and made his grumpy noise. "Well, then, you might as well come inside." He turned and went into the study.

I followed with Miranda. When we entered the study,

Merrick was standing beside my chair. The one I always used. He was gripping the back of it and jostled it a bit. "Will this chair suit?"

"It'll do just fine. Thank you for your consideration."

Merrick looked at me. "Lilliane, would you kindly fix us some tea and biscuits?"

Morning tea? Seriously?

"I'll be happy to." I helped Miranda settle into the chair. She hooked her cane over the edge of Merrick's desk and sat back.

I left.

But I wanted to listen.

No. I didn't want to hear anything they said. It was no longer my business. Never had been, really.

But I wanted to know anyway. I forced myself to focus on making the tea. Ms. B was staring, wide-eyed.

"What is going on here?"

"She saw the emergency lights last night. Came over to see how Merrick is."

"Humph." She made her own grumpy noise. "No sense. She hasn't been over before. All these years."

"Did you know about what happened all those years ago too?"

"Course I do. I know most everything. That's how it is when you're working in folks' homes as I do."

I set out the cups and saucers and took down the cookies. I paused, staring at the box. How many times had I done this over my time here?

I'd leave these behind. I'd leave them for Merrick.

After arranging two shortbread cookies each on the side of the saucers, I returned the box to the cabinet.

CRꙄꙄ

I returned to the study and set the tea and cookies on the desk.

Miranda thanked me, glanced the length of me, and said, "Merrick, you need to pay this gal more so she can afford some shoes."

Merrick laughed. I was stunned and reminded again of the change that always came over him when he dropped his hard shell and let loose. I could imagine a woman, including his Marie, being charmed.

"I have shoes. More than one pair, in fact. But I like being barefoot."

Miranda said, "Then you're in the right place. Credit to your good sense, or good fortune, or most likely the good Lord, for getting you here."

There was a sudden hitch in my giddyup. My brain stalled like an old car with no fumes left to run on. *The Lord giveth and the Lord taketh away,* per the King James Version and my recollection. I'd been given a gift, I reminded myself. Now it was time to show I had the grace and gratitude necessary to let it go.

I tried to smile, but my grimace was probably not convincing. So I left. Just like that. I fled. Because it was either that or cry.

CRSO

I ran away from the part of the beach that Miranda and I had shared. I ran away from that area because that's where Davis would expect to find me. Somehow, I knew they'd drag him in, or that odd sixth sense he had would bring him into it. I ran, as I'd done last night, toward The Point. To where the dunes rose like small hillocks topped with tall, slender grasses that waved in the breeze. But with no trees and no real shelter. Today was already hot, though the onshore breeze cut the heat somewhat.

For a while, I sat there feeling sorry for myself. Feeling confused. Feeling the dampness from the sand soaking into the seat of my shorts. It was tricky to sustain my emotional distress as that dampness spread. I knew that when I finally gave up and stood, I'd be a sight.

Didn't matter. I was headed home. I'd meet the new aide, stay tonight, then leave the room ready for her to move into tomorrow morning.

All of this would be a memory. Mostly good. Pretty fantastic, actually. The down parts, the betrayal, would fade—I'd let them. And I'd get on with my life back home.

I'd always loved Cub Creek and growing up there. I'd sort of just gone through the motions of living my life over the last few years, but I could change that. I was the only one who could. I could put the past in the past and move forward. Try new things. Take some chances. But back home where I belonged.

My shoulders tensed, and the back of my neck itched. I reached up to shrug and scratch, but then I just bowed my head.

Momma had said lots of things. Many of the things had been told to her by her own mother and grandmother. I'd added a few wisdoms and truisms of my own through the years. Many of those I'd shared in my stories in front of the kids, and often adults, on story days at the library. But she'd never taught me how to say goodbye.

I rubbed my forehead and pushed my hair back out of my face. The sandy grit on on my palms left a path across my flesh. When I heard Davis's voice, I wasn't even surprised.

"May I join you?"

"I don't see the point." *Doggone it.* If he mentioned any reference to a pun, I would hurt him.

"That wasn't a no." He sat beside me.

"Your shorts are going to get wet."

He shrugged. "It's the beach. Wet bottoms are expected."

I frowned. "Seriously?"

"Sorry, it sounded a little different than I meant it."

The angry words flowed out of me unexpectedly, shocking me. "You know he had me reading your story—correction—what I *thought* was your story. I promised him I wouldn't tell. I thought I'd start it, be able to say I tried to read it, but couldn't, and then hand it back. It would be done." I breathed. "But it was good. I contributed to the lie, but I meant well." He stayed silent, so I continued. "So how do I now hold him to a standard? A standard of truth and honesty that I failed to keep."

Still, he stayed silent.

"Now I know what your argument with Merrick was about. You were angry when you discovered he'd been sharing his manuscript and saying it was yours. And that I agreed to help him in that. Except I thought it really was yours. You had—*have*—every right to be hurt and angry that he and I were in that strange conspiracy, true or not." I pressed my fingers to my temples. "It feels too complicated to explain."

He said, "Context."

I squinted at him. "What?"

"You're missing context."

The sun seemed too bright. A cloud must've moved. With my hand, I shielded my eyes from both the light and him.

"Explain."

"You helped an old man. You made a promise, and you kept it."

"Ultimately, I was a willing coconspirator."

"True. But that's up to me to forgive, right?"

"Okay."

"And I forgive you. I'm glad you went along with Merrick. I'm glad that by doing so you helped him get over his fear of getting back to work."

"It was still wrong."

"Lots of stuff is."

"And you figured out what he was doing. That he was

lying to me too. And you didn't tell me."

"I suggested you talk to him. Ask him what he was writing."

"Not the same as being honest with me."

He shrugged. "I claim the same right to forgiveness that I extended to you."

I stayed silent this time.

He said, "Think of the two of us like good wish fairies. Muses, maybe. We saw an old man with no real life, seriously in need of a muse and a little stardust. So long as I don't have to wear a tutu, I'm okay with that."

I laughed. I tried to hold it in. I really was a terrible person if the image of Davis in a tutu was enough to salve my conscience and save my mood.

He said, "Now don't get mad at me."

"For what?"

"See that truck?"

A large black pickup truck had parked nearby.

"Yes."

"That truck belongs to Miranda's granddaughter's boyfriend, summoned by Miranda to ferry Merrick out here. You should've seen the two of them together. Miranda and Merrick. Scary folks when their goals line up, let me tell you." He gave a mock shudder, then touched my hand. "I was under strict orders to give you up to the posse as soon as I found you. I called them."

"No, I can't believe you did that."

"Had to." He shrugged. "Merrick couldn't make this walk under his own power."

I hit him. I pushed his arm and wanted to slap him.

He took my hand and held it gently, saying, "You'll have to do better than that to make me regret it. Any of it. Meeting you was worth every up and down. Or slap."

Way to make me blush and steal my words. And there was Merrick, with his bony feet, narrow and bare, and pale enough from constant shoe wearing to blind the unwary.

Someone had rolled up his pants legs for him, and a young man was keeping a hand on him and holding his cane as Merrick navigated the sand.

Frankly, he appeared delighted to be walking in the sand, though awkward. When his eyes fixed on me, his look lost the glow of delight. I started to rise, but Davis said, "Stay." Then he got up and walked the few steps over.

"Give me a hand," Merrick said to him.

It was a production. Between Davis and the young man, they helped lower the old one to the sand.

"Oh my," he kept saying, punctuated by his growly noise from deep in his throat. And when he was fully down and his long, bony feet were stretched out in front of him, he laughed. But softly. "Never thought I'd be sitting on the beach again." He gathered a handful of sand and let it sift through his fingers.

He nodded toward me. "Even if you choose not to forgive me, I'll never regret this day. It's hot, though. Might be too hot for this old man, so I'd better get on with it." He took a long pause, then said with near formality, "I'm sorry."

"For what?"

"Tough, huh?" He nodded again. "I saw this morning, on my computer, that someone had gone through the pages. Knew it was you. Knew that you knew."

"That you'd lied to me. Played me."

"That you knew my cowardice. The cowardice as concerns the world that prompted the need to conceal what I was attempting to do, and the cowardice as concerns you that prevented me from confessing. Didn't want to make you mad . . . or disappoint you." He nodded again. "Confessing and apologizing."

"You used my personal information. Information I trusted you with when we chatted. You were gathering my heartaches and grief to people your story."

He frowned. "Was I?" He shrugged. "Perhaps. I suppose I might have. I did take some of what you told me . . . but . . .

But, Lilliane, you must understand that that's what novels are. Fiction." His hands moved, his fingers splayed, as if conducting the words like music. "It's fiction. *Not* a literal retelling of someone's life or experience, but . . ." He stabbed the tip of his cane into the sand. "Isn't that what you do? When you tell your stories? You don't just talk about yourself. Where do you think your stories come from? The things your momma told you? From experience—hers and others."

He coughed. It was loud and rough sounding. I wished I had water to offer.

"We'd better get you back to the house."

"Not yet."

"Come on, Merrick. This is unnecessary."

"It is *very* necessary. You want to go back to the house so you can get on with leaving. Just like that. Just leave, like you're any old hired companion. Someone showing up to do a job and then moving on."

"Isn't that what I am?"

"Susan called. Maybe she knew you wouldn't be able to break it to me yourself. Doesn't that tell you something?"

"It's time for me to go home, Merrick. I don't belong here."

"I guess you've got folks missing you. But if you leave, we'll miss you too."

"You, and the others, will forget me in no time."

"Wrong."

"Susan has already arranged a replacement. I was going to tell you, but then Miranda arrived, and I couldn't say the words while she was there. Then everything kind of fell apart. I'm sorry about that. I apologize for the drama. The new companion is arriving this afternoon to meet you. I'll leave in the morning when she shows up to stay."

"No. I don't want her."

"Merrick, you aren't a two-year-old. You don't get to stomp your feet or . . ." I touched his cane. "Or bang your cane against the tiles. Get to know her. Give her a chance." I smiled. "I'm not that special. This new woman will have skills that I don't. She'll have aspects of personality that I don't, that you'll appreciate."

"No." He held up his hand. "Go if you must. But only for a week or two. See if going home to Cub Creek is really what you want."

"Merrick . . ."

"Go home. I'll accept this new person on a temporary basis. I'm going to be busy anyway. I have a book to finish writing. And when I'm done, you'll come back."

"Merrick."

He'd gone from flushed to pale. Despite the heat.

"Tell me one thing, Merrick."

"What?"

"Danielle."

"Who?"

"Danielle and Mike. Does she die?" I hated that my voice broke on that last word.

He stared. He frowned. He grimaced. "The story?"

"Does she?"

He frowned again, but this time he also added a soft, kind smile. "No, Lilliane. She does not. Mike and Danielle have a happy ending."

I nodded several times in relief. "One more thing . . . about the grapes? You have to change that. As it is, I'll never be able to eat grapes again. You can't do that to other readers."

His expression had gone blank. He asked, "Grapes?"

"The grapes." I touched my throat. "When Mike grabs Jeff out at The Point?"

"Ah. Grapes." He nodded. "Whatever you want."

My eyes stung.

He said, "Thank you, Lilliane."

Shaking off the tears, I said, "Thank *you*, Merrick. This whole thing—all of it—has been an amazing experience I'll

GRACE GREENE

never forget." I stood. I motioned for the young man to come forward and take Merrick's arm.

Together, we helped him rise. But then Davis stepped in and took the young man's place. We walked on each side of Merrick, to steady him in the sand. When we reached the truck, Davis lifted him up into the front passenger seat and fastened the seat belt.

Merrick looked pale and exhausted.

Davis offered me a hand up into the back seat.

"Thanks, but y'all take him back and get him a snack and a drink. After last night . . . I don't want to go down that road again. The cookies are in the upper cupboard next to the stove. He gets two. I'll walk back. Alone."

Chapter Twenty-Two

Much of what he'd said about stories was true. Not generally a literal retelling, but stories were more a mishmash of personal experience blended with the stories of others, living or historical, pushed and shaped into controlled, coherent sharing. Oral storytelling. Written storytelling. Pretty much the same, as far as I could see.

But I'd spoken to Merrick as a friend. I hadn't expected him to use elements of my life. Was it more than hurt feelings on my part? If he'd asked first, cleared it with me, would I have said it was okay?

I'd never had a job where I'd grown so entwined in the lives of my client or employer plus the lives of the people around him or her.

It felt wrong.

Wrong in a dangerous way. Like volunteering for hurt. Risky.

I'd been here for almost three weeks. My brain said it was time to return to Cub Creek. My heart said I was already on the way.

My eyes stung again. My chest felt tight.

I dipped my toes in the water, fixed my eyes on the horizon, and breathed in the ocean air like a goodbye kiss.

CR&O

I didn't feel like talking. I pulled into myself, hiding inside. I remembered my father—those times when he'd go quiet, sometimes sitting in the corner and doing nothing and Momma would bring me into the kitchen and say, "Leave him be for a while, Lil, honey. Daddy's in a quiet mood today. Go play outside until lunch." On those days, Dad didn't go to work or even come to the table to eat, but the quiet times always passed, and when they did, it seemed like he'd used them to store up all his energy and it would come bursting out. He'd get back to work in the shed, or fix equipment for pay, or take odd jobs. Sometimes he'd come home with bruises on his knuckles. Once with a black eye. But at home, he would be sweet, funny, and cheerful. So I learned to respect the quiet times. We all had stuff only we could deal with, and we had to process it as best we could.

I felt like that now. I wanted to sit in a chair in a dim corner, a corner where no one would bother me and I didn't have to think. To face the wall and go away. But I also had my momma in me. If Dad had dark threads through his personality that tied him to the earth and emotions, then Momma was light and hope and taking things on.

So when the doorbell rang and I opened the door to the new aide, I tried to be welcoming but professional. The woman was older than me, but not by much. She was wearing a white uniform and was totally done up like a nurse down to the white, rubber-soled shoes. I glanced toward the study, then reminded myself that this was Merrick and Susan's problem. Not mine.

"Judithe Smith?"

"Yes, I'm here to meet Mr. Dahl."

"Certainly. Come in."

She said, "My given name has an *e* on the end. Pronounced Ju-dith-a."

"Happy to meet you, Judith-a."

Under other circumstances I might have made a joke about having name pronunciation issues in common, but not today, and she moved past me into the foyer, not interested in small talk.

She moved strongly. Odd to think of it that way. She was sturdy looking. Deliberate. I was immediately convinced that she was dependable, but I knew she'd step on that carpet in the study and never notice how heavenly it was. Or catch the way the light filtered in through the sheers and touched Merrick's shoulder.

Like my dad's.

Almost a halo effect.

My heart hurt. *Time to go home.*

I introduced them and told her she could see herself out when she was ready to leave and that I'd be here tomorrow morning when she arrived to officially begin the job. Then I left the room to allow them to talk. I paused in the kitchen to breathe.

Ms. B walked in. She spoke, sounding combative. "Was that her at the door?"

"The new me? Her name is Judithe. With an *e* on the end pronounced like a third syllable."

"Don't matter. I'll call her Judy."

I smiled at my reflection in the fridge door. *Good luck, Judy–Judithe.*

"I'm leaving in the morning, so I won't be here on Tuesday. I'll say goodbye now."

"No need. Mr. Merrick said you're coming back in a couple of weeks."

"What? When did he say that?"

"Little while ago, whilst you were mooning around in misery."

She'd noticed?

I said, "This isn't easy for me, you know."

"I guess. But then why are you doing this thing? Leaving? Making some kind of point, I guess." She was walking away toward the counter, and that last bit was said in a muttering sort of fashion.

I didn't know if I was expected to respond or not. I simply said, "It's been a pleasure knowing you, Ms. Bertie. I appreciate all that you do, have done, for Merrick—and for me too while I was here. Thank you."

She grunted, shaking her head and keeping her back to me. I let her be and turned to leave the room.

She said, "Mr. Dahl asked me to stay a little later today to serve his supper. He asked me to tell you that he'd appreciate you sharing the meal with him."

"I don't know. I—"

"Got all that big packing to do?" She turned toward me, holding a long spoon and shaking it at me. "You can spare time for a meal."

I raised my eyebrows in mock shock. "Glad that's not a knife."

"Ha, ha, ha. Ain't you a funny one? Just be there, that's all." She added, "Awkward or no. You're an adult. You can handle it."

"Yes, ma'am." As I was leaving the kitchen, I paused and turned back. "Please understand, Ms. B, that this isn't just a fit of pique. There are other issues. Other responsibilities I have back home. I forgot them for a while, but it's time to face them. To go back to my real life."

"That's all well and fine. If you must, you must. So long as you're here for dinner this evening."

⋘⋙

As instructed by Ms. B, I walked into the study just before suppertime. No one was there. I looked in Merrick's bedroom and found no one. Stepping back into the foyer, I listened. Not a creak to be heard.

Maybe Ms. B was in the kitchen?

No, the kitchen was empty too.

I heard a small noise outside and went to the pool door.

Napkins sailed by. A sudden gust of wind had kicked up out of nowhere. The tablecloth thrashed, fighting to escape the hands that fought just as hard to hold it in place.

I dashed out to help Ms. B and Merrick before they, and the tablecloth, ended up in the pool. It was already too late for the napkins.

We laughed at the craziness, and most of our awkwardness blew away with the ocean breeze. Even when Davis came around the side of the house and joined us for the meal, we kept it light. No one brought up anything except fun stuff. Davis had little to say, and I figured that was just as well.

Ms. B excused herself, saying, "Be right back." Without her, with only the three of us together, a silence threatened to derail our dinner party. I saw relief in Merrick's eyes when Ms. B rejoined us. I turned as she approached the table and saw Merrick's gift—the secret present I'd picked up for Susan in Beaufort. Reflexively, I half rose to intercept her, thinking she'd become confused, but she kept walking toward me, her arms extended.

I didn't understand.

Merrick said, "It's yours."

"But that's . . ."

"It was a polite fiction. This is for you."

"Why? I don't understand."

He grumbled as he stood. "It's a thank-you gift. Intended to be given to you at the end of two weeks. Lucky for us, we kept you a week more."

Stunned, I wanted to force them to take it back.

Ms. B said, "Unwrap it. Be polite."

Yes, it was that simple. Courtesy.

"Thank you." I removed the paper and found a companion to the painting in Merrick's bedroom—the one of the barefoot woman running on the sand. Not the same, but clearly intended to go together. This woman, this figure, looked like she might be dancing. I'd have to take a closer look at Merrick's painting. Maybe his was a dancing woman too, and in the flurry of action and color, I'd mistaken dancing for running.

And then I remembered I was leaving in the morning. Could I possibly have forgotten that? Even for a moment?

Meanwhile, Merrick was speaking. He said, "I have a similar painting. The gallery in Beaufort was able to locate this one for you. The series was painted by an artist here in Emerald Isle. Anna Barbour."

I couldn't help saying, "But Susan said it was a gift for you."

He shook his head slowly. "No, ma'am. *The Barefoot Girl* was always meant for you."

"For me." I didn't bother making it sound like a question. It wasn't. It was a confirmation. I looked at Merrick. As if in unspoken agreement, we both squared our jaws and refused to cry.

Ms. B had already stayed past her time. I viewed that as a gift too. I said to her, "Let me help collect these dishes. I'll wash them up this evening."

She made a dismissive noise. "No, I got this."

I started to insist, but Davis asked me to take a short walk with him.

"To the ocean, if you will. But at least as far as the gazebo."

Ms. B said, "Good. Go." She took the painting back, holding it ever so carefully in her hands. "I'll carry this inside where it's safe."

"Lilliane?" Davis offered his hand.

"All right." I owed him a courteous, dignified goodbye too.

We walked quietly side by side until we reached the gazebo. We sat on the benches and surveyed the beach, the waves rushing, children chasing, and seagulls trolling for scraps. Just the beach in July. For some reason, I thought of the Fuel Up Fast.

Just life, either way, thank you very much.

I didn't wait for Davis to speak. "Remember what you said soon after we met? Discussing friendship between you and Merrick? That it was a convenient relationship? That he found your presence convenient but that if you stopped showing up, he wouldn't miss you for long?"

Davis frowned. "Yes, I said something like that, but I thought I sounded clever. Perhaps not. But it's true. It's also true that it doesn't apply to you."

"Doesn't it?" I touched his arm. "I never meant to stay. And I was never *meant* to stay. This was a two-week job that stretched beyond that. It's over now."

"You have free will, don't you? You know he wants you to stay indefinitely. Why not change the 'never meant' to 'I'll stay as long as I want to'?"

"Because I have a life and obligations elsewhere."

"Are you worried about what's happening back home? Maybe with your house or about someone special?"

"No, not necessarily. Maybe."

"What about being too emotionally involved with Merrick and the people here? Are you worried about that?"

I drew in a deep breath. "In part. I don't belong here. If I stay, then at some point my heart is going to be broken. The last time that happened was almost twenty years ago when my parents died. I'm not at all sure that I can survive another devastating event."

"But it might not happen. If you stay, you might find a lifetime of happiness. Of good things. Going back home doesn't guarantee anything."

"The homeplace calls to me, Davis."

"Is it the homeplace? Or the past?"

"Is there any difference? They are entwined." I took his hand and squeezed it. "My parents died just as I was becoming an adult. I thought I was doing fine. Now I look back and it's as if my vision has cleared. Time moved forward, but did I? Was my life there a true one? I need to go home and find out."

He squeezed my hand in return, gently. "I know you have friends at home, but remember you have friends here too, and no one is required to live in only one place, to call only one place home. Remember that. And when you do, remember us." In a softer voice, he added, "Remember me."

"I will." I released his hand.

"By the way, in the interest of full disclosure and because Merrick might put his foot in his mouth, know that he tasked me with convincing you to stay. I'm here talking to you, but not because of anything to do with Merrick. This is me and you. Maybe friends, if that's what you want. Maybe more, if you decide to give us a chance." He stood. "May I escort you back?"

I slipped my arm through his. "Thank you."

"You might also remember that you promised we'd talk?"

"We just did, right?"

Somehow, we'd moved closer. Both of his arms reached around me, one against my back and the other in my hair.

His face, his lips came close to mine, and his breath was warm as he whispered in my ear, "What you said on the beach? You still owe me that talk. Time and promises don't end with today." He brushed my lips with his. "And until you tell me otherwise, I'm still hoping to collect."

ᘒᕽᘖ

I took one last walk along the crossover to watch the last night end—and again in the morning to watch the sun rise. I took a few last photos with Gwen's camera. I wasn't sad or happy. *Bittersweet* was as close as I could come to putting a name to what was in my head and heart.

I'd placed Merrick's breakfast on his desk early so it would be there when he arose. Then I went to load my stuff in my car. No rush. For one thing, I had to wait for Judithe to arrive. She was expected at ten a.m. sharp. Hopefully, she'd be punctual, because I didn't know how long I could sustain this appearance of calm without . . . without something breaking inside me.

Chapter Twenty-Three

On Saturday morning, the doorbell rang precisely at ten. I had an odd feeling that Judithe may have stood there waiting for the hour hand on her watch to reach the ten and go *click* before she pressed the doorbell. I greeted her politely and mustered all the dignity within me to escort her to the study and say goodbye to Merrick.

I'd survived. So had he. With consummate dignity on both our parts.

Feeling numb, I went to the garage, climbed into my car, and backed out. An ordinary activity I'd performed countless times since I'd first sat behind a steering wheel and heard Momma say, "Look both ways before you pull out, Lillie." Yet the action felt . . . life-changing. Extraordinary. I drove across the street and parked in front of Miranda's house. For both the first and last time, I knocked on her door. Her granddaughter answered my knock and invited me in. Miranda was in the sunroom with her feet up. She saw me coming and said, "Too swollen today. No beach for me."

"I came to say goodbye."

"Going back to Cub Creek after all?"

"I am."

She asked with a slight smile, "Missing those trees and hills and hollows?"

I shrugged. "Yes. And missing some people. Some old habits."

"Too easy, right?"

"I don't understand. Do you mean going home is too easy?"

"Nah," she said. "Staying. *Here*. Easy living, right? You

don't trust it."

Speechless, I had to think about what she'd just said. I sat on a nearby chair. Finally, I said, "Maybe so. Too easy. I fell into it too easily. It fit too well. But I don't really belong here. It won't last. Nothing good ever does."

"Ending it before it's done is just cheating yourself of the good that comes between the rest."

I sighed. "Well, Miranda, you've given me something to think about." We sat in silence for a moment before I stood. "It's time I got on the road. It's a long trip back."

"It's *always* a long trip back. Most folks never manage to arrive back quite where they started. That's usually called *personal growth*."

"Oh, stop. You are certainly philosophical this morning. Waxing poetic too."

She grinned. "In the end, my dear girl, you must do what's best for you. Not best for your friends. Or your acquaintances. Or even your parents . . . or your memory of them. This is your turn. Your go-round. Do your thing. Whether it's in Cub Creek, Emerald Isle, Timbuktu, or someplace else—*do you.* Otherwise, all the hopes and dreams and heartaches were just a waste and a cheat." She leaned forward as much as she could with her feet still up and reached toward me. "Give this old woman a hug, and then go find your life."

We hugged, and she added, "Remember, you'll always have friends here and a place to be. Remember us. I promise *we'll* remember *you*."

CRBO

The landscape reversed itself for my trip home. Too soon, the crystal-clear light of the beach was behind me and I was in that no-man's-land of interstate, exit-ramp gas stations, and fast-food restaurants. It all zipped by, looking pretty much the same regardless of the mile marker. It wasn't until I was nearing home—had finished with Interstate 95 and merged onto Interstate 64 and left Short Pump behind—that the trees returned in force.

Instead of blue, the air that filled the open spaces here was tinted green. It was gentler. Easier on the eyes. And the hills and forests offered places of privacy, and even of vanishing. I'd loved the beach, but the feeling was undeniable—this was home.

It seemed to me that while my life had not been perfect, and in many ways and by many people might even be considered a failure, I had been the recipient of many kindnesses. I was blessed. And I was also blessed to have choices. Having choices was delightful; it was also a curse.

I tried to put those choices out of my mind during the drive home. I wanted to go home, be there in person to see if my memories were true and compared well with those in my head. To decide whether my future lay in the forests and winding roads of my hometown or in the sun and sand of the place I'd just left.

Or, as Miranda had said, *someplace else*.

ॐ

My first stop was at the grocery store for the usual things. The cashier, a sweet gal named Stephanie, greeted me. "How was it?" she asked.

"Wonderful."

"I'm so jealous. I need a vacation so bad."

"I understand that," I said, nodding in agreement.

From there, I went by Joe's garage.

He asked, "Did you have a great time?"

"Oh, sure. It was wonderful. Thanks for helping with the car. I brought you something." From the tote bag on the front seat, I pulled out a box of saltwater taffy. "For your sweet tooth."

"You know me too well," he said with a grin.

"I do indeed. And I'd like to ask your help with getting some AC units installed."

"No problem. Happy to help."

"Thanks. I'll call."

"Sure thing, Lilliane."

These were my people. This felt right.

I turned off the main road at our rack of mailboxes and navigated the dips and turns of the dirt road. I stopped at Patsey's house to collect my plant.

"You're back!" she said. "When you called to say you were staying longer, I certainly didn't expect to see you this soon. Welcome home. How was it?"

"Had a great time." I accepted the plant back from her. "Thanks for taking care of my dieffenbachia. It looks better than when I left it here."

She waved her thumb at me. "Pure green. Through and through. Got it from my granddaddy."

Next stop would be up the rutted dirt road and around the corner. *My lifelong corner of the world.* The forest that had crowded close alongside the narrow road would draw back and open up to a wide clearing, and I'd be home. Mine was the last house at the end of the road—two stories of white clapboard, a century and a half old, slowly losing its battle with time, but still defying gravity.

The blue tarp was secured to the roof. Everything looked just as I'd left it. The house was old and tired. Leaves and a couple of small branches littered the wide front porch. That porch had needed scraping and painting for the twenty years I'd been in charge of things. It had been that long since Momma and I'd sat in the rockers out here while she told me her stories, yet the porch seemed especially empty now. More so than ever. And from out here, the curtained windows looked vaguely like eyes observing my return. But those eyes existed only in my imagination, conjured up by a lifetime association with a house that had been inhabited for generations of my family, including my parents and grandparents, and people before them whose blood ran with mine but whom I'd never known. Once I was inside, the house would feel right again. Familiar and homey. My sense of disorientation would vanish.

My heart ached. Home might be welcoming, but home could also be a place of hurts.

I gathered my bags and set them on the porch while I unlocked the door. No AC, I reminded myself, so I drew in a deep breath and held it before I opened the door wide and was hit with the hot, stale air.

Thank goodness for Joe. He'd help me pick up and install those AC units. The sooner, the better. I'd splurge for upstairs and down. One each would make a difference.

I could almost feel the house thank me as I went from window to window, opening them—except for the ones that were warped or painted shut. I left the front and back doors open to help the breeze blow through and air things out.

Across the yard, the shed waited with the forest thick behind it and forming a horseshoe around the open space between the house. The house had been my mother's domain. The shed had been my father's favorite place. His refuge? Maybe. At times he'd work in there with the door open wide and the sun streaming in. Other times, the door would be closed against cold, or against interruption. Sometimes Dad wanted to be alone. For long periods of time. But he always had something he'd either fixed or created to show for his isolation when he emerged.

I touched the key pendant hanging on its chain around my neck. The memory of my father's hands ceaselessly working the wire around it, capturing the amethyst stone within the heart of it, of the twisting and wrapping and turning and twisting as he created the small sheath to hold the key. I remembered the day he'd hung the chain around Momma's neck, saying, "So you'll always be able to be with me, whenever you want to. I'll never lock you out."

That's how I'd known. Twenty years ago. The truth of

accidental versus on purpose. I knew, not because she'd dropped the book. Not even because of the blanket—that could've been coincidental. I knew she'd made the choice because she'd removed the necklace and pendant and had placed it neatly atop the book for me to find, before she . . .

Before she went with Dad. On their journey together.

Off the confines of an earthbound map.

CHAPTER TWENTY-FOUR

Joe was a gem. He got those AC units over to my house in a hot minute. LOL—I laughed at my wit. And three units instead of two. He said one was for upstairs. One was for downstairs front. The other was for the kitchen. Said he'd talked the rep into selling three for the price of two. Joe always found the deals. Sometimes I suspected I might not approve of how he made those deals. But he was Joe, and most everyone liked having him around. He was that kind of guy.

I hired a roofer—Joe's second cousin once removed—to replace the damaged plywood and roof shingles. He knew a guy who'd hire out to wash the house exterior, and I agreed. The house needed painting too, but that would have to wait. My funds were limited.

On the upside, I seemed to have an endless supply of elbow grease. I put that to good use. Currently, I was deep into pulling the rugs outside to beat the dirt out of them and cleaning the wooden floors. Next up was to wash the windows and ditch the old curtains. Less than a week home, and each night I collapsed into bed almost too exhausted to brush my teeth first. A quick stand under the shower was about the most I could manage. When Hal called and asked if I'd be interested in picking up a few hours of work at the Fuel Up Fast, I said not yet.

The day Gwen came over with her laptop, I was in the middle of washing walls in the living room and kitchen, while the roof guy was busy working up top.

"What's up, Lillie?" She looked around from her vantage point in the living room. "Such beautiful floors.

Your grandparents lived here, right? Your mother's parents?"

"Yes. I remember them, but barely."

She walked over to the kitchen to peek in. "Looking good, but this is a lot of work. You've only just returned home. You should take your time, maybe rest a little."

"No, I can't. I have to get it done now. Quickly. While I can see what needs doing. Before the old and dingy looks normal to me again."

"I know I've never been in here before, but I'm certain you never kept a dirty house. It's just old. Costs to fix it up. No shame in that. Just reality."

"I can do what I can do. I can't make it new or perfect, but I *can* make it better. That's what I'm doing now, before I fall back into what *used to be*. Into forgetting what it should be . . . or *could be*."

We shared a long moment of silence before Gwen said, "I understand. I truly do." She looked down at the computer she was holding in her arms. "Do you want to download the photos now or wait for a time when you're less engaged?" She grinned. "I confess I'm eager to see them. If they're private, though, it's okay to say. I won't nose in."

She stopped as she passed the fireplace. The painting of *The Barefoot Girl* was sitting on the dark wooden mantel, propped against the gray-and-brown stones of the chimney. I was going to hang it as soon as I decided where it belonged. Considering the walls were mostly empty of decoration, and had been for as long as I could remember, it was almost too big a choice.

"Beautiful. Did you get that as a keepsake of your visit?"

"A gift."

She smiled. "The best kind of keepsake."

"Let's go in the kitchen. I could use a break anyway, and a tall glass of iced tea. You too?"

"That would be lovely." As she opened the lid and

turned the machine on, she added, "You haven't shared much about your trip. I'd love to hear about it—whatever you don't mind telling."

I handed her the camera, and she removed the memory card.

"This should only take a moment," she said.

Before I'd finished pouring our drinks, Gwen was already exclaiming over the photos.

"These are good!" She laughed. "Oh, oops." She said, "Those are your toes. They look fuzzy!"

"What?"

"Come see."

I set the glasses on the table and looked over her shoulder.

"Fuzzy because I blurred the photo. Took it unintentionally."

"Oh, look at the ocean! A sunrise, and you've got sunsets too. Is this Merrick Dahl? Who's this man? He's very good-looking."

"Hold up," I laughed. "Let's start again."

Maybe part of my cleaning mania had been to forestall homesickness. Subconsciously, at least. I hadn't admitted it to myself until just now seeing the photos and laughing with Gwen.

"The younger man is Davis McMahon. He's a writer too, and a friend of Merrick's."

"In this photo Mr. Dahl is smiling." She glanced at me. "He looks very cranky until he smiles, doesn't he?"

"He's pretty much cranky all the time. Occasionally, his mood improves." I shook my head. "He's not a warm, cozy kind of guy. He walks a different path."

"Hmm. Probably true for all of us. He doesn't try to fit in. Might be age as much as anything else." She said, "What happened?"

I frowned. "Nothing. The days were ordinary. Relaxed, really. Good food, beautiful house, sand and sea with gorgeous views—as you've seen."

"I mean, what happened?"

"Explain."

"That you left as you did. I know that Susan was hoping you'd stay indefinitely. Per her, Mr. Dahl had only good things to say about you. In fact, he'd told her to convince you to stay regardless of cost. But you left, and rather abruptly."

"I was homesick."

"Nope." She shook her head. "I don't believe you. What happened?"

"Why do you care? Frankly, it isn't any of your business."

"Harsh. But actually, it *is* my business. I'm the one who involved you. If there was a bigger problem, if something happened, then I want to know."

"Seriously, Gwen. It wasn't anything terrible. Not really. Some of the things I'd told Merrick as a—as a friend—he put into a book he's writing. A book he lied about, then asked me to lie about his lie."

"A lot of lies."

"Indeed."

"Sounds like fiction. Then again, if he identified you or used your confidences verbatim . . ."

"He didn't. Still, I don't approve of what he did. It wasn't right. It was hurtful. He'd passed out. I found him on the floor. No idea how long he'd been there, or how long he might have stayed there if I'd been out or already in bed . . ." I shivered. "Then, after all the upset and the doctor and EMS and all that, I discovered he was the one writing the book, had been lying about it, and that he'd put some of my memories in it—yes, I was angry. It was a horrible way to discover the truth. I decided to leave."

"Lillie . . . think about it. You, yourself, use anecdotes and events from the lives of others when you tell stories. You are careful not to identify them or align them with specific people, but still . . ."

"Yes, and after I'd calmed down, I probably would've decided to stay, except . . ."

"Except?"

"To be that upset, to relive Merrick collapsing and all that—I just couldn't do it. Couldn't risk it happening again. I realized I was too involved with them. Too . . . friendly. With all of them. It was time to go home."

Gwen fell silent. She looked sad. She pointed at the computer screen, waved her hand at it. "These people became your friends."

"Yes, but I was there for a job. I forgot that somehow. It was time for me to leave."

She looked away from me but not before I saw the dismay on her face. "I'll get the photos printed out for you."

"Thank you. Let me know the cost."

She stood. Her whole demeanor had changed. The air around us felt heavier. She said, "I'm disappointed."

"Things don't always work out." I shrugged. "It was a good opportunity and a fun experience until . . . But things like that don't last."

"No, I mean I'm disappointed in *you*." She closed the lid and reached across to unplug the power cord. "Not that you are so very concerned about my opinion, and you owe me nothing, but I thought you had greatness in you." She wrapped the cord so it didn't dangle and then picked up the computer.

Stunned, I echoed, "Greatness. Greatness? *What* are you talking about?"

She stood there holding her laptop in her arms and staring at me as if . . . as if maybe deciding whether I was worth continuing the discussion.

How dare she? I felt my cheeks growing warm.

Gwen said, "I've heard that in the DNA world there is a gene they call the explorer gene. It sets some people apart from the usual run in that they are the ones who follow a path to see where it leads. Who look to see what's around the corner. Just because. That when driving home, instead of taking the usual turnoff, they keep going to see what lies over the next hill. I believe the early pioneers, the explorers, the early navigators had that gene. Instead of staying put and just doing the best they could, they followed their curiosity."

"Me? Why on earth would you think that was me?"

"It is you, freed of the past and becoming your own person." She sighed. "You came close." She shook her head. "I thought you just needed a boost. A helping hand to get started. I remember that day your father came to repair my furnace."

"You mentioned that the day we met. That you'd met my father way back when. What has that got to do with anything?"

"I was new to town. He asked where I came from and mentioned you loved poring over maps and were always asking questions." She stared into the distance with a small smile on her face. "I'll never forget how proud he was of you. He said—" She broke off.

"What?" I bit back the hysteria in my rising voice. "What are you talking about? What did he say?"

"He knew I was a nurse. I guess that prompted him to open up some. Or maybe it was just his mood that day. People can be unpredictable that way. But he said that he knew you'd go far—that the things that held him back wouldn't do the same to you. That you were fearless."

I was speechless. I was suffocating. Not like when I was under the water, but painfully. My chest hurt as if it were cracking in the middle and about to cave in. I reached up and, of course, found the pendant.

Gwen whispered, "I never said it before. I didn't tell you because I saw how you were stuck. I didn't want to make your situation more difficult, but when I saw the chance to help, that's what I did. Just that." She shook her head. "I shouldn't have meddled. I apologize for that."

Before she reached the door, she added, "You can be

angry with me for expressing my thoughts so freely. You can choose *not* to be my friend, but I am yours. I have the caring gene, if there is such a thing, and I couldn't live with myself if I didn't try to open your eyes."

She left.

I stood in the middle of the living room. So many rude words swirled around in my head. I wanted to shriek them at her. To indignantly throw her out of the house and slam the door shut behind her. But she was already gone. I heard her car start and drive away.

Greatness. That's what she'd said. *An explorer gene? Nonsense.*

My father had bragged about me being fearless? About me wanting to see the world? *Not a chance.*

Didn't Gwen know who she was speaking to? The woman who'd never left home. Who was content—or at least *willing*—to live as she'd lived for twenty years, with perhaps an occasional odd venture into the world.

I began to shake. To stop it, I hit the wall with my fist. Didn't even ding the wall, but it surely did hurt like heck. I cradled my hand, rocking my body back and forth, needing to cry and unable to.

There was a knock on the frame of the screened door. I looked over expecting to see that Gwen had returned—hopefully, wanting to apologize or to explain better—but it was the roofer.

"Ms. Lilliane? I'm all done. Roof's sound and tight now. The rest of the roof is going to need attention soon. The shingles are old, but you should be good for a while—unless another branch drops on you. I gotta say, these trees out here must be ancient. They're huge. Risky, though."

"Risky?" My voice shook a little—I was still shaken—but he seemed not to notice.

"Risky, ma'am. Yes indeed. Big branches. Tons of leaves. But beautiful. Course, anything worth having and enjoying is, right? Risky." He nodded. "Life is risky. So are trees. But we wouldn't want to do without them."

He was stumbling along, perhaps waiting for me to respond.

"Yes, of course. It's all risky. Let me get your money."

"Yes, ma'am. I'll finish cleaning up and be on my way."

The rest of the day was a haze. I sat out back as the sun set. There was a low knoll of sorts in the middle of the backyard clearing. When I was a child, I'd sit out here with my parents with our lawn chairs pulled up around a rough firepit. Some evenings, just before dark, the sky would flame up pure red, backlighting the trees and turning them shadow-black.

On this evening, with the birds calling and occasional squirrel scampering in the trees or across the yard, I felt home but more alone than I ever had.

My sleep was fitful that night. I tossed and turned, rose before dawn, and started washing the kitchen floor. As soon as the sun came up, I was out at the hardware store getting wood floor cleaner and wax. Patsey had an old electric floor buffer she was willing to loan me, though she'd looked at me a little sideways when I'd asked about it. I'd forgotten to eat. It was as if everything depended on that floor being not only clean, but shiny too.

I knew I couldn't sustain this. Gwen's words aside, whatever it was that I was trying to wash away or avoid, I had to figure it out and give it up. On the upside, the floor was looking super. Nicer than it had ever looked, as far as I could recall, so there was that.

Seven days after leaving Emerald Isle, the flowers arrived. I set the vase on the coffee table.

The card was signed by Merrick in such perfect penmanship, I stared at it in wonder. Only his name. *His autograph*. No message.

The flowers, along with the painting, added bright, colorful touches to my otherwise drab living room.

What was his intent? Was it "I miss you," or "I'm

sorry," or "Please come back"? No clue.

I was working on the floors and walls upstairs now. I'd thrown out a fair amount of junk. Only real junk. Nothing that could be of value, either through age or sentimentality. The house felt lighter. I'd been very careful with my monies, but the second check had arrived from Susan with a very generous bonus. I could move forward with fixing the furnace. Best and most amazing of all was a picture of Susan's grand twins with their newborn baby sister.

Life *will*. It finds a way to work things out. I cautioned myself to remember that it may work out, and probably all the better, if we don't get in the way.

I'd tidied the yard too. These were productive days. Making up for all the neglected days that had rolled into years and decades.

A week after the flowers arrived, a car drove up. I recognized the shiny car as the one I'd seen in Merrick's garage. It pulled into the large dirt area I called the driveway and came to a stop near a massive oak.

The windshield was tinted, so I couldn't see who was inside. Whoever was in the car sat there for a long minute before the driver's side door swung open and a man climbed out.

Davis.

CHAPTER TWENTY-FIVE

Of course it was Davis.

Hadn't I expected him?

It had taken him a while this time, hadn't it? But then, the distance between us had been somewhat greater than a sandy beach path.

He couldn't see me through the house window and couldn't know that I was watching him. But given how intuitive he was, I suspected he could feel that prickling along the back of his neck.

As Davis walked around the car, I understood that he was playing chauffeur for Merrick.

Spell broken, I dashed to the bathroom to check my face and hair. Thankfully, I hadn't been doing any dirty, sweaty work today, but neither was I dressed for company. Shorts and a sleeveless cotton shirt. Could be worse. Regardless, they'd have to take me as they found me. Their fault.

Boldly, I walked away from the bathroom mirror, down the hall, and to the front door. I swung the screened door open and stepped out onto the porch like I owned the place. LOL.

Davis smiled at me. Merrick was still standing by the car door with one hand on his cane and the other braced against the side of the car. He was frowning. Or squinting. I wasn't sure which.

"Merrick. Davis. Welcome." I looked at Merrick and the front steps, which, because of how the land sloped, had a fair number of steps. I doubted he could manage them. "If you'd like to come in . . ."

"We were hoping to speak with you," Davis said. "To

see . . . how you are doing."

Merrick broke in. "Nonsense," he said roughly. "We've come to bring you back with us. Kidnap you, if necessary."

I stood on the steps, amazed.

"Don't think I won't."

"Well, you'll probably have a better chance at accomplishing an abduction if you have a drink and a snack first."

He sighed. "Likely so. Lead the way."

"Why don't we go in the back door," I said as I walked down the steps. "It's a longer walk to go around the house, but not so many stairs."

Merrick grunted and nodded. He put his cane to work and walked past me as if he had a point to prove.

Davis stopped me, letting Merrick get a head start.

"I'm sorry for no notice. I dropped by his house this morning and found Merrick in the car trying to back out of the garage. Luckily, I arrived before he did any damage. I don't think he's driven in a long time. Said he was on his way to Cub Creek to pick you up."

"What about Judithe?"

"Gave notice." He shrugged. "Says she won't leave until her replacement is found. Hence the drive."

I shook my head. "It's a crazy-long drive for him to sit through, much less to think he can drive it himself. He can't hardly see over the steering wheel."

"Don't tell *him* that. It didn't go well for *me* when *I* tried. After attempting to argue reason, it seemed simpler to bring him."

Silly of me, maybe, but I was a little disappointed that Davis had only come along to keep Merrick from injuring himself or others. I shrugged, but only mentally. Just as well, really. I hadn't *wanted* him—rather, *them*—to come, had I? *Nope.*

Davis said, "Merrick and I have spent a *lot* of time together lately. I—"

I cut his words short, saying, "I'd better catch up with him." I took off and left Davis to follow.

The kitchen porch steps, only three of them, were immediately around the back corner of the house. But Merrick wasn't waiting there. He'd kept going and was standing about twenty feet from the shed, facing it. Dad's shed.

The corrugated metal of the shed's roof and walls had been an exercise over many years in cobbling together disparate parts—wood, metal, plastic—whatever was necessary to keep it intact. Dad had acquired new sheets for patching, and when he couldn't, he used whatever he *could* find. In recent years, when a patch was needed here or there, Joe had helped me find something that would work. The exterior of the building resembled a patchwork quilt of building materials in various shapes and sizes. The wonder of it was that while tree branches thick as trunks might drop from above, and thought nothing of damaging my house, none ever touched the shed. The winds that sometimes rolled up and over the ridge to rush across the yard occasionally grabbed at the metal sheets, but mostly didn't seem to have the power to do real damage.

"Merrick." I touched his arm to redirect him.

Where was Davis? He was wandering around the yard, staring into the woods and back up at the house. Both men were annoying me. Seemed like they were not only seeing the flaws and years of neglect but were actively looking for them.

"Merrick, the house is this way."

He resisted me. "Is that it?"

It? A shock drilled down through me. Was he here for me or for the shed?

It. The shed. Was it now an object of curiosity? My fault. I blamed myself for sharing something so private with him. How could he throw it back in my face this way? As if it were nothing more than an oddity? Anger rose up in me until my heartbeat was thrumming in my ears.

"The bomber. In there?" He looked at me with the eagerness of a child at the prospect of holding a puppy. "Is it still there?"

"It is."

"Might I see it?"

"The shed is locked." I crossed my arms. "I keep it that way."

He leaned on his cane as he examined my face. "Don't tell me it's been that way—locked—since . . ."

Davis joined us, asking, "Since what?"

I shook my head. The shake echoed down my body. I felt cornered. "No," I said.

Merrick grunted, but the noise was different than his usual. I wasn't quite familiar with it. He stepped away from me and the shed and moved several yards away to the metal chairs. They were old-fashioned and more than a little dirty. Sometimes in the late fall or winter, I'd lay a fire in the rock circle as we'd done in my childhood. A friend or neighbor might drop by. Even Joe on rare occasions. We'd share conversation and maybe something to sip on. But this was summer, so no fires. Still, it was a pleasant sitting spot in the afternoon in the shade, and because of the slight rise of land back here—a knoll of sorts—it always caught the best breezes.

Merrick lowered himself into the nearest chair, almost missing it. I moved quickly to guide him into the seat. He said, "Sorry. Stiff. Long car trip." He sat and rested his head against the hard, curved metal of the chair back.

"Stay here. I'll get you some water."

A sensation of altered reality hit me as I entered the kitchen. The same room, same appliances, Momma at the stove, Daddy in the living room paging through a repair manual or a parts supply catalog. The silence.

It suddenly hit me that I'd grown up in a house of silence. Momma or Daddy might be laughing or teasing, or

Momma might burst into a bit of song, or Daddy might tell a joke, but otherwise all was silent. No TV or radio. No other kids running and laughing. I hadn't really noticed the years of silence until this moment. It had seemed usual and ordinary. In fact, even though I had a small TV now, it was rarely on.

Maybe I was almost afraid to disturb that silence. The status quo. Might be a good thing that Merrick had settled himself out there by the fire circle.

I poured glasses of tea and added a few cookies on the tray and carried it all outside. Davis was up as soon as he saw me coming out the door and grabbed the tray from me, smiling and apologizing. But then he winked. I didn't know what the wink meant, so I pretended not to notice.

Merrick drank gratefully, downing major swallows, before gobbling a cookie. Unselfconsciously, he brushed the crumbs from his shirt. They fell onto his pants legs.

I sat in the chair next to him.

"Seriously, Merrick, what were you thinking? Did you give any consideration to how far the drive was?" I looked back and forth between them. "Did you drive straight through?"

Davis said, "Merrick slept most of the way. Should be well rested by now. Think I'll let him handle the trip home."

"Funny, not funny."

Merrick said, "In my day, I was a fine driver. That day may have come and gone. Funny how you think it's easy and you'll go out there and hop in the car and drive it like you used to—until you try." He lowered his voice. "You never think, *This will be the last time.* You know? Unless it's an occasion like a school graduation or a marriage or such. We mark our lives by occasions, but not by the everyday things, the ordinary joys and sorrows. The last time I'll kiss a girl for the first time. The last time I'll hop in my car and drive out to dinner. The last time I'll dance with my wife."

"Please, Merrick. You will make me cry." I kind of

already was.

He laughed. "There's a last time for everything. But if we're lucky, new joys and sorrows that we didn't know to anticipate come along." He touched my hand. "That was you, Lilliane. I appreciated the laughter and the stories and the rudeness you brought into my home."

"Rudeness?"

"You talk back."

"Well, if you don't want rude, then you should be more careful of what you say to people."

He grinned, then turned his attention to Davis. "What's wrong with you? You look foolish."

"Me? Nothing wrong here. I was watching those trees . . . how tall they are. Full of leaves. Makes patterns of sunlight across the yard. The breeze is nice."

I said, "Maybe we should pitch you two a tent out here for the night. I regret that I can't offer to put you up. I don't have guest rooms fitted out. I've going through and sorting things and doing some improvements, but . . ." I'd almost said that the past occupied those rooms now. I shivered.

Davis asked, "Are you okay?"

"I'm fine, but a poor hostess."

"You live here alone, is that right?"

"Yes." Alone with my memories. That about-to-cry feeling tried to return. I shook it off.

Davis said, "You need to get out more. This is a beautiful place, but it feels wrong to leave you here. Come with us. I have rooms reserved near Richmond for the night. We'll do the drive back tomorrow."

"I can't. Truly. I've done a lot of work around here, but there's much more to do." And sitting so near the shed, I was reminded clearly and with no room to argue—I could never leave here for more than a short trip or so.

"Can I see inside? I want to see the plane, and the workshop of a man who tried to build one."

I recoiled instinctively. If I'd had the power of speech in

that moment, I would likely have said words I would've regretted with all my heart, but my words wouldn't come. The question—his request—slammed around in my brain.

Hearing his question, the earnest request, Daddy would've shown him the shed. Once inside the building, and with genuine interest shown, Dad would've talked his ear off about the plane and most everything else inside. Dad would've had the radio playing in the background. The shed was almost never silent. The shed was where Dad had preferred to be. And Momma with him.

"Please."

"It's a mess. Very dusty. I only go in there every few years."

Davis said, "What's Merrick talking about? What is it he wants to see? He mentioned something about a plane in a shed on the way here. I thought he was hallucinating."

I sat back and crossed my arms. "Honestly, Merrick. You didn't come to see me at all, did you?"

"I came to see you *first*."

"I can almost believe you were charming once upon a time. Almost." I wanted to ask him, *Why?* What did it mean to him to see it? But I wouldn't. A response that he was merely curious—or just wanted to gawk at a long-gone man's dusty obsession—might break my heart.

"If this is for something you want to write, I'm not okay with that. This place and the memories that go with it are special to me."

"My writing days are finally done. No more books after this one. I'm too old to start anew."

Humph. "Well, maybe yes, maybe no. Never can tell when a muse—or inspiration—will appear."

"Do you think that's true?" In fact, he looked hopeful.

"Why not?"

He asked, "What if I promise to get your permission before sharing?"

I tried hard to give him a scathing look, and then I turned

it on Davis too. "This goes for both of you."

Davis said, "I have no idea what you two are talking about, but if a promise earns me the price of inclusion, then I absolutely do promise. Cross my heart."

Merrick asked, "Well, then?"

I touched my shirt and traced the shape of the pendant beneath it. I waited as if a message might come, but there was none. I hadn't really expected one, had I? No, but if you weren't willing to receive a message, you never could, right?

Grasping the chain, I lifted the key pendant from under my shirt.

By holding the key and the twisted wire sheath just so, a tiny push and jog to the left freed the key. A small, simple ordinary key that looked so different without the frills.

They were staring at me. I laid the key on my palm and showed it to them.

"My father made the decorative pendant to hold this key. For my mother. As a sweetheart token. He shaped the wire to represent a heart and two flowers, and when the key is in place, the chain joins with a clasp, creating a union. Like a handclasp. Hearts and flowers. Key to his heart. Symbology of the joining creating a circle? A romantic could go on and on. In practical terms, she could've sat with him in the shed any old time, as she often did, or she could've gone in there by herself whenever she wanted. But it was like giving his true love the key to something that he also loved.

"I may have mentioned, they were sweethearts from the first day they met in preschool. That never changed."

I cleared my throat and stood. "Warning. It's dusty in there. And whatever was sharp way back when is still there and sharp, so be careful what you touch."

It was just a mostly metal building, corroded and dinged over many decades. As I fitted the key into the lock, Davis knelt, brushing at something on the corner at ground level.

"Stone foundation?" he asked.

"Sure. The original small house was here in this spot on

the old foundation. My great-grandfather converted that into a shed for storing equipment and hay and such. My dad repaired and enlarged it and put it to use for his projects."

"Not just for reconstructing an airplane?" Davis joked.

"Oh, no."

My hand shook a little as I fitted the key into the lock, popped it, and removed it. I left the lock hanging in the hasp but stepped aside to return the key to safety before going any farther.

Davis, with his hands on the door, asked, "Mind if I slide it aside?"

I nodded. "Go for it."

The metal squealed on the overhead rollers, but not as much as one might expect. But the dark inside . . . it was thick and heavy with the smell of *old*. Of old dirt, old metal, old equipment oil. All the molecules trapped in the shed for the last many years emerged in an overwhelming way as smells, bringing many of my memories—good and bad—right along with them. The dust, too, but the dust held together longer on the surfaces, awaiting the least bit of breeze to begin scattering the particles, dancing and filling the air with them. Breathing really would be a problem then.

"Be careful, Merrick."

The top propeller reached into the lower rafters of the shed. It was the elephant in the room. The thing that no one could miss seeing. Tall and grand with the streaming sunshine penetrating, throwing glints off the metal like sparks amid the dust of ages now stirring.

Merrick stepped forward. I put my hand on him. "Wait," I said. "Take this cloth." It was the hand towel I'd brought out with our drinks. "Hold it over your nose and mouth. No need risking breathing in the dust and finding yourself with pneumonia."

He nodded and did as I'd asked. Then he walked forward into my father's world.

After a moment of hesitation, I followed him.

CHAPTER TWENTY-SIX

For eighteen years, my life had been one of love, of certainty that my parents adored me and I adored them, and that we three were all each other needed.

Admittedly, there were times during my teenage years when I questioned that, but those times were rare because I wouldn't have risked hurting my parents for the world.

The world. Our world.

When two-thirds of my world chose to depart without me, I was left with an old house and a shed—which I did everything in my power to protect because it was all I had left of my loved ones. By doing that, I could have nothing new because there was no room for it in my life, chained as I was to things of the past.

I stood back and allowed Merrick to enter ahead of me.

The shed was not a shed. It was a world of metal and tools and the things that made other things work, or sometimes caused them to break. The plane was the big, unmissable thing in the middle, but the cabinets that lined the walls were full of wonders, from vintage tools to rock collections and even drawers of arrowheads and prehistoric shark teeth. The walls above were a gallery of hanging things, from bike tire inner tubes, to used fan belts, to amazing works of art that my father crafted from the metals he found. Some of the metal sculptures were recognizable as representing a real creature or object. Others were abstract. Or maybe they were as they were supposed to be, needing no names to identify them.

"I asked my father once what that one was supposed to be." I pointed toward the back wall to a hanging hodgepodge of silver and darker metals, chain links, and rake tines. The piece itself was about five feet square, one of the largest of his artistic creations. "He said that was sometimes how it felt inside his head."

"When you first mentioned your father's hobby and the shed, it caught my imagination. It stuck in my brain," Merrick said.

"You could've asked me more questions about it."

He shook his head. "No. Maybe a part of me—the part that's been bored, rusting away for years—wanted to believe it was special. Unique. Not mundane enough to be an ordinary topic of conversation."

Davis said, "Lilliane. Your father was an artist. A sculptor."

"He repaired equipment. Could never keep a nine-to-five job. He was known around town as the guy who started a lot of projects but finished few. Momma loved him, though, and he loved her. They lived in the house, but this was the heart of *his* home." I shrugged. "He didn't share this with the world. He feared what the ones out there would say . . . that it would steal away the magic of it."

Davis was next to me, but Merrick was now moving slowly inside. The cloth still covered his nose. He seemed almost to be vanishing into that strange place of my father's past as he neared Momma's chair. That chair was still sitting inside and might well house a family of rodents by now. Davis, standing beside me and unaware of the internal earthquake tearing me apart, said, "This should be shared."

I looked at him with anger. "No. Dad was right. I won't open his . . . his secrets to the world. They will see him as odd, as they did before. I won't expose his memory to that."

"You can't think that he meant for you to spend your life here guarding this . . . like a caretaker." He put his hands on my arms. He tried to speak to my brain—the thinking part. "There must be options for honoring his memory and doing right by yourself, for your own life."

I shook his hands off, then held my own hands up to silence any further remarks, however well meaning. I drew in a deep breath to try to defuse the decades-old resentment trying to break through. Merrick was ignoring us, still entranced in the shed. With more calm, I called out a reminder to him, "Don't touch anything, please. That stuff is sharp. If anything falls on you, you'll be injured." I turned to Davis again. "Watch him. When you're done gawking, shut the door, please. I don't want anyone coming along unawares to see it. Close those doors securely and snap the lock tight. I'm going into the house to get cooking. I hope you don't mind breakfast for supper." I didn't wait for answers or suggestions, just left them there.

I pulled out dishes and pans, probably loudly, but nothing broke. I tossed the flatware and napkins on the table. I was scattered. My brain hurt.

I couldn't sustain the effort of normal things. I found the couch and sat with the week-old flowers on the coffee table in front of me. I hugged the sofa pillow and really just wanted to be alone. I wanted to be left alone almost as much as I was terrified of being left alone.

How much of what we did, our choices, our fears, were built on habit, on perceptions, long out of date and due for a reassessment? Joe had always complained that I fought to keep things as they were. Gwen said I was stuck in the past.

I was. I could admit it to myself, if not to them. But what was my alternative? To abandon the heart of my father's life? Where my mother made that last choice?

Was that nothing?

If it had only been memories, but nothing tangible, nothing so absolutely remarkable as the shed . . .

The back door slammed behind them. I wiped at my eyes and rose.

"I'm sorry. I didn't get started cooking. I got sidetracked."

"Good," Davis said, "because I'm in the mood to cook."

"No . . . no."

"Are you saying I can't cook? Because you really have nothing to base such negativity on."

"Can you cook? Seriously?"

"I can."

"We'll do it together," Merrick said, already pushing his sleeves up.

"*You* don't cook. I know that for sure."

"I used to. Maybe it's one of those things I haven't done for the last time after all."

Davis winked at me. "I'll keep an eye on him. Stay handy in case I need backup . . . or can't find something." Giving me a quick grin, he went into the kitchen, saying, "Merrick, how about . . ."

Before I could react, someone knocked on the door. *Now what?*

"Gwen."

She smiled through the screen door. "Is it a bad time? I saw a car. If you have visitors, I can come back later."

"What?" I opened the screened door. "I mean, are you okay?"

"No, I'm not. But I will be after you accept my apology."

In my head I was preparing to suggest that I walk outside with her to chat, but I probably looked blank because she prompted me, "Might I come in?"

Still wordless, I pushed the door open, and she stepped inside. Before either of us could speak, Davis yelled from the kitchen, "Where's your frying pan? Do you have a small one?"

Gwen's mouth opened, and her eyes widened. Her cheeks flushed a deep rose. "I'm so sorry. I—"

Clearly, she assumed he was my boyfriend. "No, it's not like you're thinking."

Davis interrupted, "What?" He leaned around the doorframe, saw Gwen with me, and stepped all the way out.

"Hello. Apologies for interrupting. I thought Lilliane was speaking to me."

Gwen fumbled her words, saying, "No, I'm the one who's interrupting, it seems. I'm so sorry."

A loud, grumpy, frustrated sound came from the kitchen. Davis frowned and ducked back in. We heard him say, "Merrick, not there. No, let me heat the pan first." In a softer voice, he said more, but I couldn't hear it clearly enough to understand.

Merrick appeared in the kitchen doorway. "Davis said you need me?"

At the sight of the old man—he'd ditched his jacket, his sleeves were rolled up his forearms, and he was leaning heavily on his cane—Gwen's rose-tinted flush spread swiftly from her cheeks to her throat and along her arms. No mistaking she was a booklover.

I touched her. "Are you okay?"

"I'm fine. Is this . . . are you Merrick Dahl?"

"Wait," I said. "Allow me, please." I pointed to Merrick. "Gwen, this is Merrick Dahl, for whom I recently worked." I pointed to Gwen. "Merrick, this is Gwen Foster, an old school friend of Susan's and to whom I owe more gratitude than I can express for having brought the two of us together."

Merrick's sharp look of suspicion morphed instantly into congeniality. I'd said it in jest earlier, but now I saw it was true. Despite ninety years of aging and a cranky personality, I could see that once he'd been very charming indeed. In fact, watching from the sidelines, it occurred to me that I'd been influenced by the ghost of that gruff charm when first we'd met.

Gwen said, "I'm so pleased to meet you."

He said, "I am greatly in your debt, Miss Foster." He all but bowed, as if ready to accept her hand if she offered it. Ridiculous.

"Seriously?" I asked.

"Are you a reader?" Merrick asked her.

"Oh, yes," Gwen gushed.

"We should discuss books."

I said, "Please excuse me. You two can chat. I'll be in the kitchen." I paused for a last remark. "Gwen, I insist you stay and join us for the meal."

CR80

Davis definitely knew his way around a kitchen, even a small one like mine. I tried to hide it, but I loved how working in the small kitchen with him was almost like doing a dance with close, complicated steps. My face felt flushed, and I pretended it was the warmth of the kitchen. Davis knew the truth. I saw it in his eyes when he asked for a ladle and I found the implement in the drawer and turned too quickly and there he was. Smiling. And when he took the ladle from me, he made sure to put his hand around mine first, moving slowly until we were both holding it.

Who knew cooking could be so interesting?

We added a fourth place setting in no time, and gathered around the kitchen table, accompanied by light and laughter and silliness. The scrambled eggs, bacon, and toast vanished in minutes, but no one seemed to notice the meal was over. Gwen seemed equally delighted to chat with Davis as with Merrick, and she cast discreet glances my way, as if somehow amazed. I shrugged. Actually, it was stranger than she knew. I couldn't remember the last time someone had shared a meal with me at this table since Joe and I divorced.

It was going to be very quiet here when they all left.

Then someone said something about metal art and a plane and a shed—and it wasn't me or Gwen or Davis. Merrick seemed not to realize what he'd done at first, but within moments he heard the silence and understood. He changed the subject quickly, but it was too late.

Gwen asked, "What metal art? I don't understand. It's in your shed?"

Suddenly, all three were staring at me.

I looked back at them steadily and said, "It's a secret."

"I don't understand," Gwen said.

"How could you understand? It was, as I just stated, a secret."

She cringed, and I felt it. Was she deserving of my anger? No.

I said, "My father worked with metal. He did repairs and such, but he also did . . . artwork. He was building things. He crafted all sorts of things."

"Your father created artwork?"

"Among other things." The unspoken tone in my voice said, *Drop it*.

She continued anyway. "He was a gentle man with complicated emotions. Your parents were a sweet couple." She seemed to be addressing Merrick and Davis now. "I was about thirty when I moved here. I met Lillie's mother when I stopped at the roadside stand and bought her jams. Delicious. I met her father when he did some work on my furnace."

I was holding my breath, willing her to stop. But she looked at me intently and took it yet one more step. "When they died . . . there was talk, of course."

To no one in particular, but to make the facts clear, I said, "They were overcome by carbon monoxide poisoning. Kerosene space heater." I ended the sentence emphatically, to quash any thought of further discussion.

But Gwen continued, "Of course. It was tragic, so it was natural for people to talk, to help them process it."

"Gossip," I countered.

She shot me a look that begged me to trust her, that she wasn't going into dangerous territory. She said, "In part, but the loss was shocking to many. I never heard any malicious gossip. Only grief and regret."

Desperately, I wanted to leave the table. I felt their curiosity in the averted eyes of Merrick, Davis, and in the pitying expression in Gwen's. I wanted to leave. Or better yet, for them to leave.

Gwen reached over and touched my hand. "Merrick and Davis never had the honor of meeting them, but your parents were a well-known part of the community. It was natural that their loss created a wound for many, so people talked. Your father was a man of many interests. Skilled with machinery, a collector of things, and a solitary man, but I never heard him called an artist, and I am amazed."

I liked how she'd described my father. Maybe it *was* okay. There was healing in her words and tone. "He never told anyone. You are right. He was a kind man. But with little expectation of kindness from others. He did what he did—whether fixing equipment or creating art, and anything in between. I mentioned it to Merrick one day, and suddenly, instead of a secret of one plus one, it's now a secret of four. I suppose it doesn't even qualify as a secret anymore."

"It slipped out by mistake because he was impressed too," Gwen said. "As for me, the only person at the table who could possibly mention this to anyone local—you can trust me, you know that." She added gently, "I'd love to see what he created. It's in the shed, you said?"

Davis shot me a look, and I nodded. He said, "You two go ahead. Merrick and I will handle the cleanup."

I started to say something sharply cynical but saw that Merrick was embarrassed at having spoken out of turn. I put my hand on his shoulder and gave it a soft pat. It was out of my hands. There was an inevitable feel to this. Fate was moving this along. Momma had said that when fate takes over, it's important to know when to pass the reins and ride along gracefully.

Merrick said, "My Marie and I shared dish duty every evening."

I squashed my harsh remarks and stood. "Okay, Gwen, come with me."

CRISO

It was still light outside and would be for another hour or two, but the sun was dipping below the tops of the trees, so the light inside the shed was very dim.

Gwen stood in the open doorway, much as Merrick and Davis had done a little while ago. A few minutes of respectful silence, perhaps? Maybe a bit of awe? The late-afternoon light was failing. Under the tree canopy it was that much dimmer. Too little light to do the art display justice. Impulsively, I did something I hadn't done in almost twenty years. I walked into the corner of the shed and found the light switch. Had the mice been at the line? Would it work?

It did. The bare overhead bulb lit the metallic surfaces, infusing the glossy surfaces with a glow and glinting brightly off the smaller, shinier knobs, bolts, and chains, and, as always, the propellers and fuselage overwhelmed it all.

Gwen's mouth was gaping. Her eyes were big as saucers. Suddenly, she jerked forward, saying, "What on earth?" But she stopped a couple of steps inside.

"Gwen?"

She swung back toward me. "So this is why you won't leave."

"It's my home, Gwen."

"No, you're the keeper of the memories. The creations." She touched my arm. "I thought it was memories and the loss, but it's literally . . ." She waved her hands at the interior. "It's all this."

She faced me full-on. "Lilliane, you can't live your life as a caretaker, for this or anything else." She put both her hands on my arms and shook me a little. "Your parents would never have wanted this for you. It's almost a perversion of love. Celebrate this. Do with it what your father couldn't do—or if he'd lived out his full years, what he might well have done himself."

"What are you suggesting? Pull them down? Break them

up?" My voice rose to a shrill level as the sentence ended.

"Give them the life they deserve. A display, maybe. In a gallery? Art collectors would buy them."

"Not for sale."

"Why, on God's green earth, not? Are they better here, dusty and unseen? Until one day the building falls apart or burns down or they are damaged by any number of things that befall the creations of humans? By leaving them here, locked away, to be destroyed by nature or found after your own death, you turn them into objects of curiosity. Celebrate them now. Don't hide them."

I pressed my hands to my head. My temples were thrumming in pace with my heartbeat. I shook my head. And yet, there was logic and merit in what she said.

Gwen said, "Don't do anything drastic, but don't procrastinate either. Unless I'm way off base, I think you've got something very special here, but you need an expert. This isn't yard sale material, and it's probably not appropriate for the usual kind of gallery either. We need someone who has more business expertise and knows the people with the info we need." That last syllable played out long and slow, and then, suddenly, Gwen said, "Let's talk to Susan and get her advice."

"Susan?"

"Sure. She'll be happy to help, and you can trust her. She knows all sorts of experts. You need someone knowledgeable who can advise you on how to proceed."

We heard noises behind us and turned to see Merrick and Davis crossing the yard, likely drawn by the bright interior. They stopped beside us. Davis put his arm around my shoulders but didn't speak. Merrick took another look. The light touching the varied surfaces—the mantles of dust, the shine of dancing reflections, the daggone propellers—it gave the whole world within the shed a surrealistic look. Or perhaps one borne of science fiction? It was a bit like being in the midst of a manic, suddenly frozen-in-time Salvador

Dali painting.

Merrick turned back toward me, saying, "Your dad went to a lot of effort to craft and create this . . . these works. Shame to leave 'em to rot." He spoke more loudly, and his rough voice was compelling. "Put the man's name on them. Name him big and bold and put it out there. Get him the credit he didn't get when he was living." He cleared his throat and spoke more softly. "That's what I'd do, anyway."

He said, "I've got to get back to my own work," but paused as he passed me, to add, "And you, Miss Lilliane Moore, need to figure it out so you can get on with your life, including coming back to work with me."

I stayed in place as Gwen walked with Merrick around to the front of the house.

Davis said, "I need to get him to the hotel. I think he's close to exhaustion."

"It's past his bedtime."

We shared a smile. Davis slipped his arms around me.

I said, "Thank you for bringing him."

"Thanks for not being angry. I could blame Merrick, but I wanted to be here."

"To see the shed?" I was joking.

"No. To see you." He brushed my face with his fingers. "I brought you a gift."

Gift? It didn't make much sense to me. Merrick was hardly a gift. But I was more interested in Davis's arms tightening around me than in questioning his meaning. Still, when his lips touched my cheek and then found my mouth, I pushed him away ever so slowly, ever so gently.

"I haven't committed to leaving here or going anywhere."

"No problem. I have GPS. I know the way now. If I'm ever invited . . ."

Gwen cleared her throat. "Kids, we can't get into the car without the key. I left him sitting on the front steps, but if you don't hurry, he's going to be asleep and you may have to carry him."

We did as instructed. Merrick was awake but sagging. Davis helped him into the car, and with a last embrace for me, he said, "I'll see you soon, either way."

As they drove away, Gwen and I waved them off.

Gwen said, "I'll be back early tomorrow with the computer. We'll use the camera to take photos of your dad's sculptures. Having pictures may help Susan figure out if she can help or refer us to someone." She put her hand on my arm. "Please don't be offended that I'm saying *we* and *us*. This is your business all the way. I just want to be helpful."

I nodded, still feeling odd about all this.

Gwen said, "You must talk to Susan. Get a feel for options and things to consider—if, that is, you choose to move forward with investigating the possibilities." She lowered her voice, as if someone might overhear. "Just imagine seeing one of your dad's metal sculptures hanging on the wall in the library . . . or maybe in the town hall?"

Her excitement was contagious, and I felt a delighted buzz at the idea of it all. A buzz of destiny? Maybe so. Maybe one ending would begin another, new, life story.

Gwen turned to me. "Don't be angry, but might I be there for the conversation? I won't intrude without being asked, but it might be good for you to have someone right at hand to bounce ideas and questions off of."

"Excellent idea. But don't get too excited, Gwen. It's possible that Susan will say there's no market for this."

Gwen shook her head slowly as she smiled. "No, I feel very certain about this. But as I said before, my instinct tells me this isn't standard gallery fare. It's something very special. Let's not get ahead of things, but don't talk yourself out of discovering the possibilities."

After Gwen drove away, I went back to the shed. I was dazzled by the artificial light hitting the metals and other dusty surfaces. How much more would these shine and stun if the dust of decades was brushed away? I pressed my hands and forehead to the metal of the fuselage. I found Dad's old stepladder in a dark corner and carried it near the large piece—the one Dad had said was how it felt inside his head sometimes. I climbed up to touch the varied surfaces, textures, and shapes that made it special.

The work to the left of it looked like a shield that a steampunk Viking might've held. The creation on the right looked more like a fancy hubcap had smashed into a toolbox and merged with an assortment of nuts and bolts and springs.

If I stretched, I could just brush it with my fingertips. The last person to touch these had been my father. Now me.

Until today, no one but my mother, father, and I had ever come in here, as far as I knew, but still he'd made a gallery of sorts. Maybe he would've wanted more for these, if he'd been able to move past whatever had held him back? Or maybe he'd hoped someone would do it for him? Instead of having his daughter guard them, along with his memory and that of her mother? Maybe he'd hoped for more. For better. Maybe he'd wanted more for me too.

Susan might have connections that would help.

The more I thought about it, the more I found the possibilities compelling.

I put the ladder back in the corner, turned off the light, and locked the shed up tight. I patted the door, then walked away. The yard was dark, especially near the woods, but for me it was a friendly dark. I feared nothing here. The moon was peeking through the upper boughs of the taller trees and lighting up the knoll and the firepit. as I returned to the house by myself.

So quiet. Silent. But peaceful. The glow I'd felt inside remained. Regrets had flown, at least for now. Likely, not far. They were sitting somewhere, maybe up in those trees, waiting to return, but for now, they kept a respectful distance.

As I walked from the kitchen into the living room, a detail caught my eye. Something was out of place.

A package wrapped in brown paper was on the coffee

table under the vase of wilting flowers. It had about the same dimensions as typing paper, such as one might have found in recent weeks inside a manila envelope, but thicker. Much thicker.

My breath caught. I knelt and moved the vase aside to reach the package. It hadn't been there *before* supper.

A parting gift?

So many gifts today.

I slipped my fingers under the folded ends, releasing the tape. A stack of paper, practically a whole ream of it, secured with a thick rubber band, was revealed. I riffled the pages and saw so many words, pages and pages of print. Except the first page.

The first page had fewer: *The Book of Lost Loves by Merrick Dahl and Davis McMahon*. Beneath the title and names was a single sentence: *A Story of Infinite Heart— dedicated to Lilliane Moore, a beloved friend, without whom this book could not have been written.*

There was a sheet of notepaper too, covered with Merrick's impeccable old-school script.

Lilliane,

With immense pleasure, and great trepidation, I submit this manuscript to you for your review. Please be aware that this is a draft still in need of work, is as flawed as the human hands and hearts crafting it, and requires your input. Davis and I have partnered to get this draft done as quickly as possible, and I am eager that you will now do your part— and add your magic—to help us tell this story.

No grapes were harmed in the crafting of this story. I promise.

Respectfully, I request that you please move this submission directly to the top of your TBR stack.

Yours truly,

Merrick Dahl

Written below in a different, scrawled hand was:

P.S. I miss you. Please give us a chance. Davis

TBR stack. *To be read.*

I smiled. It would go right to the top, no doubt about that. But for reading later—maybe tonight or maybe tomorrow—after I'd been able to fully process today's events.

Even so, my fingers thumbed the edges of the stacked paper. It would be so easy to simply slip the last pages out and sneak a peek at the ending.

I yanked my hand away as if it had been slapped.

Oh yes, I'd read this. And while I was interested in whatever ending Merrick and Davis had come up with, it was about the story. Whether written or spoken—the unfolding story was the heart of the tale. I wanted to go on that journey from start to finish. To be surprised.

As for my own journey, I didn't need a map or a story to chart my way. I was seeing the path laid out before me now—with a little help from my friends, both old and new.

I hugged the manuscript. Merrick and Davis had delivered it in person. For me. Gwen was bringing the camera back in the morning to take pictures of Dad's sculptures to send to Susan. Again, for me. Through their eyes, I was seeing the past suddenly reborn and shining with new possibilities.

Beach clothes. Yes, I was going to need more.

My life here at Cub Creek? I needed that too.

The crisp coastal light and onshore winds bearing mysterious, exotic scents, or the green smell of growing things, a gentler light and cozy hollows—I could have them both.

I was ready to see what was over that next hill and around the corner—the best of all worlds in a map solely my own, a not-yet-drawn map of my world and of my life.

Epilogue

Juggling the manuscript and a cup of tea, I headed upstairs intending to enjoy a little reading time in bed. Until I stumbled. And then I saw myself tumbling down the steps and hitting bottom hard, so I grabbed for the railing and the only thing that tumbled was the manuscript. I saved the tea and myself, but the manila envelope hit the stairstep and ripped down the side. Some pages spilled out, falling onto the steps below me.

After setting the teacup and saucer on the step, I began reclaiming the loose pages. As I gathered them up, I couldn't help but see what was written. These were words I'd already read, words that had set me into a dizzying spin of emotion back in Emerald Isle while sitting at Merrick's desk the night that he'd collapsed.

> Though he didn't know what was wrong with Danielle, every instinct he owned insisted that something was dreadfully wrong. Something more than cheating or falling for someone else.
> In that moment, he heard her . . .

I broke off reading as I remembered what had already happened. Mike and Jeff had had an argument out at The Point with Jeff telling Mike that Danielle was throwing him over—for Jeff—and that she'd asked Jeff to break the news to Mike. Mike had been really angry. He'd decked Jeff, had nearly choked him, before racing to Danielle's boathouse, anxious to reach her before Jeff caught up.

Presumably he'd wanted a chance to persuade Danielle otherwise ... but the force driving Mike had seemed dangerous to me. A mix of violence and desperation? Perhaps. I remembered that part of the story through the overwhelming distress that had been swirling around me, specifically, as I'd read about that idling car and the hose feeding from the car exhaust into the house. My stomach had lurched then, and it did now, and my heart rate was ramping up again now despite myself. Despite the good will and lovely day today. Despite knowing this was only a story, a mere work of fiction. Yet my eyes found the page again anyway. They sought out the words, and I read:

Jeff's words wouldn't quit echoing in Mike's head.

Life might be random, but when something didn't make any sense, it didn't make sense—that simple. There must be more. A reason. An explanation he could understand. He reached up to rub his temple—where the headache had lodged that morning when Suze had called, and now it wouldn't quite go away. The chain of the necklace scratched his skin. Had tangled itself around his fingers. He tried to pull free of it, and the links snapped.

How long had Dani been involved with Jeff? Almost from the beginning, as Jeff had said? No, Mike didn't believe that.

Jeff had a checkered past. Dubious at best. But he'd never done anything this extreme before.

Mike dropped the necklace into his shirt pocket but clutched the book more tightly, suddenly feeling at a loss ... sensing that something was wrong. Dreadfully wrong.

Something more than cheating, or Dani simply falling for someone else.

Was it a smell? Perhaps an instinct?

No matter. He'd check here at the boathouse first. If she wasn't inside, he wouldn't give up. Not this time.

He lunged forward, grabbing for the doorknob. In that moment, he heard her voice. She was calling his name. But not from inside the boathouse.

His hand still on the doorknob, he paused and looked back.

"Don't, Mike! Don't! Step away."

She was running toward him with her arms outstretched. He heard fear in her voice. But it was when she fell, flat-out on the ground, and popped back up as if it was unimportant, that stopped him. She was running again. He was mesmerized. His hand dropped from the doorknob just as her arms reached him. He'd thought an embrace was about to happen, that all his dark thoughts had been proved pointless and full of crap, but as her hands touched him, she grabbed at his shirt, at his arm.

"Come away, Mike."

For a moment, he was distracted by the distant sound of sirens, now growing louder.

"Danielle, what's—"

"Now, Mike." Her voice was low and beseeching. "With me. Step away."

He allowed her to move him. Her fingers tightened around his arm as they moved. She kept talking. "It was Jeff. He tricked me. I believed him when he said you were no good. That I was no good for you. I'm so sorry, Mike. I understand now that he wanted more from me, more than I could give. He wanted you out of the way."

By now they were near the main house, and he was noticing the scratches on her arms and dirt on her hands and cheeks. From the fall.

"Are you all right?"

She smiled and touched his face gently. "I'm fine now. He tricked me, sending me to your house while he was sending you here to the boathouse." As the first emergency vehicle came into view, she said, "I found a note that appeared to be written by you, that you'd set a bomb, rigged the boathouse to blow when that door opened. That you'd planned to kill the two of us rather than lose me."

She whispered, "I knew that wasn't true. You wouldn't hurt me, and you wouldn't choose that path for yourself." She dug her fingers into his arms. "I don't know if he actually set a bomb of some kind, but he was so . . . He wanted you out of the way. I believe he's insane, Mike."

Mike laughed and she looked confused, but he put his arms around her and hugged her so hard, her feet left the ground.

A police officer and emergency workers were walking their way and moving fast. Danielle pushed at him, demanding to know why he was laughing. "This is serious. This is tragic. This is—"

He pressed a quick kiss to her lips to stop her because they were about to be interrupted and he had something to say.

"Dani, stuff happens. Bad or good, stuff comes and goes. The police will deal with Jeff. We—you and I together—will take care of us and make each moment worth living." He repeated, "Together." He knew in his heart that the only future worth seeking was the one you were willing to fight for each day of your life.

I stopped reading, stunned.

There was no mention of tubing. No idling car.

Merrick changed the story. He changed the story for me to give me a happier ending.

Instead of Mike rescuing Danielle, Danielle had stopped Mike from falling victim to Jeff's jealousy.

Merrick and Davis wanted feedback? Oh, yes. I had feedback.

But for tonight, I had dreams to dream and hope to warm my heart, and in the morning . . . all things would be possible.

The End

AUTHOR'S NOTE:

Beach Rental, the first book in The Emerald Isle, NC Stories series, was published in 2011, but it wasn't the first novel I wrote. That first novel, *Cub Creek*, set in Louisa County, Virginia, was not published until 2014. *Beach Rental* had a delightful beach setting and was mostly romance with a little suspense, while *Cub Creek* was set amid the forests and rolling hills of rural Virginia and had more mystery and suspense with a little romance. *Beach Rental* led to *Beach Winds* and *Beach Wedding*. *Cub Creek* grew to include *Leaving Cub Creek* and other single title books that share the setting: *The Memory of Butterflies* and *The Wildflower House* series, and *The Happiness In Between*.

I love both settings and the characters in each.

After writing *A Light Last Seen* in 2019, I was ready to work on a new beach book, but 2020 had arrived and unhappy things had happened and the virus was upon us. The book I was now trying to write kept going very dark. Meanwhile, a new character was whispering to me—Lilliane Moore—but she was in Cub Creek, not at the beach.

For several months I persisted with that first manuscript, but finally put it aside and got to know Lilliane. Guess what? She'd never been to the beach. She'd never seen the ocean. I took her to the beach in *A Barefoot Tide* and had the joy of experiencing the ocean and shores of coastal Carolina right along with her for the first time all over again. It was wonderful.

Also, Lilliane works as an aide for the elderly Merrick Dahl, though she isn't a skilled nurse and considers herself more of a companion. Many of the qualities I found in her were those I found and respected in most of the aides who cared for my mother during her journey through Alzheimer's. I admired their willingness to do whatever was needed for the fragile and oft confused elderly residents, and the best of them managed their jobs with grace, kindness and practical assistance. My mother was blessed to have the same core caregivers for most of her years in the memory care facility. I will never forget them. Lilliane's job in this fictional story is less intensive than what most aides experience in real life, but you'll see many of the best qualities shown by these strong women in Lilliane as she interacts with Merrick.

A Barefoot Tide is my 2020 story—a story that gave me comfort—and I'm more pleased than I can express to be able to share it with you and all readers.

One last note: You can't drive on The Point during beach season, and even during the months that you can, a permit is required. Just letting you know so you don't get into trouble. As Merrick might say, *Fiction allows for a flexible representation of life ~ not a literal retelling.*

Thank you for sharing the ride with me.

~ January 2, 2021 Grace Greene

QUESTIONS FOR DISCUSSION

1. Was Lilliane fearless? Or simply stubborn? Or was she, at heart, a practical person who tried not to let personal feelings rule her? How might her parents' personalities and her childhood have contributed to how she interacted with others?

2. Lilliane felt secure and loved until she lost her parents. What are your thoughts about the choice her parents made when Lilliane was eighteen?

3. Both Miranda and Gwen played strong mentor roles in Lilliane's adult life. Each shared unique strengths and insights into dealing with life. What role do you believe each played? How did that mirror the dual settings in the Lilliane's life? The rural, small town setting of her childhood, and most of her adult life? Versus the coastal setting?

4. Lilliane struggled between the past and future. Between duty and emotional damage and being able to move beyond them. What do you think will be her decision about her future?

Thank you for purchasing

A BAREFOOT TIDE

I hope you enjoyed it! If so, please consider leaving a review to help other readers find a book they'll enjoy.

Please visit me at www.gracegreene.com and sign up for my newsletter. I'd love to be in contact with you.

If you enjoyed *A Barefoot Tide*, I'd like to recommend the sequel, *A Dancing Tide*, or one of the other books listed on the last page.

ABOUT THE AUTHOR

Photo © 2018 Amy G Photography

Grace Greene is an award-winning and USA Today bestselling author of women's fiction and contemporary romance set in the countryside of her native Virginia (*The Happiness In Between, The Memory of Butterflies, the Cub Creek Series,* and *The Wildflower House Series*) and on the breezy beaches of Emerald Isle, North Carolina (*The Emerald Isle, NC Stories Series*). Her debut novel, *Beach Rental,* and the sequel, *Beach Winds,* were both Top Picks by RT Book Reviews magazine. Her most recent release (2020) is *A Light Last Seen.* Her 2021 release, A *Barefoot Tide,* brings together both the Cub Creek books and the Emerald Isle, NC books.

Visit www.gracegreene.com for more information or to communicate with Grace or sign up for her newsletter. Connect with Grace on Facebook here: www.facebook.com/GraceGreeneBooks

Other Books by Grace Greene

BEACH RENTAL   (Emerald Isle Novel #1)

<u>RT Book Reviews</u> – TOP PICK

"No author can come close to capturing the awe-inspiring essence of the North Carolina coast like Greene. Her debut novel seamlessly combines hope, love and faith, like the female equivalent of Nicholas Sparks. Her writing is meticulous and so finely detailed you'll hear the gulls overhead and the waves crashing onto shore. Grab a hanky, bury your toes in the sand and get ready to be swept away with this unforgettable beach read." —*RT Book Reviews TOP PICK*

<u>Brief Description</u>:

On the Crystal Coast of North Carolina, in the small town of Emerald Isle...

Juli Cooke, hard-working and getting nowhere fast, marries a dying man, Ben Bradshaw, for a financial settlement, not expecting he will set her on a journey of hope and love. The journey brings her to Luke Winters, a local art dealer, but Luke resents the woman who married his sick friend and warns her not to hurt Ben—and he's watching to make sure she doesn't. Until Ben dies and the stakes change.

Framed by the timelessness of the Atlantic Ocean and the brilliant blue of the beach sky, Juli struggles against her past, the opposition of Ben's and Luke's families, and even the living reminder of her marriage—to build a future with hope and perhaps to find the love of her life—if she can survive the danger from her past.

CUB CREEK (Cub Creek Series #1)

<u>Brief Description</u>:

In the heart of Virginia, where the forests hide secrets and the creeks run strong and deep ~

Libbie Havens doesn't need anyone and she'll prove it. When she chances upon the secluded house on Cub Creek in rural Virginia, she buys it. She'll show her cousin Liz, and other doubters, that she can rise above her past and live happily and successfully on her own terms.

Libbie has emotional problems born of a troubled childhood. Raised by a grandmother she could never please, Libbie is more comfortable *not* being comfortable with people. She knows she's different from most. She has special gifts, or curses, but are they real? Or are they products of her history and dysfunction?

At Cub Creek Libbie makes friends and attracts the romantic interest of two local men, Dan Wheeler and Jim Mitchell. Relationships with her cousin and other family members improve dramatically and Libbie experiences true happiness—until tragedy occurs.

Having lost the good things gained at Cub Creek, Libbie must find a way to overcome her troubles, to finally rise above them and seize control of her life and future, or risk losing everything, including herself.

A LIGHT LAST SEEN (A Cub Creek Single Title)

Brief Description:

Chasing happiness and finding joy are two very different things-as Jaynie Highsmith has discovered. Can she give up searching for the one and reclaim the other? Or is she fated to repeat the mistakes her mother made?

Jaynie Highsmith grows up in Cub Creek on Hope Road acutely aware of the irony of its name, Hope, because she wants nothing more than to escape from it and the chaos of her childhood. Desperate to leave her past behind and make a new life, she is determined to become the best version of herself she can create. But when she does take off, she also leaves and forgets important parts of her past and herself.

The new life is everything she wants, or so she thinks until she finds herself repeating the same mistakes her mother made. Is Jaynie destined for unhappiness? Is it *like mother, like daughter*? Did running away only delay the unhappiness she fears she is destined for?

Seventeen years after leaving home, Jaynie needs a *new* fresh start and returning to Cub Creek is critical, but she promises herself that the visit will be as short as possible and then she'll be out and free again. However, a longer stay may be vital to her future because if she has any hope of changing her destiny, Jaynie must reconcile the past she turned her back on with her present.

BOOKS BY GRACE GREENE

Emerald Isle, North Carolina Series
Beach Rental *(Book 1)*
Beach Winds *(Book 2)*
Beach Wedding *(Book 3)*
"Beach Towel" (A Short Story)
Beach Walk *(Christmas Novella)*

Barefoot Tides Two-Book Series
A Barefoot Tide *(Book 1)*
A Dancing Tide *(Book 2) Coming October 2021*

Beach Single-Title Novellas
Beach Christmas *(Christmas Novella)*
Clair *(Beach Brides Novella Series)*

Cub Creek Novels ~ Series and Single Titles
Cub Creek *(Cub Creek Series, Book 1)*
Leaving Cub Creek *(Cub Creek Series, Book 2)*
The Happiness In Between
The Memory of Butterflies
A Light Last Seen

The Wildflower House Novels
Wildflower Heart *(Book 1)*
Wildflower Hope *(Book 2)*
Wildflower Christmas *(A Wildflower House Novella) (Book 3)*

Virginia Country Roads
Kincaid's Hope
A Stranger in Wynnedower
www.GraceGreene.com

Made in the USA
Columbia, SC
06 February 2023

11823903R00178